A MOMENT

IN TIME

LONE STAR BRIDES

BOOK ✤ TWO

DISCARD

A MOMENT
IN TIME

TRACIE
PETERSON

BETHANYHOUSE
a division of Baker Publishing Group
Minneapolis, Minnesota

© 2014 by Peterson Ink, Inc.

Published by Bethany House Publishers
11400 Hampshire Avenue South
Bloomington, Minnesota 55438
www.bethanyhouse.com

Bethany House Publishers is a division of
Baker Publishing Group, Grand Rapids, Michigan

Printed in the United States of America

Library of Congress Cataloging-in-Publication Data

Peterson, Tracie.
    A moment in time / Tracie Peterson.
       p. cm. — (Lone star brides ; book two)
    Summary: "With so many obstacles in her path, will Alice Chesterfield find sanctuary in her new life on the 1890s Texas frontier—and a chance at love?"— Provided by publisher.
    ISBN 978-0-7642-1216-1 (cloth : alk. paper)
    ISBN 978-0-7642-1059-4 (pbk.)
    ISBN 978-0-7642-1217-8 (large-print pbk.)
    1. Single women—Fiction. 2. Family secrets—Fiction. 3. Man-woman relationships—Fiction. 4. Frontier and pioneer life—Fiction. I. Title.
PS3566.E7717M65 2014
813'.54—dc23   2014003385

Scripture quotations are from the King James Version of the Bible.

Cover design by Gearbox
Photography by Steve Gardner, PixelWorks Studios

14 15 16 17 18 19 20   7 6 5 4 3 2 1

Chapter 1

Alice Chesterfield could feel the intensity of the man watching her. Not just any man. She knew very well who it was and why he continued to hound her steps. Gathering her brown wool skirt in hand, Alice did her best to avoid the muddier spots in the road as she crossed to the small fabric store on the opposite side. Her heart pounded wildly. Her breathing seemed to catch in her throat.

Would he follow her there? Would he dare? She had been plagued by this stranger—this man who'd been responsible for upending her world—for over a year now. The wind picked up just as she reached the door of the establishment and chilled her to the bone. At least she told herself it was the wind that caused her shivers. Forcing herself not to look back, Alice raised her chin and slipped inside.

Stay calm. Don't let this disturb you any more than it already has.

A small bell over the door heralded her entrance. The warmth of the room was welcome, but it did little to help the icy fingers that seemed to run down Alice's spine. Reaching her gloved hand out to touch a bolt of blue cotton broadcloth, she closed her eyes and drew a deep breath.

"May I help you?"

Alice jumped at the voice and opened her eyes to find a matronly woman standing at her right.

"We don't have much in stock, as we're closing our doors on Friday."

Alice nodded. So many of the smaller businesses had folded since the banking crisis struck earlier in the year. "I'm looking for needles. The mercantile was out and suggested you might have some."

The woman shook her head. "Sold the last of them on Monday. I have some pins and plenty of thread, but as you can see for yourself, my shelves of fabric are pretty much exhausted. I can give you a good price on this broadcloth."

"Yes, well . . . thank you. I don't really need any fabric." Alice steadied her voice as she glanced out the window to see if the man was still there. He was.

"I haven't seen you in here before." The woman frowned. "I would have remembered you . . . your scar."

Alice put her gloved hand to the scar that ran from ear to chin on the right side of her face. "I . . . well . . ." She didn't know quite what to say to the woman's open rudeness.

"Such a pity it should have happened. Your old man do that?" She watched Alice carefully. "I used to be married to a man who carried a knife. Thought nothin' of threatening me with it from time to time. Eventually he threatened the wrong man, and now I'm a widow."

"No," Alice said, shaking her head. "I'm not married."

She glanced over her shoulder at the man who continued to wait for her on the other side of the street. "I was attacked—a year ago."

The woman didn't miss a thing. "That the man?" she asked, nodding her head toward the stranger.

Alice realized this woman might well be her salvation. "Yes. At least he was responsible. He calls himself Mr. Smith, and he's been following me since I left home."

"Well, I won't brook any nonsense," the woman stated, moving back behind the counter. She pulled up a shotgun. "Like I said, I was married to a man who got his way at the end of a knife. I just won't have it."

"I wonder," Alice said, moving toward the counter, "is there another way out of here?"

"Of course there is." The woman pointed. "You go ahead through that curtain over there, and it will take you through the storeroom and into the alley behind my store. I'll keep an eye on the no-account, and you get on home."

Alice looked at the older woman with gratitude. "You are a blessing from the Lord."

"Bah, I don't know about that," she said, squinting her eyes to study the stranger. "I do know about mean-tempered men, however. Now, get on with yourself."

"Thank you." Alice hurried through the curtain and made her way to the back door. The alley was a muddy mess, but she didn't care. Picking her way through the ruts left by numerous delivery wagons, Alice slipped between buildings and disappeared.

She all but ran the rest of the way home. It wasn't that Mr. Smith didn't know where she lived, but she would feel a lot better once she was safely behind the locked doors of the Wythe house.

Hard times in the financial world had altered the stately

beauty of the upper-class estates that lined the road. Many of the wealthier Capitol Hill residents had closed their houses and moved away. With silver devalued and the mines shut until further notice, Denver had suffered a tremendous blow to its economy. No one knew that better than the stuffed shirts of this elite neighborhood.

Reaching the red stone and brick house she'd come to call home, Alice hurried up the back steps and burst into the kitchen, not even bothering to remove her muddy boots. Thankfully, there was no one there to chide her. The housekeeper and butler had resigned their positions the month before, and due to the financial situation, Mr. Wythe had not seen it possible to fill their jobs.

Alice didn't really mind. At eighteen, she was willing to work to get what she needed. She'd certainly never had a maid to wait on her hand and foot, even when her father was alive. Instead, she was the one required to work. Mrs. Wythe—Marty—had been kind enough to let Alice stay on with them. She'd hired Alice, without references, as her personal maid, and over time the relationship had developed into something more. Now, despite Marty's being able to pay only a small pittance, Alice remained for the comfort and assurance that she was cared for by someone.

"I thought I heard you in here," Marty declared, coming into the kitchen. "Were you able to . . ." Her words trailed. "What happened? Was it Smith again?"

Alice knew it would be impossible to hide her fear. "He fell in step behind me almost from the start. I tried to lose him in the shops, but he watched me too carefully. Finally, I just accepted that he would trail me wherever I went and pretended not to care. With the help of a woman at Bennett's Fabrics, I managed to get away unseen."

Marty crossed her arms in contemplation. "Of course it won't stop him. I think it's time we speak with the authorities."

"But what will we tell them that I haven't already explained?" Alice asked. "They know all about him but don't care. They said they were much too busy with the increase in crimes. People are desperate."

Marty narrowed her eyes. "That's no excuse. Of course crime is increasing with so many people suffering financial ruin. Even so, it's not right that a young woman can't feel free to walk down the street without being accosted. Next time, I'll drive you myself, and we'll see if Mr. Smith is inclined to reacquaint himself with my shotgun."

With her muddy boots discarded, Alice put them on the back porch and then hurried to clean up the mess she'd made on the floor. Marty had already retrieved the mop and pail. Alice took them from her and smiled. "I'm supposed to be the hired help."

Marty laughed. "Those days are long gone, as you well know. I can't help but wonder when Jake will walk through the door and tell me the bank has closed its doors. He knows his job there hangs by a thread. Mr. Morgan told him the banks were falling into failure like dominoes lined up in child's play." She shrugged. "I don't know what to expect from one day to the next. But then, I suppose no one does."

Alice nodded and worked to clean the floor. "I know I've said it before, but I think it's time you stop worrying about giving me any money for pay. I'm blessed just to get to eat and have a bed to sleep in. You should just put that money aside for emergencies. That's what I've been trying to do."

"Yes, well, I was going to address that subject with you. My money is pretty well dried up. I could write to my sister and brother-in-law in Texas. They still haven't paid me for the ranch, but I know they're most likely hurting, too."

Shaking her head, Alice opened the door and emptied the bucket outside. There was an icy bite to the air and she shivered. Looking quickly around, she saw the unmistakable outline of a man near the stable. She hurried back into the house and slammed the door closed. Locking it, she looked to Marty. "He's out there."

"Not for long." Marty took off and returned momentarily with her shotgun. "I think I should have a little talk with him."

"But it's nearly dark," Alice protested, "and Jake, I mean Mr. Wythe, isn't home yet. What if Mr. Smith decides to call your bluff?"

Marty smiled. "Who said I'm bluffing?"

Alice put her hand on Marty's arm. "Let's just pray instead. He'll leave soon enough, and if you threaten him, he'll just come back later."

"I don't appreciate being made a prisoner in my own home," Marty replied. "Even if you could give him what he wants, he needs to know he can't push people around."

Alice thought back to the man's demands. The night he'd sent his men to waylay her father, it had seemed they were to be victims of a simple robbery. But the attack turned out to be more than expected. One man had sliced Alice's face to motivate her father, and when her father protested, he was shoved to the ground, hitting his head and dying almost immediately. Alice was hospitalized and was sick for weeks afterwards with a fierce infection. When she regained consciousness and eventually her health, Alice prayed that would be the end of the ordeal. Mr. Smith, however, had appeared not long after the incident to ask about an envelope that should have been in her father's satchel.

"I wish I had what he wanted. I wish I could find a way to rid us both of his threatening presence."

"Men like that are never satisfied. Your father was delivering gold certificates for the bank. Mr. Smith believes they should be his, but we know that isn't the case. However, since no one knows where those certificates got off to or even where the envelope might be, Mr. Smith will have to accept his plight. You can't get blood from a turnip."

Alice put her hand again to her face. "But you can get it out of people. I would never forgive myself if harm should come to you or Mr. Wythe."

Marty placed the shotgun on the top of the wooden worktable. "No harm is going to come to anyone. Not if I can help it. Now, as you pointed out, it's getting late. Let's get the stew from yesterday heating. When Jake gets home we're bound to hear all the worrisome news, and Mr. Smith will be nothing more than a minor thorn in our flesh."

★

Jake ate like a starved man and Marty once again felt guilty that they were still in Colorado instead of Texas, where Jake would rather be. Her husband longed to return to ranch life, but Marty stood in the way of that happening. Though they both had been born and raised on Texas ranches, Marty and Jake had opposite feelings toward those settings. Jake's parents had been forced to sell off the family ranch when the drought of the '80s had caught up with them. It had ripped a part of Jake's heart away, and he had mourned the loss ever since.

While I couldn't leave Texas quick enough.

Marty toyed with her bowl of stew. She had been widowed in Texas, and although she once owned a ranch and could have made all of Jake's desires a reality, she'd kept the truth from him—until recently. Even now when he talked of returning to Texas so he could get work with friends or maybe even at her brother-in-law's ranch, Marty cringed and changed the subject. She had hoped that in selling her ranch to her brother-in-law, the matter would be closed for good.

She smiled at her husband, pretending her past mistakes didn't haunt her. She had asked for his forgiveness and the Lord's, as well. But she just couldn't seem to forgive herself. Especially now.

"Has Mr. Morgan said anything more about closing the bank?" Marty asked.

Jake looked up from the piece of bread he'd been about to break in half. "No. He's hangin' on like a man breakin' in a new bronc." His Southern drawl rang clear, as it often did when Jake let down his guard.

"There's a chance he might be able to pull through?" she asked, trying not to sound too desperate.

"There's always a chance," Jake said with a look of seeming indifference. Then he offered her a smile.

It was one of the first she'd seen in days. "You seem hopeful."

He shrugged. "I guess there's not much else we can be. I figure we have to have hope. I know God hasn't forgotten us down here. Someone reminded me today about the depression of '73. Things were bad then, too, and we fought our way outta that one."

"Mr. Brentwood at the orphanage mentioned that, as well," Marty countered. "Apparently his father was some type of investor back then and lost most everything. He managed to rebuild his business, however, and that was what gave Mr. Brentwood the money to start the orphanage." Marty had taken to volunteering at the orphanage frequently, especially since the economical problems had forced Brentwood to let go of so many workers. "He also reminded me that God sometimes allows things to happen that we can't begin to understand in order to benefit us later."

"We can be assured that God will never forget us," Alice agreed, "although sometimes it does seem He's distracted."

After losing the butler and housekeeper, Marty had insisted Alice join them for meals and be an extended member of the family. At first the girl had been uncomfortable with the idea, but she was gradually getting used to it.

For several minutes the conversation waned. Marty finished her bowl of stew, and though she could easily have eaten more, she settled for what she'd eaten. Jake would need another serving, and there wasn't much left.

"I hope you won't mind," Jake said, putting his spoon in the empty bowl, "but I arranged with a man today to take some of the furniture from the house. He'll be by tomorrow to crate it off."

"Let me refill that for you, Mr. Wythe," Alice said, jumping up.

"Thanks. I have to say it makes a mighty fine meal on a cold night." He smiled at the younger woman and then looked back to Marty. "Anyway, like I was sayin', he'll be here tomorrow."

Marty tried to hide her frown. She knew this was probably a sign of things to come and didn't like it. If Jake felt it necessary to sell furnishings, he'd probably had his salary reduced once again. She tried to force a smile. "I think that sounds wise. We certainly don't need so much stuff. With winter nearly upon us I thought perhaps we should close off the third floor all together. Alice can sleep in one of the second-floor bedrooms. It should help dramatically with the heating."

"I agree," Jake replied as Alice placed the bowl of stew in front of him. "Thank you, Alice. Next time, though, I can just fetch it myself."

Marty turned to Alice. "Jake and I were just talking about closing off the third floor. It's hard enough to heat the downstairs bedrooms, and we figure it will save on the overall heating of the house. You can take one of the second-floor bedrooms in the same wing as ours. That way we can also close off the other unused rooms."

Alice nodded. "That's perfectly acceptable to me. I'll arrange it tonight. Did I also understand that Mr. Wythe is selling off furniture?"

"Yes." Marty looked to her husband. "Just some of the things we don't really need."

It wasn't the first time Jake had sold something from the house. In the beginning he'd only handed off his own meager possessions for cash. Now he was actually going to sell things that could be considered as belonging to the bank.

Paul Morgan, the bank president and distant relative of J. P. Morgan, had presented the furnished house and mortgage to Jake, along with a promotion to bank manager. He had been carefully schooling Jake to eventually take a position of higher regard and wanted the Wythe family to be part of the socially elite. Marty couldn't help but wonder whether the man would be accepting of Jake's present plans, especially knowing they were months in arrears with the mortgage payment.

Jake had assured her that with his cut in salary, Morgan had promised that the mortgage would be covered by the bank as part of his pay. Marty didn't say so at the time, but she'd never had a good feeling about this arrangement, since there was nothing in writing.

"Thanksgiving and Christmas are nearly upon us," Jake declared. "It would be nice to have a little money so we can at least celebrate with a nice meal." He once again smiled. "Not that this stew and bread isn't just as satisfying. Even Cook didn't make anything that tasted this good, but I thought maybe we could buy a ham or turkey."

Marty remembered some of the outrageously rich meals they'd shared in the early days of her marriage to Jake. They weren't even to their first anniversary, yet they'd gone from feast to famine. Marty's sister, Hannah, had taught her that money would always be fleeting and a person shouldn't ever put their trust in such a temporal thing. Even so, it was a very necessary thing, and Marty had to admit, she missed it.

"Can we sell the house?" Marty asked without thinking.

Jake said nothing for what seemed an awfully long time. "I've asked around, but no one is buying. No one wants a house that's clearly above the normal man's means."

His serious expression gave Marty cause to wonder if there was more to it than Jake was letting on. "I didn't know you'd asked around."

"I was plannin' on tellin' you about it," he admitted, "but only if it looked like a real possibility. I didn't want to get your hopes up."

"I see." Marty looked to Alice and then back to her husband. She offered him a smile. "I guess that isn't what God wants for us then. If He had plans for us to sell this place, then He'd also send a buyer our way. We'll just have to trust that He has something else in mind."

"I agree," Jake said with a tired sigh. "In the meantime we'll just sell what we have to and get by the best we can."

"Living frugally is something I know very well," Marty assured him.

"Me too," Alice agreed.

Jake nodded. "I know. But . . . I . . . well, it's not what I wanted for any of us." He looked as if he might say something more but got to his feet instead and once again smiled. "I sure didn't mean to put a damper on supper. I'll stoke up the fire in the sitting room and maybe we can retire there. Then I'll read the Scriptures before we head upstairs."

Marty said nothing to Jake, but once he left the room, she turned to Alice. "Something's not right. There's more to this than he's saying."

"Maybe he'll tell you later tonight . . . in private," Alice replied, gathering up the dishes.

"I'd just as soon he tell me now instead of letting me wonder about it."

"Something else you might consider," Alice said with a pause. "We could move our bedrooms to the first floor and close both the second and third floors."

"There aren't any bedrooms down here," Marty said, and then it dawned on her what Alice was getting at. "But we have the two sitting rooms, the library, and the music room. We could certainly convert two of those into bedrooms. It's not like we need them for entertaining."

"Exactly."

"I'll mention it to Jake. I think he'll go along with it, as well. We'll have to figure out how to get things moved around. I wish Samson were still with us." Samson was the former stableman and driver, and Marty missed his presence when it came to moving furniture . . . and to intimidating the irritating Mr. Smith.

Marty helped Alice with the cleanup, but all the while her mind raced with thoughts of what was going on inside her husband's head. It was only as they put away the last of the clean dishes that Marty realized she'd said nothing to Jake about the reappearance of Mr. Smith.

I don't suppose now would be a good time to tell him.

She looked at Alice and forced a smile. "Well, we might as well join Jake." She pulled off her apron and hung it on a nail by the door.

"I'll be there shortly," Alice replied. "Let me put water on for tea."

Marty met Alice's gaze. The young woman clearly felt the tension. She had become Marty's dearest friend, and yet there was still so much the two women kept hidden away. Maybe it was better that way. Maybe if the worst came about and they had to part company it would be easier to bear.

"I doubt it," Marty muttered.

"What?" Alice asked.

Marty shook her head and turned for the door. "It wasn't important. Just me grumbling. Tea sounds wonderful."

She hurried away before Alice could press for more details. Sometimes life here was like juggling balls at a circus. Keeping everything in motion required not only skill but complete concentration. Unfortunately, Marty wasn't at all certain that she had enough of either one to get through this crisis.

Chapter 2

"What exactly are you saying?" Marty asked her husband. Just days earlier he had assured her there was hope for the bank and his position, but now everything had changed.

"I'm saying that as of today, I'm no longer employed. Morgan closed the bank. He's taking what he can and reinvesting elsewhere."

"But what does that have to do with us living here?"

Jake looked her in the eye. "The house is in foreclosure. The bank owns it now. There's nothing left for us to do but leave. I figure we can take what's ours and head to Texas."

"No! I'm not moving to Texas," Marty said, a little angrier than she'd intended. "I don't understand any of this. Mr. Morgan didn't even give us a warning. He said that everything was fine, that the house was included as part of your salary. How can that be changed now?"

"Sweetheart, I wish I had better news. Truly I do. But you can't make something outta nothin', and that's all that's left."

"But it's not right." Marty began to pace. Surely this was

nothing more than another nightmare. She would wake up any moment now.

"Nothing about this financial mess is right," Jake replied. "The government has devalued silver, the railroads are almost all in receivership, and the only man in the country with any ability to dig the government out of its grave is J. P. Morgan. I was told in strictest confidence that J. P. Morgan will most likely end up loaning the government money to continue running its day-to-day operations."

"How can any one man be that rich?" Marty asked, sitting down rather hard. The news regarding the bank's situation wasn't unexpected, but she'd never anticipated that they would have to make an immediate move. Where could they go?

"I guess he played his cards right." Jake replied with a shrug. "Mr. Morgan at the bank said J. P. Morgan is a financial genius."

"Then perhaps he should share some of that genius with everyone else," Marty said, shaking her head.

"It's to his benefit to share his money and get some hefty interest payments on it," Jake said. "But be that as it may, we have to make plans, Marty. I know life isn't what you wanted it to be, but I have to go where there's work. I have friends in eastern Texas, and you have family near Dallas. Between the two places, I ought to be able to find something."

Marty felt discomfort in the pit of her stomach. Why was this happening? Why couldn't they just go on living in Denver? Maybe she could get a job . . . and Alice, too. Alice would be happy to help, just to have a place to stay.

"We can get jobs here," she told him, jumping to her feet again. "I'm sure there is something Alice and I can do. After all, we aren't helpless socialites." She walked back and forth as she thought. "I can sew, cook, clean, take care of children. I'm sure to find something."

"Well there isn't much here for *me*," Jake said. "I only know two things—banking and ranching." He laughed. "Who would have thought a man could have two such opposite skills. My life ain't exactly predictable."

Marty stopped in midstep. "Jake, I know you understand my feelings about Texas. They haven't changed." She didn't want to make him feel guilty for his plans, but she had to make him choose another path. "Why don't you get in touch with my brother Andy? He's ranching in Wyoming. You could write to him and see if he needs some help."

Her mind whirled with thoughts. She didn't want Jake to go back to ranching. The dangers were too high and the payoff too minimal. Even so, if she talked him into writing to her brother, that would at least give her a little time in which she and Alice might be able to secure jobs. If they were both working, maybe Jake could relax a bit and find some menial task to put his hand to. It was worth a try.

"I don't know anything about ranching in Wyoming," Jake replied. "I know Texas."

"But ranching is ranching, isn't it?"

He shook his head. "You know as well as I do that the elements are completely different. Now, stop with this nonsense." He sounded firmer than he had earlier. "I'm gonna do what I can to support you. I figure you and Alice can stay here in Denver while I go to Texas. Once I get established I'll send for you both."

She looked at him in surprise. "And where do you propose we stay? You've already told us we have to vacate the house. I don't see that affording us many choices."

"Well, that's what I really wanted to talk to you about.

See, I spoke with Mr. Brentwood at that orphanage you like so much. I happened to see him on my way home and told him what had happened. He suggested you and Alice could come stay at the orphanage and help out there in exchange for room and board. I told him I thought that would work well."

"You decided that without even talking to me first?" she asked in a rage. She wasn't really mad about the prospects of living at the orphanage. God knew she loved the children and was completely devoted to helping them through this bad time. She'd been sharing whatever she could with them ever since the country's crisis began. What angered her most was that everything was spinning out of control, and she had no say in it.

"Marty, listen to me," Jake said, coming to put his hands on her shoulders. She tried to move away, but he'd have no part of it and held her fast. "Marty, we aren't the only ones sufferin' here. The rest of the country is hurtin', too. We knew it was only a matter of time."

"For you to lose your job and the bank to close, yes. To lose our home and have to relocate to Texas, no. I didn't bargain for that."

He gave her a lopsided smile, which only served to irritate Marty all the more.

"None of us exactly bargained for any of this." He sobered. "Now listen to me, please. I've been looking around the city for work since this summer. I knew there'd come a time when my job would be no more. There's nothing here. There are hundreds—no, thousands of men without work. Denver doesn't offer a whole lot of opportunities just now."

Marty relaxed just a bit. "I know that. I'm not naïve."

He nodded. "No you aren't. You're a reasonable woman when you want to be, and I need you to be that now. My friends, the Vandermarks, live in eastern Texas and have a logging business. I figure they can hire me on for a time."

"Logging? But that's just as dangerous as ranching, maybe more so," Marty countered.

Jake shook his head. "You can't keep me from harm by hiding me from danger, Martha Wythe. I'm a man and I have to do what is right for me. I know you're afraid. I know you hate Texas, although I don't pretend to understand why."

"But you've gone to college. You have an education. You should be one of the men helping to change this country and solve the problems we're in. You don't need to go back to branding and driving cattle to market. You're worth more than that."

"Now, wait just a minute, Marty. Are you suggesting that ranching is less important work than sittin' behind a desk? 'Cause if you are, then I must disagree. You know full well that ranching is an honorable and necessary way to make a living. Some of the finest and smartest men I've known were ranchers. You're just worked up because of the news, but I won't have you talkin' like ranching is somehow demeaning. You grew up with it, and it benefited you nicely. Kept you fed and clothed and in some ways brought us together."

She started to speak, but he put his finger to her lips. "I know. You lost one husband to a ranching accident in Texas and you fear losin' another. But, Marty, we both know that's not the way things work. God is either gonna take me home or leave me here to work out livin' my life. We've gotta trust Him for the answer."

"I do trust Him," Marty declared. "But I don't trust that this is the right decision."

"Because you don't trust me?" he asked. His voice was full of sorrow.

Marty considered the question. Was that the problem? Did she lack the ability to trust Jake? To trust him to do the right thing for both of them? Jake had never done one thing to break the trust between them, while Marty on the other hand had lied about owning the ranch in Texas, about selling it back to her brother-in-law, about so much. Certainly she'd done her best to make up for it. She'd finally told the truth, and Jake had forgiven her and trusted her. Didn't she owe him the same?

"I trust you," she said, nearly choking from the emotions rising up in her. "It's not about trust."

"Isn't it?" He studied her for a moment. "I love you, Marty. You know that. I wouldn't do anything to hurt you, but you have got to let me be the man of this family and make decisions that I think are best."

"But you don't care about my desires," she said. "If you did, you wouldn't talk about Texas."

"Texas isn't the problem, Marty, and we both know it."

She stiffened. "Meaning what? That I'm the problem?"

He shrugged. "As my grandmother used to say, 'If the shoe fits, you might as well kick yourself with it.' You know as well as I do that your brother-in-law and sister would have us back on the ranch in a heartbeat."

"They've never said any such thing." She pulled away. "You're just assuming on their good nature."

"I'm not assuming anything. I know from the way you've talked about them that they're God-fearing people. They wouldn't see you go in need, and because we're married, they wouldn't see me go in need, either. And I'm not talkin' about a handout. I could work for them, Marty. I would work hard, and you could be back amongst your family again."

Marty searched her mind desperately for some excuse to reject such a resolution. "And what . . . what of Alice?"

"She could come, too. You know that I care about what happens to her. She's too young to be on her own. And that Smith character is just a step away from causin' her harm. Think about that, Marty. Put your selfish desires aside and think about Alice. Texas could mean freedom for her. Freedom from the fear of Smith and his cronies."

Marty hated being made to feel guilty for her fears. She bristled and narrowed her eyes. "Go then. Go to Texas or wherever else you choose. Just don't expect me to follow."

She left him staring after her and fled for the quiet of the kitchen. Shaking from head to toe, Marty hovered near the stove for comfort. But the heat hardly seemed to permeate her body. The cold she felt came from the inside and nothing could warm it.

★

The following day Marty allowed Mr. Brentwood to show her and Alice to a large room with two single beds.

"This used to be one of the rooms for the older children," he told the ladies. "Of course those orphans are gone now. Some, as you know, to your sister's place in Texas, and others . . . well, they were dispersed to the streets or wherever we could find temporary homes. Anyway, there used to be eight beds in here, but I had to sell some of those. Didn't even get a pittance of what they were worth."

Marty knew very well about the hardships Mr. Brentwood faced. The orphanage had once housed over fifty children and now maintained no more than fifteen. Even that number taxed Mr. Brentwood's meager funds.

"I strung a rope in the corner from one wall to the other. It's good and secure. I figured you could hang clothes from it or make a curtain for changing behind."

"This looks fine," Alice said, pulling Marty from her thoughts. "I'm sure we will be quite comfortable."

Marty met the man's worried look. "Yes. It will be fine." She wanted to give him a smile of reassurance but had none to offer. Just that morning she had told her husband good-bye. She'd offered him neither her encouragement nor her love, and only now was beginning to feel guilty for her actions.

"Frankly, I'm glad to have your help," Brentwood admitted. "I have plenty of room for you here. Even the food will stretch to include two more mouths. What I don't have is time for all the needs of the children or money for staff. You will both be very valuable to me in that sense. With you here, I can leave you in charge while I go appeal in person to some of the churches and charities that have helped us in the past. There may not be much to be had in the way of donations, but anything is better than nothing."

Alice stepped forward. "I have managed to secure a job waiting tables. It's only part-time work and won't pay very much. I'm happy, however, to contribute what I can to help with the food purchases for Marty and me."

"That's most generous, Miss Chesterfield." Mr. Brentwood offered her a warm smile. "Now if you'll excuse me, I'll let you two get settled in while I return to the classroom."

Marty nodded but said nothing more. She looked around the stark room that would become her home for no one knew how long. Without thought, she plopped down on one of the beds. It wasn't anywhere near as comfortable as the goose down mattress she'd shared with Jake.

"I suppose we could have it much worse."

Alice turned and met her gaze. "Much worse . . . believe me. This is truly an answer to prayer, Marty. I know you aren't happy about it, but at least we're safe here. Mr. Brentwood and the children will help keep us from being so easily accessible to Mr. Smith. With Mr. Wythe gone, we were bound to be vulnerable to Smith's attacks."

Marty knew the truth of it, but she didn't want to admit it. Admitting it gave credence to Jake's choice, and that was something she couldn't do. He hadn't cared about her feelings. He hadn't listened to her pleadings or even taken into consideration her ideas for alternatives. It caused her great pain to know that her desires weren't important to him.

★

Robert Barnett settled back in the saddle and waited for his father to catch up. The day was chilly but otherwise not too uncomfortable for working out on the range. He and his father had just finished checking on the herd in the north pastures and knew it wouldn't be long until they'd have a great many new calves. New calves equaled more stock, and more stock meant more financial security—at least eventually. With the country suffering a depression right now, Robert knew they might well have to sit on the herd for a long time before being able to sell at a reasonable price.

Of course, profit wasn't everything, and Robert knew his father to donate animals to some of the charities and poorhouses. Kindness and concern for his fellowman was something Robert's parents had instilled in him from the time he was a little boy.

"There will always be someone less fortunate than you," his mother had told him on many occasions, *"and you must remember that what you do for them is serving the Lord himself."* Robert always took that to heart—maybe too much so. He was always finding some poor soul to take on as what his mother fondly called his "special project."

His father's bay made good time closing the distance between them. William Barnett rode a horse as if born to it and had made certain his son could do the same. Robert couldn't help but admire his father's daring as he put the horse into a fast gallop and jumped the narrow ravine that divided the two sections of the north range.

"Ma would have your hide if she saw you do that," he said as the bay came to an abrupt halt about ten feet away.

"Your mother isn't out here, and I'll have *your* hide if you say anything to her about it," his father replied.

Robert grinned. "Yeah, well, I'd just as soon not have a tanning from either of you. So I guess I'll keep my mouth closed. What'd you find?"

"Most of the herd has stayed together on this side," he said. "There's a good mix of brands—Atherton's, Watson's, and ours for a good start. I saw a few head that belong to some of the smaller outfits, as well. We'll get 'em all sorted out at roundup."

Nodding, Robert turned his horse toward the south. "The cows seem to be in good shape. Most look to be expecting. Hopefully the weather will hold and we'll have a mild winter."

Father drew up alongside as they made their way back toward the ranch. "The talk at the Grange was that it would be."

"You been hangin' out at the Farmer's Association again?" he asked with a grin. "What will the other ranchers think?"

His father laughed. "My guess is they're listenin' to whoever will help them keep their stock alive and well fed.

"Plenty of good feed out here." Robert scanned the open grasslands. A carpet of brown and gold had replaced the rich greens of summer. He breathed in the surprisingly dry air and smiled. This was his home, his land. His parents had long ago told him of their plan to pass it on to him, and in turn he had developed a deep love of all that he could see.

"That smile on account of the party tonight?" his father asked.

The comment pulled Robert's thoughts back to the immediate. "Not exactly."

"I thought maybe you were thinking of a particular young lady. You know the holiday season is a good time to propose."

"I know that everyone figures that's where my mind is most of the time," Robert replied.

"Well, it's long been figured that you and Jessica Atherton would marry. Now that she's just had her nineteenth birthday, I thought maybe you two would be makin' an announcement." His father threw him a wry smile.

"Yeah, well, folks have been figurin' a lot of things that aren't necessarily so," Robert countered. "As far as I'm concerned, Jessica is too young and too spoiled."

"She'll grow up fast enough. Besides, you're twenty-seven. You ought to settle down and start a family. You're gonna need a good number of sons to help you keep up with this spread."

Robert considered the comment. It wasn't that he didn't want to have a family, especially a wife. He'd long been desirous of that very thing, but he loved Jessica Atherton like a sister, not a woman to marry.

"Pa, I . . . well . . . Jess and I don't have a lot in common. I care about her, don't get me wrong."

He shifted his weight in the saddle and realized his back and shoulders were weary of the ride. By the look of the sun's position he'd been in the saddle for nearly eight hours without many breaks.

"What are you sayin', son?"

"I'm sayin' that I don't know that I can marry her. She

doesn't want a ranching life. She's told me over and over that she wants to live in a big city with loads of servants and free time." He shook his head. It was hard to even imagine such a life and how a man might fit into the scheme of things. "I know some people expect us to marry. Mostly her ma and mine, but honestly, I don't know that I want to spend the rest of my life with her."

"Marriage is a real important thing, son. You don't want to be toying with the girl's affections if you don't intend to do the honorable thing." His father's weathered face bore considerable concern.

"I've never toyed with her affections, Pa. I haven't even kissed her." He felt his face grow hot. The topic had suddenly become embarrassing. Truth was he'd not kissed any girl other than his mother and sisters. He'd had plenty of chances, but his mother and father had always put into his heart the need for chastity and caution when it came to stirring up romantic feelings.

"I didn't mean to suggest you hadn't treated her right. I just want you to be sure that you don't lead her on."

"I don't think Jessica loves me any more than I love her. We're just like brother and sister or good friends. And I hope we will always be that—after all, we grew up knowing each other's families. We're all close, and I don't want to lose that."

His father nodded. "Well, make sure of your heart. I know you've long taken up the affairs of the broken and wounded. Don't let your heart be swayed by guilt or worry over what folks will think. She'll recover a lot faster if you just lay it on the line with her. I don't want to see either of you compromising or giving in just to keep the other from feeling bad."

"I just don't know for sure what I'm supposed to do."

"Have you prayed on it?" his father asked.

"I have. I still am."

William Barnett smiled. "Good. I'm glad to hear it. Maybe tonight at the party you'll get a feel for what you're supposed to do."

"Christmas seems a bad time of year to tell someone you aren't gonna marry them, especially when everyone figures you will."

"Christmas is still two weeks away, and the truth is never something to be delayed. Think about it, son. You may have more feelings for her than you realize. Might be that the expectations are what's clouding your heart. Give it to the Lord and see where He wants to take you."

Father was right, of course. He always offered wise counsel, and Robert would do well to heed it. Still, he hated to hurt Jessica. She might be a pampered child, but she was still deserving of genteel consideration, and he did care about her. Putting the matter to the back of his mind, Robert gave his father a grin and touched his spurs to his mount.

"Right now He wants to take me home to some of Ma's great cooking. Race you back!" His sorrel gelding shot forward in a streak of red.

Chapter 3

Alice gave a quick glance in the mirror to check her blond hair before heading out to wait tables at the Denver Daily Diner. She'd been blessed to get a job so quickly, despite her scarred face. The owner, Frank Bellows, told her that it didn't matter to him. The clients he catered to were mostly rough and rugged railroad men whose aim was to eat quickly and get back to work. She could still hear the words of Mr. Bellows: *"You're still kind of pretty—enough to entice them to buy an extra piece of pie. Just keep your face turned to the right and maybe they won't notice the scar."*

But Alice knew that wasn't enough. The scar was still noticeable, although after a year it was finally starting to fade. Marty's idea to use whale oil on the scar had helped in a most remarkable way.

Touching her fingers to the line that ran from just below her earlobe to her chin, Alice couldn't help but relive the horrible moment. Memories of the night her attacker cut her

31

flooded her mind. She could almost smell his putrid breath and the stench of cigarettes.

"Place is filling up, Miss Chesterfield. Best get out there," Bellows said as he passed her on his way to the storeroom.

"Yes, sir." Alice pulled on a pinafore-style apron and tied it securely. She was grateful the man had been willing to take a chance on her, and she didn't want to let him down.

In the dining room the counter was already full. Some of the men had been waited on by Mr. Bellows and were happily focused on their meals, but others were waiting for attention.

She smiled and approached the counter. "Who's first?"

"Me," a burly man in oily denim announced. "I'll take the beef sandwich special—three of 'em." He drew out a large handkerchief from his pocket. Wiping his face, he quickly added, "Cup of coffee, too."

"Sure thing," Alice said.

"I'm next," a skinny but equally dirty man said, motioning Alice to the far end of the counter. "Give me a bowl of gravy and biscuits, a ham steak, and a glass of milk."

Alice jotted down the order and hurried to the next man. She took five orders in all before turning them over to the cook. By this time even more men had crowded into the small diner. It looked to be a very busy day.

Without regard for her aching back or sore feet, Alice maneuvered amidst the hungry men, dealing out menus and coffee like a gambler might deal cards. She smiled and for a time forgot about her scarred face. The men were hungry and didn't seem to care all that much that she was damaged. They were mainly interested in filling their empty bellies and getting back to work before the lunch whistle blew. No one wanted to risk losing a job in this economy.

"Order for four more beef sandwiches," she announced, putting two tickets on the cook's counter.

The man glared at her. He wasn't at all the pleasant sort. "I only got two hands," he told her.

Alice didn't wait to comment. She had a half dozen pie orders to deliver, and since desserts were something she had sole responsibility for, she didn't want to take time out for conversation.

By the end of the lunch rush, Alice felt like she had barely managed to meet the demands of the men. There was a great deal of improvement needed before things would run smoothly.

Hurrying to gather the dirty dishes and clear the tables, Alice nearly ran over Mr. Bellows. He reached out to steady her. "Whoa there, li'l gal."

"Sorry. I should have been looking where I was going."

He nodded toward the now-empty dining room. "You did a good job there. I have to say you surprised me."

She smiled. "Thank you. I know I'll get better with time."

"Tell Joe I said to get right on those dishes after he puts another batch of roasts in the oven."

Alice nodded and hurried with an armful of plates and cups to the kitchen sink. Joe, the cook and dishwasher, stood to one side of the room picking his teeth. He noticed her and frowned.

"Ain't no end to it."

Feeling self-conscious as he continued to stare at her face, Alice motioned toward the dishes. "Mr. Bellows asked me to tell you he needs those dishes done as soon as you get the roasts in the oven."

"I know my job. Nobody's gotta tell me." He pushed his hand back through his greasy hair. The man's slovenly appearance was only worse after working the noon rush.

Alice didn't like him, nor did she like the way he always seemed to be watching her. She didn't mean to be so judgmental, especially at their first meeting, but the way he watched her reminded her of Mr. Smith—almost as if he were studying her for some troublesome purpose.

Alice thought to apologize for offending the man, but she didn't want to encourage conversation, so she simply deposited the dishes on the counter and returned to the dining room for more.

With the tables finally clean, Alice set to sweeping the floors. She was just finishing when Mr. Bellows appeared in his coat and hat. "I'm taking the noon monies to the bank. We did good today. I'm sure you made some decent tips."

There hadn't been time to check, but Alice did feel the considerable weight of change in her skirt pockets. Mostly it was pennies, but even those added up. "I suppose so," she murmured.

"Good. I hope so. This job don't pay much, so those tips are gonna make all the difference. That'll encourage you to be extra nice to the fellows."

"Is it always this busy at noon?"

Bellows shrugged. "Not always. A lot of the married workers bring their own lunches and might stop by for hot coffee. Others are single and don't have anyone to look after them. Many who used to work for the railroad shops here are out of work now. It's anybody's guess as to when things will turn around. I figure the word got spread about you being here and most came out of curiosity. With any luck, they'll be back.

"When you've finished cleaning up in the front, you can head out. Tell Joe I'll be right back to handle any customers."

Alice nodded and watched Mr. Bellows leave. She was weary to the bone but glad to have a chance to earn a little money. She hurried to finish wiping down the counters and was just about ready to leave when she noticed Joe watching her again. Remembering Mr. Bellows's comment, Alice cleared her throat.

"Mr. Bellows said he'd be right back and will handle any customers once he returns." The man gave a brief nod but said nothing. He kept watching her with his piercing gaze, leaving Alice most uncomfortable.

A sense of dread crept up her spine. She hesitated a moment. "Is something wrong?"

He smiled. "Just wondered if you'd like to step out with me tonight. There's a good place a few blocks away where we could hear some music and maybe dance. Good food, too. I know you made some tips today, so maybe you could treat me to a cold beer or two."

The man's comment left Alice confused. "You . . . you want me to buy you a beer? Or two?"

"Sure and maybe some supper." He laughed. "I can't leave until after the roasts and pies finish baking, but I figure we could have ourselves a little fun."

Regaining her composure, Alice undid the ties of her apron. "I don't think so. I have responsibilities."

"You ain't married. I heard you tell that to Bellows. So you can't have that much to be responsible for." He once again pushed back his oily hair, as if it were the only thing out of place on his person. "I know how to show a gal a good time, and I can clean up good."

"I'm sorry. No." Alice hung her apron and went to retrieve her coat. "I'm expected at home." She pulled the coat on and hurriedly buttoned it. Then, retrieving her bonnet and securing it over her hair, she made her way toward the back of the kitchen.

Joe deliberately blocked her path to the door. "You're kind of uppity for a gal who's all marked up like that. Ain't like you can rely on your looks to get yourself hitched. You be nice to me, and I might even think about lettin' you be my steady gal. I don't much mind the scar, since you got a fetchin' backside."

Alice couldn't keep the surprise from her face. Her eyes widened and she stammered for words. "I . . . you can't be . . . Oh my . . ." She stopped attempting to make sense. "I have to go." She looked past him to the door, wishing she could somehow will herself outside. For a moment she feared he might try to force her to stay.

However, with a grunt, Joe shrugged and stepped away. "You'll change your tune soon enough. Ain't gonna be just any man who'll want you around—leastwise not the marryin' kind. No one's gonna want a wife lookin' like that."

Alice hurried past him and out the back door before he could say another word. The man was abominably rude, but she knew he was right. No decent man would want a disfigured woman. Tears came to her eyes, stinging as the December wind hit her face. She did her best to control her emotions, but this time of year was especially hard. It was only the second time she'd faced Christmas without any family of her own.

Pulling her coat tight, Alice fought to regain control of her thoughts. Joe was just one of those unpleasant sort of men who preyed on vulnerable women. His nonsense needn't upset her any more than it had. Alice was fully capable of taking care of the matter, and if he got out of hand, she would tell Mr. Bellows. Hopefully the proprietor would be so pleased with her service that he wouldn't brook such nonsense from his cook.

With her emotions back in check as she approached the orphanage, Alice vowed to put the matter behind her. It was just one incident, and now that Joe knew how she felt . . . well . . . they could put the discomfort aside and do their jobs.

Inside the orphanage Alice caught the aroma of freshly baked bread. It gave her a sense of security and welcome. Marty was a marvel at baking. Her biscuits were always light as a feather and her cinnamon rolls the best Alice had ever tasted. Making her way to the kitchen, Alice paused in the doorway to breathe in the scent as Marty peeked into the oven.

"Ah, you're here at last," Marty said as she pulled several loaves of bread from the oven.

"Yes, it was a busy lunch, and it took time to clean up afterward."

"I can well imagine. The railroads might be suffering, but life goes on, eh?" Marty put a pan of biscuits into the oven. "Supper will be in an hour. You probably want to go freshen up."

Alice nodded. "I do. I'm worn to the core. The job is much more difficult than being a maid for you." She gave a laugh. "I'm afraid Mrs. Landry was right—you spoiled me for proper work."

Marty joined in the chuckle. "She's Mrs. Brighton now, as you will recall, but I believe she was wrong. There isn't a spoiled bone in your body. Now take this kettle of hot water and go give your feet a good soaking." Marty wrapped a towel around the handle and pulled it from the stove. "You'll feel better in twenty minutes. Oh, and don't forget to add some peppermint oil to the water."

Alice took hold of the kettle. "I don't have to do that, Marty. I can stay here and help you prepare supper."

"I insist. There will be plenty of work for you to help with another day, but tonight you need to take it easy. Now go."

She didn't have the strength to argue. Instead, Alice made her way to the bedroom and did as Marty had suggested. The hot water was soothing to her aching feet, and she eased back into the chair and closed her eyes. The scent of peppermint wafted up from the steam, reminding her of her childhood.

"Can I have some candy?" she had asked her mother once when they'd been shopping. Alice couldn't have been more than five or six, but the memory was quite clear.

"Of course," her mother had answered, reaching for three peppermint sticks. *"You are my little princess, and you can have most anything your heart desires."*

Alice couldn't remember the details of her mother's face, but the scent and sweet taste of peppermint always reminded her of her mother. Pity the woman hadn't truly cared for her daughter. The last time Alice had seen her mother and little brother was now just a dim memory.

Since she was young, Alice had been told she favored her mother considerably. They both had blond hair and blue eyes, while Alice's younger brother, Simon, favored their father, with brown hair and blue eyes.

Alice had thought there'd been a special bond between mother and daughter. But since her mother seemed to have little difficulty deserting their home in the middle of the night with Simon in tow, Alice knew she couldn't have felt very strongly about her daughter.

How could a mother just walk away from her child? How could she leave Alice to fend for herself? To face abandonment and bitterness? Alice's father had been a bear to live with in the early days after Mother left. He'd raged against her mother, declaring her a heartless woman who had no concern for the pain she'd caused Alice. Father had lectured Alice daily about all of her mother's shortcomings. Little was mentioned about Simon, yet Alice missed him with all her heart. He had been her only sibling, and though he was eight years her junior, she had loved him dearly.

After a few months, Alice's father seemed to settle into their new life. He kept guarded watch over Alice, even hiring a woman to walk her to and from school. He gave strict orders that Alice never go outside without him. She wasn't sure why he demanded this but eventually decided he was afraid something might happen to her and then he'd be alone.

Alice continued to watch and hope that her mother and brother would return to them. She spoke of them whenever her father appeared to be in a good mood and often asked if he thought they'd ever come home. He always told her it was a hopeless desire.

In spite of her father's negative thinking, Alice would hurry home from school and ask if there'd been any word from Mother. She saw a mixture of pain and resentment cross his expression as he replied that there wasn't. Alice had longed to comfort him, but it seemed the only way to do that was to say nothing at all—to pretend Mother and Simon had never existed. It wasn't something she could easily do. She wanted them to come home. She wanted her father to go out and find them.

"Do you think maybe the sheriff could find them?" she had innocently asked her father one morning nearly a year after her mother's disappearance.

"No," her father had said adamantly. "He won't be of any help to us now. I've had word about them."

"You've heard from Mother?" Alice could still remember the feeling of hope. Her heart had been wrung like a wet towel, squeezing out the pain of loss and betrayal of abandonment until all that remained was the desperate desire of a child to see her mother again.

"I'm sorry, Alice. Your mother and brother are dead."

He said the words so matter-of-factly that for a moment they didn't even register. Alice forced meaning into the words, however, and her eyes filled with tears. "Dead? How? When?"

She thought her heart might actually stop beating. "Dead?"

"It was some sort of epidemic. I'm sorry. They died quickly and the authorities sent me word. That's all I intend to stay about the subject."

And that was all he would say. No matter Alice's pleading to know more, her father was determined that they put the matter behind them. To his dying day, he refused to ever allow Alice to mention her mother or brother again. It was as if they had simply been eradicated.

Chapter 4

Christmas morning found the orphans awake before dawn. Marty could hear them whispering and giggling from their separate dorm rooms. The boys were especially noisy in their space. Since there were ten boys and only five girls, it made sense they would be louder.

"I think we'd better hurry," Marty said, tucking her blouse into her skirt. "They don't sound any too patient."

"Given the promise of presents and goodies, you can hardly blame them," Alice replied. She finished braiding her hair and tied it off with a ribbon.

"Church comes first, though, and they know that full well."

Marty took up a jacket to match her dark blue wool skirt. Slipping her arms into the added warmth, she couldn't help but wonder if it had snowed again in the night. She could still remember her first Colorado snow and how she and Jake had thrown snowballs at each other. The memory caused her heart to ache. How she missed him.

But she didn't want to miss him. She wanted not to care

that he was gone. God had been her mainstay through these difficult weeks, but Jake was never far from her thoughts. Now she would face Christmas without him. Without any word from him. Marty frowned.

"Is something wrong?" Alice asked.

"Nothing that hasn't been wrong for a while now."

"Mr. Wythe?"

"Jake. Just call him Jake," Marty insisted. "And yes, I suppose there's no sense in pretending otherwise."

Alice smiled. "It's only because you love him so dearly."

Marty buttoned her jacket and turned away to take up a handkerchief. "My love means very little to him. But let's not fret over things we cannot change. It's time to ready the children for the morning service. Hopefully they've managed to start dressing themselves."

She headed out of the room, hoping Alice would let the matter drop. She didn't want to talk about Jake and how much it hurt to be without him.

Mr. Brentwood was already busy with the boys. "We were out early to clear the walkways of snow," he told her. He had most of the ten wearing their clean Sunday clothes and was working to get everyone to comb their hair. Marty had to smile at the question posed by seven-year-old Wyatt.

"Why do we have to wear our Sunday clothes again today? It's Monday."

"But," Mr. Brentwood replied with infinite patience, "we are going to church again to celebrate the birth of our Lord Jesus. Remember what we talked about yesterday?"

Wyatt looked at the other boys, ranging in age from four to eleven, and nodded with a sigh. "We gotta go to church two times 'cause it's Christmas."

Marty smiled. "And you want to look your best."

"Can God see us even when we're not wearin' our best?" ten-year-old Thad asked.

Mr. Brentwood straightened from combing the hair of a rather rambunctious four-year-old named Benjamin. "God can see us everywhere—all the time."

Thad shrugged. "Then why does He care which clothes I wear? He's already seen the others."

Marty ducked her face to avoid the gaze of the children. She thought she might well burst into laughter at any moment and pretended instead to fuss with her buttons. How the children lightened her weary heart.

"God doesn't really care which clothes we wear. We're doing this to honor Him—to show Him that we're willing to take extra care to clean up and look our best for Him." Mr. Brentwood cleared his throat. "Now, remember what I said. We will eat our breakfast and open gifts when we return. If you misbehave in church, you will miss out on the fun. So remember the rules about being in God's house: No talking. No running. No fussing or fighting. We owe God our respect."

This sobered all ten of the boys in the wink of an eye. They nodded, assuring their compliance. Marty raised her gaze and nodded, as well. "You all look very nice. I think we should make our way downstairs and get our coats."

The boys hurried to line up. Wyatt came to tug on Marty's jacket. "Can I walk with you?"

Marty smiled. The boy had become one of her favorites. "Of course."

"Me too?" six-year-old Sam asked. His little brother, Benjamin, nodded rapidly in agreement. They had been in the orphanage for about five months, dropped off by their father after the death of their mother. They always seemed to crave Marty's attention.

"You too. In fact, I'll be right there with all of you," Marty declared. "I love to celebrate Christmas and sing carols. You know, we could probably sing a Christmas carol on the way to church."

"I think that's a splendid idea," Mr. Brentwood said, beaming Marty a smile. "Let's sing 'Silent Night.'"

They were joined downstairs by the girls and Alice. When everyone had their coats and hats on, Mr. Brentwood led the way. Marty mused that the children were rather like a group of little ducks waddling after their father.

The children sang at the tops of their lungs, a little off-key but nevertheless filled with joy. Marty couldn't remember when she'd enjoyed Christmas so much. Indeed, she'd nearly forgotten that just five years earlier she'd been made a widow when her first husband, Thomas, died on Christmas Eve.

How did the day get past me?

Marty fell silent as she considered the matter. The last year had been such a busy time. It wasn't that she hadn't contemplated her years with Thomas or the tragic accident that claimed his life, but her marriage to Jake had changed her focus. Jake's kindness and gentle nature had eased her pain and filled some of the empty holes. Not all of them, of course. She would always remember Thomas. Her love for him was something special. But so, too, was her love for Jake. Maybe that's why it bothered her so much to imagine that he didn't care about her feelings.

She had hoped to hear something from him by now. Especially since it was Christmas. But there hadn't been any word at all. Marty found herself regretting the harsh words she'd spoken to him before their parting. She wished she could take back the ones spoken in anger—in fear, really.

What am I afraid of?

She almost laughed out loud at the question. The answer wasn't at all difficult. *I'm afraid of losing Jake like I lost Thomas.*

But haven't I already lost him?

The question haunted her throughout the church service, and the joy she'd originally felt for the celebration waned. She was at war with herself. She hadn't really lost him. But she had refused his solution. What obedient wife would do such a thing?

But he knows how I feel about Texas. And now it's more important than ever before.

"Wise men from the east followed the star," the minister declared. "They followed it because they knew what they would find at the end of their search. They knew they would find the Christ child."

The children fidgeted but didn't make a sound. All the normal problems of sitting too close to each other or of needing to share a comment were banished at the thought of missing out on the Christmas festivities.

"So what is it that *you* are searching for?" the minister asked.

Marty felt the question prick her conscience. *What am I searching for?* The uneasiness that had threatened to engulf her since Jake's departure reared its ugly head as if to answer.

You want everything your own way, a voice seemed to accuse. *You are so unworthy of anyone's love. You are selfish—a liar—a schemer. Even God has cast you aside.*

Marty frowned and lowered her head. She felt tears come to her eyes. Was it the devil who tormented her? Had God given up on her? She hadn't been willing to see Jake's side of the disagreement. Certainly he could have sought ranch work in Colorado, but there was something to be said for returning to those who already knew you and knew your abilities.

"Sometimes we search for what has been lost," the minister continued. "But sometimes it is we who are lost and who are searching to be found. Maybe you have lost your way today. I want to encourage you to remember that it was through the birth of Jesus that we were given hope. It is through Jesus that we are found. Believe in Him and be saved. Believe that Jesus came as a babe in a manger, innocent and pure. Believe that He grew into a man who took on the guilt and filth of your sins and mine and died upon a cross. Believe!"

The choir stood to sing, and Marty silently prayed that God would help her to make better choices—to be obedient to both Jake and to God. It was a prayer she had prayed many times before. *I want to do what's right, Father. I want to live in a way that would be pleasing to you. Help me, please. I know I can't face the future without you.*

★

The children were happily stuffing themselves with sweets and playing with their Christmas gifts when Mr. Brentwood approached Marty and Alice.

"I believe the wooden blocks and dolls were a success," Marty said, smiling. She and Alice had worked to create five rag dolls for the girls, and Mr. Brentwood had arranged for the wooden building blocks to be cut and sanded. Painting them had been a time-consuming project, but Marty and Alice had mastered the task in love.

"I believe you are right. That is the joy of having nothing—even something small seems a great treasure. Speaking of which, I have something for you," he said, smiling at Marty in particular.

"For me?"

He nodded and handed Marty a neatly folded shawl. "I couldn't afford wrapping for it, but I knew you'd understand."

Marty unfolded the material to reveal a beautifully crafted piece. "This is lovely, Mr. Brentwood, but I don't understand." She looked to him and saw his eyes light up and his smile broaden.

"It was knit by a poor Irish woman. She was selling her wares near the capitol, and I thought, well, I thought the color would be wonderful for your . . . eyes."

Marty looked at the light blue yarn and nodded. "I love it." She glanced at Alice. "The workmanship is quite impressive."

As if remembering that they weren't alone, Mr. Brentwood handed Alice something. "I purchased this for you."

Alice smiled at the dark green scarf. "How lovely. You are too kind. I have nothing to exchange, I'm afraid."

"I wouldn't expect a gift from either of you. Your presence here has been a wonderful gift for me. I don't know what we would have done without you," he said, looking at Marty. Then he quickly added, "Both of you."

"We feel the same way about you and the orphanage," Alice replied before Marty could find her tongue. "Being allowed to stay here has been quite beneficial."

"Indeed it has," Marty said, growing a little uncomfortable. She hadn't thought about it before, but now she couldn't help but wonder if Mr. Brentwood was coming to depend on them too much. After all, as soon as she and Alice could figure out what their future held, they would need to be on their way.

"I'm quite blessed," the man said as he rubbed his hands together. "With you here, I can take a little time to solicit funds for the orphanage. I plan to do so immediately after today. People tend to be in a giving mood around Christmas. If I can secure pledges of monthly support, I can rehire at least one worker. For instance, I could offer you a salary, Mrs. Wythe."

"Nonsense," Marty replied. "I am working for room and board. That's more than fair. What you need is your former staff. They are better trained at the workings of an orphanage."

"But the children clearly love you," Mr. Brentwood said, glancing over his shoulder. He looked back at Marty and Alice. "You have made them feel loved and cared for."

Marty didn't want to ruin the day so she let the matter drop. In time, she would remind Mr. Brentwood that her presence at the orphanage was only temporary.

"Now, if you'll excuse me," Marty said, "I have work to do. The children need something other than sweets and sandwiches and it will soon be time for supper." She made her way to the kitchen, still clutching the shawl. Alice was right behind her.

"Is something wrong?" the younger woman asked once they were alone.

"I can't really say." Marty carefully placed her gift on a chair and went to put on her apron. "I suddenly felt uneasy. I'm worried that Mr. Brentwood is coming to depend on us too much. I fear he will expect us to remain here forever."

"At least you," Alice said, raising a brow. "He cares for you."

"He cares for us both," Marty protested. She took down a mixing bowl. "Would you retrieve the chicken and broth we put in the icebox and get it warming on the stove? I'm going to make dumplings."

Alice hesitated. "Marty, you do realize that his feelings for you are different than they are for me. I might only be eighteen, but I can see that the man adores you."

Marty laughed. "You're being silly, Alice. He's just grateful for the help. I gave money and time to his cause. That's what he loves."

Alice took hold of Marty's arm but then just as quickly let go. "I suppose I could be wrong, but I've seen the way he looks at you. He doesn't look at anyone else that way. I think he's fallen in love with you."

"He's knows full well I'm a married woman. Goodness, he made these arrangements with Jake. Mr. Brentwood is an honorable man—a godly man. He wouldn't dream of defiling me that way."

Alice shrugged. "I don't think he has defiling in mind, but I do think he has deep feelings for you."

Marty turned away and placed the bowl on the counter. Alice was young and impressionable. No doubt her girlish ideals saw romance at every turn. Opening the flour bin, Marty retrieved a large sifter full of flour. She hoped that Alice would put the silly notions from her mind and realize that Mr. Brentwood held nothing more than respect for her.

★

Alice decided to leave well enough alone. She had planted thoughts in Marty's mind, and now she would pray that Marty would understand the truth before it was too late. Alice had no doubt that Mr. Brentwood was relying on Marty to ease the pain of having lost his wife not so very long ago. Perhaps he wasn't even conscious of what he was doing.

Supper passed by easily with the weary children almost happy to head for bed when the hour finally came. Mr. Brentwood gathered everyone together for prayer, and afterward Alice and Marty got the children tucked in for the night. With their work done, the women settled down before the fireplace in their room and breathed a collective sigh.

Marty quickly picked up a shirt to mend, while Alice took up her crocheting. Outside, the wind had picked up and chilled the drafty room. Alice paused in her work to add another log to the fire. She thought of Christmases when she was little. She'd been happy then with both mother and father to offer love and care.

I miss them both—so much. Walking to the window, Alice pulled back the curtain and looked out into the night. There was a slight glow coming from the windows of the house next door. It offered enough light to reveal it was snowing again.

"The first Christmas I can remember was right after my father went away," Marty said, as if Alice had asked a question. "We didn't yet know that he was dead. I was five years old and my sister Hannah—she was much older than I—she raised me after my mother died. . . ." Marty paused.

Alice returned to her chair by the fire. "Yes, I remember. I've always thought that a tremendous blessing."

"It was." Marty smiled. "That year she made clothes for my doll, and one of the dresses was an exact match for a dress she made for me. I thought it was the most wonderful thing in the world. That is, until I saw my brother's present." She shook her head. "Andy got a horse and saddle. I was so jealous. Especially when he commented that he was a real rancher now. I declared to everyone that I was a real rancher, too. I told them I had a horse and could rope. I was always given to lies and exaggerations."

"What did your sister do?"

"She reminded me that I was being untruthful. I remember telling her that I had spied a horse in the pen that I liked a lot and decided that one was mine. She told me that the horses belonged to Will, and I couldn't just go picking one out and deciding it was mine." She smiled, remembering.

"That Christmas was very special, in spite of Pa's absence. I felt safe and happy. Maybe Pa's being gone was part of the reason. He wasn't a very happy man. Hannah told me that after Mama died he changed completely."

"My father changed after my mother went away, too," Alice remembered. "He had always been a very strong man—focused on his work and dedicated to whatever task was before him. He was sometimes rather stern with us, and I remember he could be quite angry at times."

"Even before your mother left?"

"Yes." Alice closed her eyes for a moment. "But I remember Christmases before my mother went away. A special one was when my brother Simon was just three or four. We weren't rich, by any means, but we had plenty. That year mother bought Simon a wooden train set. He loved it and scooted it across the floor for hours on end." She laughed lightly. "He would make chugging noises and toot like a train whistle."

Marty put one shirt aside and picked up another. "Boys make a lot more noise than girls do. Or rather, I suppose I should say *different* noises than girls do."

"Yes." Alice felt the memory fading.

"What did you receive for Christmas that year?"

Marty's question brought back the images. "I got a new china doll with the most beautiful satin gown and a wonderful bonnet trimmed with feathers and lace. She had long brown ringlets that spilled down her back. She made me wish I had brown hair." Alice met Marty's gaze. "I don't know what ever happened to her. I suppose she might have been sold with most of our other things after the attack."

"I'm sorry. I can't imagine how hard that must have been for you."

Marty's words betrayed her affection for Alice and it made the younger woman smile.

"It would have been awful enough to have suffered such a heinous attack, but to wake up in the hospital and realize all that you'd known was gone . . . I can't imagine how hard that would be."

"It was difficult," Alice admitted. "I felt so ill from the infection and was very weak. The doctor wasn't certain I would recover. My friends from church were good to visit and to encourage me to keep fighting. But I knew Father was dead, and since Mother and Simon were, too, I figured the best thing for me would be to die, as well. I knew there was nothing to go home to. Later, when I found out there wasn't even a home left, I was truly lost in despair."

"I can only imagine the nightmare of losing everything."

Alice shook off the thoughts. "It's Christmas, and we really shouldn't be sad. We've a warm place to sleep, food in our stomachs, and despite the crisis going on all around the country, we are safe. If not for the threat of Mr. Smith's constant harangues, it would be nearly perfect."

"Yes, well, hopefully with the new year, Mr. Smith will lose track of you entirely. He hasn't come to the diner, has he?"

"No. Not yet, but I have to admit I am in constant expectation."

"At least then you won't be surprised by his appearance," Marty offered.

"I suppose I'm more surprised when each day passes and I don't see him lingering off in the shadows somewhere."

Marty reached over and patted Alice's still hands. "God will see us through. He will protect you. I feel confident of His watchful eye on you and me."

Alice nodded and gave a sigh. "I just wish God would

remove Mr. Smith from our lives completely. I have nothing to give him. No possible means of helping him find what he feels is his." Alice thought of the things Jake had told her. "I can't imagine my father as being corrupted enough to forge gold certificates. Someone must have threatened him to make him choose such a path."

"Well, given Mr. Smith's threats to you, do you doubt that might be the case?"

Alice shook her head. "My memories of those days seem even more blurred than those of long ago. It's as if the accident robbed me of thought. Even so, I remember my father's nervousness at the time—and his fearfulness. It wasn't like him at all."

"Men often do things they don't want to do . . ." Marty started and then fell silent.

"You're thinking of Mr. Wythe . . . of Jake."

Marty nodded. "Yes, I suppose I am. He never wanted to be a banker. His father pressured him to finish his university studies and make a different plan for his life. Jake, however, wanted nothing more than to be a rancher."

"And return to Texas," Alice said more than questioned.

"Yes."

Alice offered Marty a look of sympathy. "God will provide the answers and direction. We have to remember that, whether it's in our dealings with Mr. Smith or with Jake."

"Or with Texas," Marty murmured.

"Yes," Alice agreed. "Or Texas."

Chapter 5

Marty decided that the time had come to part with the last of her finer clothes. She had tucked away her two last gowns in a trunk, hoping to somehow hang on to them. They were her favorites, but with a new year upon them, there were new needs.

Sickness abounded and medicines were necessary to help the children recover. The doctor's expenses alone ate away at the monies Mr. Brentwood had budgeted for the month of January. Marty felt it was her duty to sacrifice these last treasures. What good were two gowns packed away in a trunk to neither be worn nor displayed?

With Mr. Brentwood busy teaching the children, Marty and Alice each took one of the luxurious gowns in a folded bundle and headed to the dressmaker's store near the Capitol Hill neighborhood. There was a small shop at the front of an establishment where the woman often advertised remade clothing as well as new pieces. It was here Marty had sold her other gowns and hoped the woman might take these, as well.

Snow covered the lawns and walkways like icing on a cake. The sun on the vast white sea caused the snow to sparkle and gleam. It was almost painful to the eye.

"I certainly never knew anything like this in Texas," she said, her warm breath making clouds in the cold air.

"I like to imagine the warmth," Alice said amidst the chattering of her teeth.

"Everything looks so clean, so untouched." Marty marveled at the landscape. "And isn't it something how the snow muffles the city sounds?" They had just reached the shop and, anxious to leave the cold behind, hurried inside.

"I didn't think to see you again," the middle-aged matron declared. She wore her hair in a tight bun and looked quite severe, yet Marty knew her to be very friendly.

"I don't imagine I will be back after this. I have brought you my last two gowns. They were my favorites," Marty declared, placing one of the gowns on the counter.

The woman eyed the silk material and lace and smiled. "It is most beautiful. I know a woman who would pay very well for this piece. She has purchased several of your gowns."

Alice put the other dress on the counter, as well. "How can anyone afford such opulence at a time like this?"

The woman made a *tsk*ing sound. "Remember, not everyone was solely dependent upon silver. There are a good many folks who put their money into more profitable situations." The woman unfolded the dusty rose gown that Alice had brought.

"The workmanship is so perfect. I remember Mrs. Davies very well. Pity she took ill and died. Her talent will be sorely missed."

Marty nodded. "Yes."

The woman continued to look over the pieces. She finally

drew her glasses down on her nose. "I will give you five dollars for both."

"Ten," Marty countered. This was their routine, and she wasn't afraid to barter.

"Seven," the woman replied.

"Eight." Marty smiled. "I must help buy medicine for the orphans. You wouldn't want to deny them, would you?"

"Ah, you will be the end of me. If I weren't confident of reselling these to my client, I would show you the door." Nevertheless, she smiled. "Eight it is."

Marty collected the money and let her hand trail one last time along the rose-colored silk. "Those were interesting and glorious times, but I shan't miss them. Not really."

Alice followed her outside. "Not even a little?"

Marty laughed. "It was quite amazing to try my hand at living the life of ease and opulence, but it wasn't for me. I need to keep busy. I was always kept busy as a child—probably to keep me out of trouble more than the true need of having me work."

"It served you well," Alice said. "Look at all you are capable of doing. You sew and cook, you can handle reading and writing. My handwriting is terrible, but I do love to read."

"I can also handle a team of horses, brand, and rope, and ride as well as any man," Marty declared. "And that isn't exaggerating." She gave a laugh. "I was determined to match my brother, Andy, at anything. Even so, women on our ranch worked just as hard as the men. We kept massive gardens and canned and smoked food. We had chickens and milk cows, even a few of our own pigs, although the men preferred wild boar and would go east to hunt them every fall."

"It sounds like a very fulfilling life. I think I would like the wide open spaces." She glanced westward toward the Rockies. "I find the mountains beautiful but foreboding. I've never cared much for the cold weather and snow." She shivered. "I think I would like your Texas."

"It's not mine," Marty snapped. She gave Alice an apologetic look. "I'm sorry. For all the good I knew in Texas, I knew equal parts of sorrow and heartache."

"Losing your husband when that bull gored him must have been the worst."

"It was one of the worst," Marty admitted. "The miscarriages of my unborn children were equally sorrowful. I always wanted a big family—Thomas did, as well."

"I'm sorry, Marty." Alice touched her arm, and Marty stopped walking. "I know losing your babies must have been a terrible thing. Maybe one day God will give you and Jake children. You mustn't let the past keep you from being hopeful for the future."

The icy cold wind whipped at their long wool coats, but still Marty did not move. She looked Alice in the eye. "I'm pregnant."

"What?" Alice's eyes widened at the news. "Truly?"

Marty nodded. "I spoke with the doctor when he came to care for the children."

"Does Jake . . . does Jake know?"

Marty swallowed a feeling of guilt. "No. I thought there was a possibility before he left, but I didn't want that to be the reason he stayed. I plan to tell him, but since we've had no word . . . well . . . I don't have any way to get in touch."

Alice's surprise seemed to leave her speechless. Marty knew the young woman couldn't possibly understand the fears that filled Marty's soul.

"Well, it seems to me," Alice finally began, "that maybe

you should go live with your sister. You don't want to be doing a lot of heavy work while you're carrying the baby."

"I also don't know about risking travel and the problems that living in the South can bring."

"What do you mean?"

"It is said that the further south you live the greater the chance you have of miscarriage," Marty replied. "The doctor told me he believed such things were 'Pure hogwash,' to quote him, but there are those in the South who believe that the closer one lives to the equator, the stronger the pull of gravity. They believe it can pull a child right from the womb. I lost several babies in Texas. I don't think I can risk another."

"Oh, Marty, I'm so sorry. I know this is hard for you, but it's also such a happy thing."

Marty looked away and fixed her gaze down the snowy street. "I want to be happy, but I'm so afraid. I want this child very much."

"Then we will do what we can to ensure you remain healthy. Did the doctor offer any advice?"

"Nothing beyond the normal things: no heavy lifting, caution when walking in the snow and ice, eat beneficially and regularly."

"Have you told Mr. Brentwood yet?"

"No, I don't plan to tell anyone. At least not for a while. Honestly, Alice, I don't want anyone to know. I'm not that far along—not even starting to show. I'd rather just wait and see what happens. If I get past the next month, then perhaps I'll say something."

"But what about Jake? You will tell him, won't you?"

Marty bit her lower lip and said nothing. Alice took hold of both arms and turned Marty to face her. "You have to tell Jake. He's your husband—the father. He has a right to know."

She was right. There would be no avoiding the subject if Marty proved capable of carrying the child to delivery. But so many miscarriages, so many disappointments stood between her and the ability to share this news.

"When the time is right," Marty finally whispered. "Then I'll tell him. For now, you must swear to me that you'll say nothing."

Alice hesitated a moment but then finally gave a nod. "I'll say nothing . . . for now."

★

Alice couldn't help but dwell on the news throughout the rest of the day. Marty was going to have a baby. The thought delighted and terrified her. She had to find a way to get Marty and Jake back together. A woman in such a condition needed her man, and Marty definitely needed Jake.

Not only that, but Alice feared the emotions that were growing in Mr. Brentwood. Marty might be blind to his devotion, but Alice could see that he had lost his heart to Marty. She knew him to be an honorable man, just as Marty had said, but she also knew that honor could give way under the pressures of life. Wasn't that what had happened to her mother and father? Honor certainly hadn't kept them together.

Alice walked in silence alongside Marty as they made their way down Fourteenth Street to catch the tram. As they approached the corner of Sherman Street, however, Marty took a turn.

"Where are you going?" Alice asked.

"I thought it might be nice to walk through the old neighborhood. Just to see what's what and whether anyone is still there," Marty replied. "I heard that the Tabors lost all of their money in the panic."

"Everything has changed in such a short time," Alice said, shaking her head. Many of the grand homes were deserted—their wrought-iron gates locked tight. Gone were the bustling activities of visiting and sharing in one another's luxuries. The Queen City of the Plains had sadly succumbed to the devastating financial epidemic sweeping the country. Poverty was an infectious disease.

"Do you suppose the people will ever come back?"

Marty shrugged. "Jake said these things always seem to run in cycles. Those who were diverse in their investments will ride this out like they have before. Others will be destroyed."

A carriage approached from the opposite direction, and Alice recognized one of the city's socialites, Mrs. Kountze, staring out her carriage window. Their opulent mansion at Sixteenth Avenue and Grant Street was said to be the most ostentatious and grand of all Denver homes. Alice knew Marty had attended several affairs at the Kountze estate, yet the occupants of the carriage did not so much as signal the driver to slow.

"Glory is fleeting, but obscurity is forever," Marty murmured.

"What does that mean?" Alice questioned.

Marty smiled. "It means that we are once again nothing more to the Kountzes than the dust beneath their feet." She smiled. "Napoleon Bonaparte once said it. He had his glory and fame, his wealth and successes, but also his failings and defeats. I suppose that is a part of everyone's life in one degree or another."

Alice nodded. "It certainly was so in my life. I always fancied I would marry a man who was amply positioned—perhaps a bank employee like my father. I thought I would be a wife and mother and live in relative comfort." A tiny laugh escaped. "Guess it was only one of my many mistaken assumptions."

"We have all had them," Marty admitted. "Some of us more than others."

Alice took hold of her arm. "Come on. Let's get out of here and catch the tram home. I'm freezing and you need to take better care of yourself now that you're to be a mother."

Marty gave Alice a look that suggested being a mother might well be yet another mistaken assumption. Alice refused to let Marty's worries control the moment, however. "When we get back to the orphanage I will make you some hot tea."

Marty smiled. "Or I will make you a cup. We are equals now—sisters really. No longer employee and employer."

Alice smiled. "Sisters? I like that idea. I've always wanted a sister."

★

That evening, Marty sat watching flames dance in the bedroom hearth. She absentmindedly placed her hand over her stomach and pondered the possibilities. Would God allow her to carry this child to term? She was already further along than the previous times.

She thought of Jake and wondered if he would be happy at the news. No doubt he would be delighted. He had once mentioned wanting children. It was strange how their marriage had come about from a simple newspaper advertisement, but now it was more precious to Marty than she could have ever imagined.

We were only going to be good friends, she remembered. Companions who would ease the loneliness of having lost their spouses. Companions who would say and do all the proper things expected of them by society.

Marty remembered the snubbing she'd received by the Kountzes earlier in the day. It wasn't the first. There had been several occasions when she'd been downtown and her former so-called friends had turned away as if ashamed. Marty was not from a famous family or a well-moneyed background. Her Texas family was better off than many, but only because they had worked long and hard at ranching.

Thoughts of Hannah and Will came to mind. She knew she owed her sister a letter. Hannah had written the week before to beg Marty to come back to Texas. Marty had told her of Jake's decision to head to Texas for work while she remained behind in Denver with Alice. Hannah didn't like the idea and thought it much too dangerous. She even said that Will had a position for Jake and that Marty should tell him right away.

"But I can't tell him if I don't know how to reach him."

It was over a month since he'd gone and still she had no word. Perhaps he had been killed or wounded. Maybe he had given up on Marty and simply disappeared.

"And if he has, what will I do then?" she whispered to no one.

The thought of being alone—truly alone—frightened her. Here at the orphanage in the company of so many, Marty was too busy to feel lonely. But what would happen when she began showing? Would people assume a dalliance with Mr. Brentwood? Even Alice thought there were feelings on his part, though Marty was certain she was wrong. Still, two women living at the orphanage with a widower was hardly the best of circumstances.

Time was slipping away, and Marty knew it wouldn't be long before she would be forced to make a decision. Why did these things have to be so hard? Why did she always have to face the worst of it alone?

But you aren't alone. The whispered words fell across her heart like balm.

She smiled and drew in a long deep breath. "No, I'm not alone. I have the Lord. I have Alice." She gently rubbed her stomach. "And for now . . . I have you."

Chapter 6

Robert Barnett always enjoyed the ride over Fort Worth way. Today was no exception. The weather was beautiful and the humidity low. He preferred Fort Worth to Dallas, even though the ride was longer. Fort Worth was like wearing a pair of comfortable boots and old jeans, while Dallas felt more like donning your Sunday best. It was all a matter of preference, he supposed. As Robert recalled, his younger sisters preferred Dallas.

"Looks to be a good turnout for the sale," his father said, interrupting Robert's thoughts.

Robert had also noticed the swelling crowd. "You gonna buy some of those Aberdeen Angus this time around?"

"I'd sure like to. I've heard great things about them. They're a hardy bunch, and the calves are thicker, heavier at weaning time. Seems we ought to at least give it a try. Wanna stay away from those Durhams, though. I read in the *Journal* there are too many birth defects with them. Last thing we want is to put a bunch of calves down."

"I'm guessin' we'll find both here at the sale." Robert had been attending cattle sales with his father for as long as he could remember. Sometimes his mother even came along and enjoyed a day of shopping, but not this time. "I have to say I'm partial to the flavor the Angus-longhorn crossbred gives. I think we'd do well to incorporate the breed into our herds."

"Seems most folks here agree with you." A number of men were already gathered around the Black Angus sale pen. "Guess I'd better be ready to part with a good bit of money."

A year ago the Stock Raisers Association had changed their name to the Cattle Raisers Association of Texas and headquartered themselves in Fort Worth. Robert was glad to hear about the change now that they were able to participate with the group on a regular basis. Such associations were beneficial and made ranchers stronger as they stood together. This association had seen them through the closed-range issues, the drought of the '80s, and the recent economic failures and drought of the '90s. Issues of disease, the introduction of new breeds, and innovations for raising profitability were also addressed. Robert found the information of great use, as did his father.

"Where'd Mr. Atherton and Mr. Reid get off to?" Robert asked after his father finished the business of registering with the salespeople.

"Lookin' at horses. Brandon Reid is always lookin' to improve his herd. The man's gained himself a reputation as an expert on horseflesh."

Robert nodded. The mount he rode today was sired by a Reid stallion. The sorrel stood sixteen hands high and was a mix of Thoroughbred and American Paint. Robert had never known a cow horse with better instinct. The gait was easy, too. Robert could sit for hours in the saddle. He'd owned the horse since it was a colt and had been the only one to break and ride him. Aunt Marty had teased him about the horse he affectionately called Rojoe, a play on the Spanish word *rojo*—meaning red. When Robert had first learned to read Spanish, he had insisted the word was pronounced with a strong J sound instead of the H the Spanish used. Marty had given him such a hard time about it that it had become a running joke.

"We'll all meet up for the discussion on increasing profits. I can't say there's much hope during this panic, but you never know," Robert's father said, moving to remount his black. "Meanwhile, I'd like to take a look at some of those Angus."

The day passed in a flurry of activities. Robert went with his father to consider the Angus, after which the older man was determined to buy a young bull and three breeder cows. They looked into some of the other breeds, listened to the lectures on how to survive the lack of water and decent range grass, saw some of the new barbed wire available for fencing, and heard a highly regarded veterinarian speak on a new dip to eradicate Texas tick fever.

Robert listened as his father made deals on new watering tanks and lumber for building another barn and pen, as well as other supplies. Sometimes William Barnett allowed his son to barter for some of the ranch needs, but most often Robert simply accompanied his father. He had learned a great deal by keeping his mouth closed and his eyes and ears open. It was to his benefit that his father handled business and helped Robert establish relationships and connections in the industry.

Of course the Cattle Raisers Association was in and of itself a school of training for the men who sought to make a living raising Texas cattle. The state's weather could be ruthless and unforgiving—sending droughts, floods, tornadoes, and even blizzards. The ranchers had endured a great deal over the years, and only by helping one another learn from their mistakes, banding together in difficult times, and making changes to how operations were managed had they thrived.

"Ready to grab something to eat?" Tyler Atherton asked Will.

Robert felt a little uneasy around the man many presumed would one day become his father-in-law. He'd grown up as just another one of the Barnett children, but as his mother conspired with Tyler's wife, Carissa, to put Jessica and Robert together, Robert felt Mr. Atherton watched him with an especially critical eye.

"I'm starved," Robert's father said. "Where's Brandon?"

"Tied up right now with some horse trading. Said he'd join us across the street." Atherton motioned to one of the larger restaurants set up to accommodate the cowboys and ranchers.

Will nodded and the threesome headed out. Robert couldn't help but wonder if the topic of his marrying Jessica would come up. Mr. Atherton and his father weren't usually given to such conversational issues, but Robert couldn't be sure.

They placed their orders for fried chicken dinners, which came complete with biscuits, gravy, and grits. Robert hadn't realized how hungry he'd gotten until the serving woman placed a huge platter of chicken and one of biscuits in front of them. She quickly followed with bowls of gravy, grits, and another platter of biscuits.

Robert's father paid the woman and then turned to Tyler. "You wanna offer grace, or are we gonna wait for Bran?"

Tyler grinned. "If he don't know when to come to dinner, that ain't my problem. Let's pray."

Will offered a short blessing before the trio dug in. Robert sank his teeth into a crispy chicken breast and smiled at the most satisfactory flavor. He was on his second piece when Brandon Reid finally showed up. Brandon eyed the diminished platter of chicken.

"Looks like I barely made it in time."

"You know how it is," Tyler teased. "A man's gotta do what a man's gotta do."

"And we had to eat," Will added with a grin.

Brandon wasted no time in gathering food to his plate. "Well, while you three were sitting here stuffing your faces, I made a great deal for some new horseflesh. Craziest animals you've ever seen—got a curly coat."

"Why'd you want to go with that?" Tyler asked.

The question seemed to take Brandon by surprise. "Well, I figured if it was smart to diversify your cattle breeds to make them stronger and fatter, maybe I could come up with a new hardy breed of horse. These curlies are stout but have really great spirits. They aren't afraid of anything. Could come in mighty handy in a cow horse."

"Gotta give you that," Will said, grabbing up another biscuit. He immediately sopped it in gravy and bit off a huge chunk.

Robert listened to his elders talk about their purchases and endeavors until the conversation turned to him.

"So what about you, Robert? You find anything worth buyin'?" Tyler asked.

Robert looked up from his plate. "Saw some great Angus with Pa. Should be interesting to see how they do, although they don't seem much suited to our climate. From what the man said, they have a hard time with the heat."

Tyler nodded. "But Angus have a good reputation for cross-breeding with the longhorns. Should improve the stock. Instead of twelve hundred pounders we'll get upwards to two thousand."

"Well, given the talk we just heard," Robert's father began, "I'm beginning to wonder if we shouldn't consider opportunities to invest in slaughterhouses back east. Seems Texas cattle are getting noticed, and it might be one way to diversify our investments. Law allows for Texas cattle to be shipped by rail and immediately slaughtered. They aren't seeing any spread of tick fever that way. So what if we were to set up our own slaughterhouse on the rail line, say in one of the eastern cities?"

The older men got caught up in the positives and negatives of such endeavors while Robert got lost in his own thoughts. He would be twenty-eight come April. It was time to settle down and establish his own ranch. His father had said it more than once. He needed to get serious about marrying and starting his own life. Pa had even commented that maybe Robert would like to buy his aunt Marty's ranch. It wasn't real big, but it did abut the land Will had already given him. Robert had even been checking in on Marty's place in her absence.

It would be a good idea, he supposed. After all, Marty's land already had a house and outbuildings. Robert's land had nothing. He would have to start from scratch—build his own home, barns, pens. On the other hand, if he made a deal with his father for Marty's place, he would immediately be in debt. Both situations had their drawbacks.

"You seem mighty deep in thought, son." Robert looked up to find his father watching him. "You got something on your mind?"

Robert gave a chuckle and pushed back his empty plate, as if he'd been contemplating nothing more important than a game of cards. "Nothing worthy of our discussing. Guess now that my belly's full I wouldn't mind a nap." The older men laughed.

"You're startin' to sound like us," Tyler declared, "and you're way too young for that."

"I reckon so," Pa threw in. "Besides you don't even have a wife and children to wear you out like we do."

Robert shifted uncomfortably. "Maybe that's 'cause I'm smarter than you guys." He grinned and tucked his thumbs in his belted waistband.

"Or just a coward," Brandon Reid said in a good-natured manner. He returned Robert's grin and then looked to Tyler. "That little gal of yours has scared him to death."

"Jessica can do that to a man, for sure," Tyler replied. "The good Lord knows she keeps me awake nights worryin' about her."

Robert feared the conversation was going to turn to him and Jessica. He was squirming in his seat when a very tall, broad-shouldered man approached their table with hat in hand. "Mr. Barnett?"

"William or Robert?" Pa questioned.

"William," the man answered.

"That's me," Robert's father said, getting to his feet.

"I'm Austin Todd, field cattle inspector."

William Barnett extended his hand. "Glad to meet you. These are some of my associates—Tyler Atherton and Brandon Reid. And this is my son, Robert."

Austin tipped his head. "Pleasure."

"Mr. Todd." Tyler stood. Brandon did likewise and Robert followed suit.

"Is there a problem?"

"Not at all," Austin replied with a smile. "Mr. Nystrom over at the sale barn told me I could find you here. He described you right down to your boots. I was hoping I could talk to you for a minute. He said you might have some land for sale."

———————— ★ ————————

Alice handed Marty two letters. "He's written," she said, pointing to the top letter.

Marty glanced down. "I'm almost afraid to see what he has to say."

Uncertain if Marty wanted to be alone, Alice said nothing for a moment. Finally she started for the door to their room, but Marty called her back.

"Don't go. This will no doubt affect you as well as me." She drew a deep breath and opened the letter. A five-dollar bill with President James Garfield's profile fell to the floor.

Alice bent to retrieve it and handed the money to Marty. "Jacob sent you money. Must mean he's found work."

Marty took the bill and scanned the letter. "He's working for his friends the Vandermarks, but they can't keep him. There isn't enough work to go around because lumber sales are in a slump. He plans to leave there at the end of the month and go to my sister and brother-in-law's ranch." She looked up from the letter. "He hopes they can hire him, and he wants us to join him there."

Alice smiled. "We've talked about doing just that. But you don't have to include me. Mr. Brentwood would probably let me stay here if I would work full time for room and board."

"I don't know what to do," Marty said, looking at the money and then back to the letter. "He says he misses me and loves me more than life. He plans to send me more money in his next letter. If William will hire him, he's going to ask them to advance enough money so that we can buy train tickets."

Alice could see that Marty was anything but comforted

by the news. She wished she could still Marty's fears, but she had nothing in the way of words that might assuage her friend's concerns.

"At least you've had word," she said, taking the chair beside Marty. "And he loves you despite how you parted. You both miss each other so much, Marty. It seems reasonable that you would join him."

"I . . . I know."

"But you're afraid," Alice said, knowing the truth. "For the baby."

"Yes." Marty raised her gaze to Alice. "I'm terrified. I don't want to miscarry."

"I wish I could promise that you wouldn't, but of course I can't," Alice admitted. "I do know what fear is like, though. I live with it every day. Mr. Smith seems to delight in frightening me. But that's fear for myself and not for an unborn child."

"My fear is for myself, too," Marty said, shaking her head. "I just don't know if I can handle this, Alice. I don't know if I can go back to Texas. I know that I miss Jake. I know that I want us to be together. I even want to see my sister and Will again."

"But you don't want to see Texas."

"It's not even that. I found myself wishing I could enjoy the warmth of Texas again when the room turned so cold the other day." She smiled. "I guess I don't hate Texas as much as I hate what I've experienced there."

Alice took hold of her hand. "We need to pray about this, Marty. There isn't anything we can't ask God about."

"But I already know that God expects me to honor my wedding vows and be with my husband. I know God wouldn't have a child be without his or her father. I know what's expected of me. Praying about it won't change that."

"Maybe not, but perhaps it will change your heart." Alice patted her hand. "Marty, you have done nothing but care for me since we first met. You have shown me grace and love. Despite Mr. Smith's threats, you've stood by me, and because of that my heart has changed and I have new hope. You've proven to me that a person's heart can change and life can be better, even when circumstances do not change. I think God can do the same thing for you."

Marty seemed to consider Alice's words, and Alice found herself praying that God would give the older woman peace about the situation. She wanted Marty to be at peace, and she also hoped that if they left Denver for good Alice could once and for all be rid of Mr. Smith.

"I will pray about it, Alice. I know what you're saying, and I want to accept that truth." She looked at the other envelope in her hand. "No doubt Hannah will be advising the same thing. I told her in my last letter that Jake had gone to Texas. She'll be beside herself that I'm alone in Denver."

Alice shook her head. "You're *not* alone, Marty. Whether you stay here or go there, you're not alone. I'll stay with you—if you'll let me. We're sisters now, remember?"

The two women shared a glance and then a smile. Marty nodded. "Yes. Sisters."

Chapter 7

Alice hung her apron on the peg by the kitchen and rolled her aching neck to ease the pain. She had been busy at the diner since arriving that morning, and now, to her relief, it was time to head back to the orphanage.

Joe hadn't said much to her since she'd refused his proposition that they spend time together. Alice was glad that he hadn't challenged her on the matter. He seemed a bit stand-offish, but otherwise cooked the orders and performed his other kitchen duties without further complicating her life.

Mr. Bellows complimented Alice daily on her hard work and serving abilities with the customers. Alice knew the diner's business had increased and hoped it was because of her good service. In the throes of a busy day she had little time to think about her scar, Mr. Smith, or even her concerns about Marty. But when the day concluded and she began her long walk home, those thoughts always returned.

Bundling up in her coat and wool bonnet, Alice headed out onto the snowy street. Overhead the skies threatened to deliver even more of the wet, white annoyance. She tried not to let the cold discourage her, however. She'd made nearly a dollar in tips that day and felt on top of the world. She had been able to set aside a little bit of change here and there after tithing and hoped that eventually the money would help get her and Marty to Texas. The rest of her earnings went to help defray expenses at the orphanage.

Mr. Brentwood always seemed grateful for the assistance, but Alice knew he was gravely worried about the situation. While he'd managed to secure some funds, he was unable to solicit the amount needed. It seemed the winter of 1893 to 1894 would go down as one of deep poverty and hopelessness in Colorado.

Alice was only halfway home when the hair on the back of her neck prickled. She felt an icy sensation run down her spine and knew without looking that Mr. Smith had somehow found her. She could feel his gaze and wondered where he was. Looking around as casually as she could, she pretended to notice a book in the window of one of the general stores. She thought about going inside and seeing if she might escape out the back as she had done that day in the fabric store but knew it was fruitless. Smith had a way of always finding her.

For a moment Alice considered confronting him. She thought of telling him that she would go to the police and have him arrested. Maybe the threat would dissuade him from his constant haunting. But that would require her to be close enough for conversation. And Alice wanted no part of that.

She picked up her pace just a bit. It would do her little good to appear to be running from the man. No, it seemed to her that if she pretended not to notice him, he might keep his distance. Perhaps he didn't know exactly where she lived. Maybe he'd found her completely by accident. But she doubted it.

Maybe heading to Texas wouldn't help. Maybe he'd follow me there, as well.

Yet Texas held great appeal to Alice. She reasoned it to be a calmer setting, for cattle and crops, rather than silver, seemed to hold court there—at least according to Marty. Surely life in the South would be better than here.

Keeping her focus on the path before her, Alice prayed that Smith would keep his distance. Lost in her prayers, she nearly jumped out of her skin when a man called her name. She steadied herself and drew in a deep breath before turning.

"Mr. Brentwood!" She let out a sigh. "You startled me." She put her hand to her breast as if to slow her racing heart.

"I apologize for that, Miss Chesterfield. I saw you heading home and wondered if you would like to ride. I have my carriage just around the corner."

"Thank you. That would be wonderful."

He led her to the single-horse conveyance and helped her up. Alice settled in as Mr. Brentwood climbed in beside her and pulled a woolen warmer from beside him. "Here, this will help with the cold."

She smiled and spread the blanket over her lap. "Did you have business in town today?"

"I did," he said, snapping the reins. "I am happy to say I procured a charitable donation to help with the rent on the orphanage. We will be secure for another three months."

"That's wonderful news."

"Indeed. I'm also given hope that there will be an offering from one of the churches to help with the cost of coal and electricity."

"That's good to hear. I don't suppose it's easy to get assistance these days."

"No, not at all. Although I have appealed to several of the

women's organizations and hope to offer a small program to encourage donations. I thought we might have the children learn a song or two that they could perform. Maybe even have an affair at the orphanage itself to encourage godly people to come and share anything extra that they might have."

Alice considered this a moment. "Such as food and clothing?"

"Exactly. Or perhaps kerosene and candles. After all, electricity is certainly not a necessity. I've long thought to eliminate it—at least temporarily."

"Is it less expensive to run on kerosene?"

"Yes, but also more dangerous. Children aren't always cautious of fire hazards. I suppose that's why I've delayed in giving up electricity."

"So you plan to ask people to donate everyday items that will allow for the running of the orphanage. I think that's wise. Then if people can't afford to give money, they might give something else useful."

"They could even donate items we might be able to fix and sell. I have long considered the possibility of training the boys to make repairs to various items and resell them. Perhaps I could have a shop right there at the orphanage. The older children are certainly capable of helping."

"I think that's a wonderful idea. Marty and I could help with mending old items for resale. The shop would be a wonderful way to help support the orphanage and the community—especially if you weren't to charge outrageous prices like most of the town businesses."

"Do you think Marty—Mrs. Wythe—would approve?" he asked with a quick glance at Alice.

She heard the hope in his voice. "I think she would, for as long as we are here. Her husband has asked us to join him in Texas."

"But you're needed here," he said, sounding most desperate. "Mrs. Wythe has said nothing of leaving."

"I know. She is waiting for the money her husband plans to send, and then we will purchase train tickets."

Mr. Brentwood frowned. He seemed to consider the matter for several blocks before changing the subject entirely. "How do you like working at the diner? I have to say I was quite impressed with your donations to our food budget."

"I don't always care for it, but it does allow me a means of helping. I know the money is much needed and I don't mind the hard work." They turned a corner and the orphanage came into view. "I keep praying that the economy will improve, but it would seem that most of the men believe this is only the beginning."

Mr. Brentwood nodded. "I fear they are correct. I also fear for the children. I've been asked to take on more orphans but have had to refuse. I know the state orphanage is overflowing, as are many of the other church-run houses. Every day I see children, as well as adults, begging on the street. Some of the children are much too young to forage for themselves."

"It's sad that people feel they can cast their children aside like unwanted trash."

"Many of the parents are dead, and there's no one to take the little ones."

"Dead? I thought most of the children were abandoned."

"Some are, but sadly suicide is on the rise. One of the ministers was just telling me today that many people have given up. Of course winter brings with it more sickness, and some have succumbed to that. But winter and despair also increase those feelings of hopelessness. Some folks aren't strong enough to endure the pain." He pulled the buggy around to the back and came to a stop. He jumped down and helped

Alice from her seat. "I'll be in directly after I see to the horse. You might tell Mrs. Wythe that I'd like to speak to her in my office. I'd like to know how soon she might . . . when you two plan to leave us."

"I'll tell her," Alice replied. She wanted to say something more. Something regarding his obvious feelings for Marty, but she held her tongue. It was probably best that she not assert her opinion just yet. Marty was a grown woman and fully capable of taking care of the matter herself.

★

Robert glanced up from the repairs he was making to espy a rider heading toward the house. The man rode well and looked to be completely at ease with the day. Dusting off his gloved hands, Robert straightened and made his way to the front yard in order to greet the man.

"Howdy," he called as the rider came to a stop.

"Howdy yourself," the man greeted with a smile. "I was wondering if Mr. Barnett was around."

"I'm Robert Barnett."

The man dismounted and extended his hand. "Jake Wythe. I'm married to Marty."

Robert couldn't help but smile. "She's my aunt. I've heard a great deal about you. Pleased to meet you." They shook hands. "Ma told me you might be headed our way. She had a letter from Marty sayin' as much. I know she'll be glad to meet you—Pa, too."

"I hope they'll still be glad when they hear why I've come. I'm in need of work." His frank admission seemed almost apologetic.

"They already know about that. I believe Pa has been planning to hire you on since Aunt Marty wrote and told him you needed work. Come on with me and I'll introduce you. Pa's just out back of the barn plotting out an additional building for hay. You can tie your horse off over here. We'll tend him after the introductions."

Jake tied the animal to the fence. Robert led the way around the pen and to the back of the barn. "Ma said that you'd been in the East working."

"Sure have. I got friends over near Perkinsville. They own Vandermark Logging and I worked for them a spell. But with all the changes goin' on over that way, they weren't even sure how long they'd be in business. A fella named Temple has bought up some seven thousand acres of timber and plans to start up his own sawmill. Might just put the Vandermarks in a bad way."

"Do you prefer loggin' to ranchin'?" Robert asked.

"No." Jake was matter-of-fact and to the point. "I grew up third-generation Texas rancher. We had a place just south of here, but Pa had to sell it during the drought. Didn't set well with me losing my inheritance, but I learned to give it over to the Lord."

"It's best that way." Robert noticed his father and called to him. "Pa, look who's come. It's Aunt Marty's husband, Mr. Wythe."

"Jake," the man interjected. "Just call me Jake."

William Barnett came forward and extended a hand. "It's good to finally meet you. I have to say when Marty told us she'd remarried, I was skeptical." He gave Jake a head-to-toe assessment before smiling. "Looks like she chose a good Texas man."

"I am a Texan, to be sure, and me and the Lord try our best to keep me on the good side." He grinned. "I've heard a lot of great things about you and Mrs. Barnett."

"You can call me Will. I'm sure my wife will want you to call her Hannah. Come on to the house. Speaking of my wife, I'll never hear the end of it if I don't get you two introduced right away."

Jake nodded. "I'm hoping you might be able to put me to work. I know ranchin' like the back of my hand. I grew up workin' every aspect."

"I heard you were a banker," Will said with a grin. "A banker rancher."

Jake laughed. "Guess you could call me that. My pa insisted I finish my education after he sold off the ranch. I worked a time in eastern Texas loggin', then joined my folks out in California. Got my education and went to work as a teller and then moved on to Denver, where I was promoted and eventually managed a branch for Paul Morgan. When the bank failed, I thought only of returning to ranch work."

"I can't imagine that set well with Aunt Marty," Robert threw in. He knew his aunt had soured on ranch life after losing Uncle Thomas.

"No, it didn't, but your aunt is a practical woman. I'm hopin' I can get some work here and send her money to come."

"We'd like nothin' better," Robert's father admitted. "We've been hopin' you'd show up sooner rather than later. Hannah's been half beside herself to get Marty out of Denver and back down here. We don't much like her livin' there alone."

"I don't either. There didn't seem to be a whole lot of choices, though. She wouldn't come and I couldn't stay."

Robert thought there was a hint of regret in the man's voice but said nothing. They entered the house through the back porch. Robert saw his mother look up from the table where she was kneading bread. Her face lit up at the sight of his father. Even after all these years Robert could see that his parents were still very much in love.

"Well, who have you there?" she asked. Wiping her hands on her apron, Robert's mother came from around the table to greet them.

"Hannah, this is Marty's husband, Jake."

Robert watched his mother assess the man only a moment before smiling. She stepped forward and embraced Jake, much to his surprise.

"You are a sight for sore eyes. So glad you finally came our way. You know you should have come here first."

Jake nodded as she let him go and stepped back. "I know I should have, but I didn't want to impose."

"Nonsense. You're family. Now, you come with me, and I'll show you your room."

"I left my things outside with my mount."

Robert noted his mother's nod in his direction. "I'll take care of it," he volunteered, knowing full well what his mother expected. Once Jake and his mother had disappeared, Robert turned back to his father.

"Seems like a nice fellow."

"He does. Can't imagine Marty marryin' a foul-tempered one."

Robert nodded. "You suppose she'll come home now?"

"I don't see why not. She can't hardly live separate from her husband, and now that he's here, she knows her place is here, as well."

"You figure they'll take back her ranch?"

"I hope so. I never wanted her to give it up in the first place, and since her husband is a Texas rancher by birth, it seems only right."

Robert didn't mention that he'd actually had hopes of

buying Marty's ranch for himself. After all, he had his own land and his folks certainly didn't mind him staying on with them. Fact was, he preferred the idea of his aunt returning. It was good to have family close by, and he had always liked the idea of them working the land as one.

"It'd be good to have her home," Robert admitted. "Then if we could just get Uncle Andy back with his family, it'd be perfect."

"I hear you, son, but your Uncle Andy seems to be content to ranch in Wyoming with his wife's family. He wrote just the other day, and I've been meanin' to tell you about it. He wants to sell off his land here, and I thought maybe you'd like to have his acreage. He plans to stay in the north."

Robert considered the land that lay to the north of his own. "That would be good."

"There's no house or buildings for you, but it will give you an even better setup. Good water there, and Andy already cleared one area for building on. I figure you could put up a small place of your own when you had a mind to do so. It'll put you in a good position—closer to the Athertons."

He suppressed a negative comment and turned away. "Guess I'd better fetch Jake's things and get his horse put away. Feels like temperatures are droppin'."

His father said nothing, but Robert knew he probably wondered at the way he avoided discussing the future. No doubt he would bring the matter up in time. And when he did, Robert couldn't help but wonder what he'd say.

Chapter 8

Alice loved Sunday afternoons. They were a time for rest and relaxation. The children were given time off from chores and schoolwork, and Alice wasn't required to go to the diner for work. She and Marty always managed to start the day off with a nice breakfast and then Mr. Brentwood would share his thoughts on a Scripture passage, as he did every morning.

When everyone was dressed and hair combed, they would head off to church as a group and return afterwards to eat a lunch of leftovers from the day before. Everyone was then encouraged to have a time of rest. The little ones always protested, declaring they weren't tired and didn't need to sleep. They were always, amusingly enough, the first to fall asleep. Alice thought it comical to watch the way they fought napping. It reminded her of how she often fought against the rest that God offered her. So many times she had declared her ability to bear up under the load, to keep pressing forward, when all God wanted for her was rest.

"Have you seen Rusty?" Marty asked, coming into the kitchen.

Alice was just taking the last batch of sugar cookies from the oven. They were to be a surprise for the children when they awoke.

"I thought he was taking a nap."

Marty shook her head. "I thought so, too, but he's not there."

"Perhaps he needed to relieve himself."

"Maybe, but he usually comes and gets me to go with him to the outhouse." Marty frowned. "This isn't like him. He's generally too afraid of his own shadow to wander off very far."

"Maybe since the day was so nice, he snuck out to play," Alice suggested. "After all, this is the warmest day we've had in some time. To a four-year-old it probably seemed like summer."

"I suppose I should go speak with Mr. Brentwood."

"Speak with me about what? Umm, cookies." He winked and looked beyond Marty. "Perhaps I might sample them for you?"

Alice laughed. "There's a plate of them on the counter that have already cooled."

Mr. Brentwood crossed the room and helped himself. "Now, what was it you wanted to talk to me about?" He took a bite and smiled in satisfaction.

"I can't find Rusty," Marty declared. "I thought all the boys were in bed, but when I went to check, Rusty's bed was empty."

"That is strange. I remember him enjoying his lunch. Cabbage soup is a favorite of his."

"Yes, and he had two bowls," Marty replied. "Then we noticed he had muddy boots, and you told him to go clean them and leave them by the back door."

Mr. Brentwood nodded. Alice tried to recall if she'd seen the boy after he'd cleaned his boots, but nothing came to mind.

"I'll start looking for him. You're sure he didn't climb into bed with one of the other boys? He sometimes does that when he has a bad dream."

"No. He's not there. I made sure of it before I started searching for him." Marty looked quite worried.

Alice pulled off her apron. "I'll check out back. Could be he woke up and slipped out without anyone noticing."

"I'll check in my office and the classroom," Mr. Brentwood said, taking another cookie with him. "Although once he gets a whiff of these cookies, I doubt he'll be in hiding much longer."

Alice took up her shawl and headed outside. Most of the snow had melted due to the warm Chinook winds. The January day was deceptively enticing, but Alice knew from experience not to trust the moment. By nightfall it would no doubt be freezing cold, and by tomorrow they could once again find themselves buried in snow.

"Rusty! Rusty, are you out here?" she called. She looked around the play area, bending to inspect the old crates Mr. Brentwood had arranged for the children to use for play. There was no sign of the boy.

She went to search in and behind the outhouse but again found nothing. Looking back at the orphanage, she tried to imagine where she might hide if she were a four-year-old boy. Just then, however, she heard a giggle coming from behind her. She turned and saw the bushes move.

"Rusty, is that you? Come here this minute."

The boy peeked out from behind the seemingly dead brush. "We're playin' hide-and-seek."

"It's naptime and you were supposed to be in the house asleep," Alice chided.

"I waked up," Rusty said, holding up his hands in surrender.

"You need to go find Mr. Brentwood and Mrs. Wythe and let them know that you're all right." Alice took hold of the boy's shoulders and turned him toward the back door.

"Can Mr. Smith come, too?" the boy asked.

Alice froze. "Mr. Smith?"

A low chuckle chilled her to the bone. She turned to find her enemy watching her with a leering stare. He tipped his hat. "One and the same. Me and the boy, well, we had us a nice time together, didn't we, Rusty?"

The child grinned. "Mr. Smith said he can come back and play with us anytime he wants."

"Rusty, go inside and let them know you're all right." Alice's knees wanted to give way, but she forced herself to remain strong for the child's sake. She stared hard at Smith, hoping—praying—he might feel some sort of intimidation.

"I don't have anything for you," she said. Anger stirred inside and she clenched her jaw tight.

"I know that envelope has to be somewhere," he said. "Something that valuable ain't gonna just disappear."

"Well, it has. You have no choice but to stop this madness. I can't give you what I do not have." She put her hands on her hips. "You have followed me all over this city, and I'm sick of it."

He laughed again. "Then find my envelope. I have a feeling you know exactly where it is. I think you're keeping it for yourself."

Alice narrowed her eyes. "I know why you want it. I know about the counterfeit gold certificates. Mr. Wythe explained what he could find out about it. I wouldn't give them to you even if I could find them."

Smith crossed the distance between them and grabbed hold of Alice so quickly she didn't have time to react. His iron-like fingers dug into her tender arms. "You'll find them and you'll give them over or . . ." He let his words trail and nodded toward the door where Rusty had just gone. "Or next time it might not be hide-and-seek I play with that boy."

"You're a monster. I'll warn all of the children to be on the lookout for you. Not only that, I'll go to the police!"

His grip tightened. "You do and there will be blood on your hands."

Alice could imagine him stealing one of the children and hurting them. "I don't know what you expect me to do. I've told you before, everything my father owned, everything that you didn't take that night, has been sold. The house was sold before I even got out of the hospital. It was handled by friends and colleagues of my father in order to pay for his funeral and my hospital expenses. Whatever was in the house, with exception to a few of my personal items, was sold, as well. There's nothing left. Threaten all you like, but there's nothing!" She was nearly hysterical and knew she had to get a hold of herself. Forcing air into her lungs, Alice lifted her chin in a defiant pose.

It seemed that perhaps Smith finally believed her. He loosened his hold but didn't let go. "What about the house? Maybe your pa had a secret compartment where he hid such things."

Alice shook her head. "If he did, I didn't know anything about it."

"Well, maybe you need to find out." His expression once again became fierce. "You go there. Go to the house and find out if your pa hid anything away."

"The house sold. Other people are living there. I can hardly just show up at their doorstep and demand entry."

"You'd better do just that," Smith replied, finally letting go of her arms. "In fact, you'd better go and do that today if you know what's good for you. I'll come see you at the diner in the morning."

He left so quickly that Alice was still trying to think of what to say to him when she realized he was gone. For several minutes she stood frozen in place. The man was clearly insane. Perhaps the desperate times had done this to him; then again, maybe he had always been this way.

Gathering her skirts in her hand, Alice wondered how in the world she could heed his demand. The house she had shared with her father was on the other side of town. She couldn't hope to walk there, visit the people, and walk back before nightfall. Yet if she did nothing, Smith would come back and hurt one of the children.

Perhaps Mr. Brentwood would loan her his carriage and horse. She bit her lower lip and entered the back of the orphanage, wishing she had a better plan. How could she explain the situation to Mr. Brentwood? It would be hard enough to tell Marty what had just happened. Marty would want to go after Smith with her shotgun, which would be quite impossible since the shotgun had been sold off with most everything else.

"Where is he?" Marty asked when Alice stepped into the kitchen.

Alice noted Marty had a cast-iron skillet in her hand and had been headed toward the door. "Rusty told you about Mr. Smith?"

"Yes, and I intend to put this skillet up against his head. How dare he involve a child in his schemes."

"I know. And that's not the half of it."

Marty frowned. "What else is there?"

"He plans to be back—to cause harm if I don't do what he's commanded."

"Which is what?

Alice squared her shoulders. "He wants me to go back to the house I shared with my father and look for hiding places where Father might have put the envelope and gold certificates."

"The man is crazy," Marty said, lowering the pan. "How can he imagine there would be anything there after all this time? If someone found those certificates, they would endeavor to use them for their own survival."

"I don't know of any place where Father could have hidden them, but I am determined to go and put this thing to rest once and for all. I'm going to go to the house right now if Mr. Brentwood will lend me his horse and carriage." She lowered her voice and stepped closer to Marty. "I just don't know what excuse to use or if he'd allow for it."

Marty nodded. "Leave that to me. We'll go together. Mr. Brentwood will let me have use of the carriage. He's offered it to me many times."

"I don't want to drag you into this, Marty." Alice felt her eyes dampen. "You've already gone through too much, and now you have the baby to consider."

"Shh. Say nothing. There's no reason to worry. We will go to the house and speak to the new owners. I'll simply tell Mr. Brentwood that it's come to my attention that a friend of mine is in need. That much is true." She put the skillet on the stove. "I'll tell him we have need of the carriage and that we will be absent from the orphanage for a time. There are plenty of leftovers for their evening meal."

Within a matter of minutes Alice was in the carriage house with Marty. She felt helpless to assist Marty with the harnessing of the horse and feared for the mother-to-be.

"I wish I could handle that for you. I couldn't live with myself if anything happened to the baby."

"I'll be fine," Marty assured her. "Women in my condition have been harnessing and unhitching wagons, handling horses, and doing much more for centuries. I'm sure it will be all right. Besides, this old nag barely has enough energy to pull the buggy. She's not going to be any trouble to me."

They made their way across town with Alice directing Marty to the old neighborhood. The houses there were far less opulent than those on Capitol Hill, but clearly nicer than those in some of the poorer parts of town. When Alice saw her childhood home, she felt something akin to sorrow rush through her. She hadn't been back there since the night of the attack.

"That's it—right there. The one with the pine tree on the side." She swallowed hard and silently prayed for strength.

"It looks like a lovely place to grow up," Marty said, pulling back on the reins. "Whoa." The mare complied without protest. Marty got down and tied off the reins. "Do you want me to come with you?"

"Yes. Please. I'm . . . I don't know what to say or to do."

"We'll just have to wait and see," Marty said, pulling Alice up the walkway. "Do you know the people who bought the house?"

"No." Alice had never asked, nor had anyone bothered to tell her. Having been desperately ill for so many weeks after the attack, she had hardly cared what happened to the house or her things.

They knocked on the door and waited. Alice imagined her mother opening the door to them with a warm smile and a loving embrace. Many had been the time Alice had returned from school to find her mother awaiting her arrival in just such a manner.

"Hello?" A woman looking to be in her midforties greeted them.

"I . . . ah . . . well," Alice stammered and looked to Marty.

"This is probably going to sound strange to you, but I'm Mrs. Martha Wythe and this is Alice Chesterfield. Alice used to live here."

"Oh," the woman said, seeming to notice Alice's scar at the same time. "Your father was killed, wasn't he? You were injured, but we never knew what became of you." The woman's expression became quite sympathetic. "I remember being told all about it from the owner."

"The owner?" Marty asked. "Don't you own this house?"

"No," the woman said. "I rent it. My mother and I live here. Won't you come in?"

Marty and Alice stepped into the house. For a moment Alice gazed around the room and let the memories wash over her. The front room looked much the same, although there was now a piano by the front window.

"So what can I do for you, Miss Chesterfield, Mrs. Wythe? Oh goodness, where are my manners. I'm Sylvia Ingram. My mother, Matilda, is napping just now or I would introduce you."

"That's really all right, Mrs. Ingram," Marty said, much to Alice's relief. "Our visit here will seem rather . . . strange, but I beg your indulgence."

The woman's expression changed to one of concern. "I hope I can help."

"As you probably know, Alice was severely wounded in the attack that killed her father."

The woman nodded and glanced at her cheek. "Such a pity."

Marty quickly continued. "The house was sold while she

was still in the hospital, and Alice never knew what happened to their things or this place."

"Poor girl. I'm so sorry you had to endure such a terrible tragedy."

"We were wondering," Marty said, glancing at Alice, "if there was anything left behind. Something perhaps that had been hidden away and not sold."

"Particularly papers," Alice said, finally finding her voice. Mrs. Ingram seemed so calm and kind that she lost some of her fear. "It's most important I find my father's papers—his personal effects."

"Oh, my dear child, there was a box of personal items. They were upstairs in the attic, tucked back in an alcove."

Alice looked to Marty with hope of what they might find. "And do you have them still?"

The woman frowned. "I'm sorry. No. I sent them on to a relative whose address was amidst the papers. I didn't realize you were still in town."

"A relative?" Alice questioned, feeling her heart sink. "I don't know of any relatives—not still living."

The woman shook her head. "I can't remember the name. It was unusual, but I'm certain the last name was the same as yours." She thought for a moment and then raised her finger toward the ceiling. "Aha. I have a letter. After I sent the box, the recipient responded to thank me. Oh, wait. I remember now. It was from your mother. I have it still."

Mrs. Ingram hurried from the room without further ado, leaving Alice to stare openmouthed after her. She felt as if someone had hit her hard in the stomach. Her mother was dead.

"What in the world is going on?" Alice whispered and looked to Marty for encouragement. "My mother is dead. This can't be."

"We should know soon enough, Alice. Don't worry. At least we know now that there were some papers and personal effects that have been sent on to someone. We will find out to whom they were delivered and see about retrieving them."

Mrs. Ingram was gone for nearly ten minutes before reappearing, waving the letter in hand. "Here it is. I knew I'd kept it. It's from Ravinia Chesterfield—your mother, I believe."

Alice nodded slowly and took the letter Mrs. Ingram offered.

"Goodness, but it seems like forever since that letter arrived. You can read it for yourself. Of course, you may have it. I don't even know why I hung on to it. She wrote me to thank me for the box of things and for telling her about your father's death. She asks about you and your whereabouts in the letter. Seems your father wouldn't let her have anything to do with returning home."

Alice removed the letter from the envelope and began to read.

Dear Mrs. Ingram,

Thank you for informing me about my husband's demise and sending me his personal papers. We have been estranged now for many years, and much to my heartache, Mr. Chesterfield would not send me word of himself or our daughter, Alice, and neither would he allow for my return. If you know of her whereabouts, I would be much obliged if you would share the information. She is very dear to me, and I hope to be reunited with her.

Sincerely,
Ravinia Chesterfield

94

Alice handed the paper to Marty. "My mother . . . my mother is alive!"

Marty glanced at the paper and then back to Mrs. Ingram. "When did you receive this letter?"

"Oh my, it's probably been a year now—maybe not quite. I wrote her back to say that I didn't know anything about her daughter. I told her that I knew her husband had been murdered and that her daughter had been injured, and I thought . . . well . . . I was almost certain you had died." The woman gave her an apologetic look. "I do hope I didn't cause your poor mother undue heartache. Perhaps you can write her yourself and let her know that you're alive and well."

Alice felt the room begin to spin. She couldn't breathe and the world was going black. The last words she heard were Mrs. Ingram's.

"I'm certain your mother will be delighted to know you are safe."

Chapter 9

"Don't you think you should write to her?" Marty questioned Alice later that night after everyone had gone to bed.

In the darkness she couldn't see her friend's face, but she knew it was no doubt still twisted in an expression of confusion and pain. Poor Alice. The girl had taken quite a shock at the news that her mother was still alive.

"I don't know." Alice's simple statement echoed in the silence of the room.

"Well, it seems to me that there is far more to this than either of us understands. It would seem that your mother wanted to be in touch with you, wanted to see you, but your father—"

"My father loved me!" Alice interrupted. "He was a good father."

"I . . . I'm sure he was, Alice." Marty tried to choose her words carefully. "But obviously there were issues, problems that perhaps kept him from being a good husband."

For several minutes neither said anything. Marty wondered

if she'd overstepped her bounds with the younger woman. Alice was only eighteen and she hardly understood the problems that could exist between a husband and wife. Marty thought of Jake and the issues they were struggling with.

I miss him so much. How I wish you were here, Jake. I wish I could tell you about our baby and about my fears.

"I don't know what to do," Alice finally whispered. "It was so hard to accept her leaving and then hearing that she and Simon had died." She gasped. "Do you suppose my brother is alive, too?"

"Quite possibly," Marty replied. "How old would he be now?"

"Ten. He probably doesn't even remember me."

Alice's tone was so forlorn that Marty spoke quickly to assure her. "Oh, I'll bet he remembers you very well. That was only five years ago. I have vivid memories from when I was five."

Marty waited for Alice to say something more and when she didn't, Marty decided to make some suggestions. "If you're worried about it, I could help you by writing to your mother first. I could explain what has happened—even ask her about the gold certificates. We have her address on the envelope of the letter."

"She lives in Chicago."

Rolling to her side and pulling her blankets close, Marty considered the matter for a moment. "That's not that far by train."

"This is like some kind of nightmare and good dream all in one," Alice said. "I always prayed that my father was wrong and my mother and brother hadn't died. Now that I know they are alive, I also know that my father lied to me. He betrayed my trust in him and purposefully lied."

"He must have thought he was protecting you."

"From my mother? My little brother?"

Marty tucked her hand under her head. "Alice, why did your mother leave your father?"

"I don't know. Father always said it was because she wearied of being a faithful wife."

"Did they fight?"

Alice said nothing for several long minutes. Finally she whispered her reply. "Yes. But never violently. I mean, my father could say some really horrible things, but he always . . . usually . . ." She fell silent as if remembering something important. "Sometimes he apologized afterwards."

"Sometimes apologies aren't enough to diminish the pain," Marty replied and thought of ways she had hurt others or been hurt herself. She had always been taught to forgive, but it was sometimes hard to do so and to heal from the pain. "Do you suppose . . . I mean . . . is it possible he was violent when no one could see him?"

"I don't know. I feel like I don't know anything anymore. I thought he loved me. I thought he wanted good things for me, but instead my whole life has been built on a lie. Everyone lied."

"But your mother said she was stopped from seeing you. That suggests to me that she never wanted to end the relationship. It seems to me that she didn't lie but was forced out of your life. Maybe she didn't leave of her own accord."

"She snuck out in the night and took my brother with her. My father didn't know about it, because the next day when we learned the truth, he was half crazy with anger and grief. I remember that morning very well."

"Why didn't she take you?" Marty asked without thinking.

"That is the question that has haunted me all of my life.

Perhaps it was because my room was upstairs and she was afraid of waking my father. Maybe it was because I was my father's favorite, and she knew I'd be safe in his care. Or maybe she didn't love me as much as she did my brother."

"Or perhaps she feared she couldn't get away if she took you both. It's really hard to say what her reasons were, but now you have a chance to find out."

"I'm not sure I want to know anymore."

"Alice, I'm so sorry. I'm sorry for the shock this is to you. I'm sorry for the bad memories it's stirred up and the problems it's created. I want you to know that I am here for you in any way I can be. I will do whatever you need me to do."

"Thank you. Right now . . . I just want to think on it. I'm sorry, Marty. I can't talk about this anymore."

"That's all right, Alice. I understand."

And she did. She knew what it was to have a burden so complicated that it couldn't be shared with another person. But it could be shared with God. Marty hadn't always thought that to be true, but she did now and started to pray in earnest for her friend.

★

The next day after Alice left for her job at the diner and the children were settled in with their studies, Marty took the opportunity to speak with Mr. Brentwood in his office.

"Willeen is looking after the classroom," Marty announced. "I wondered if we might talk a moment." She knew the twelve-year-old would be able to manage the children should they have any questions, and this would give her a chance to explain Alice's situation—and maybe her own.

"Of course." Mr. Brentwood jumped to his feet with a

beaming smile. "I've always got time for you. Please come in and have a seat."

Marty nodded. "I wanted to let you know about yesterday."

"Your friend in trouble?"

She smiled. "It was Alice, actually. I want to explain it, although I'm not sure Alice would want me to say much about it. I feel you deserve an explanation, however."

"Go on," he said, closing the ledger in front of him.

Marty took a chair and settled in. "You know that Alice was wounded the night her father was killed. I believe we told you that much."

He nodded and sank back into his chair. "I heard her telling the children about it, as well. Such a horrible thing for one to experience."

"Yes, well, a man has been threatening her ever since. We don't know the man's true identity, but he calls himself Mr. Smith."

"The same Mr. Smith that Rusty spoke of yesterday?"

Marty gave a slow nod. "I wanted to tell you about it then, but we had to hurry in order to . . . well . . . let me back up."

She did her best to explain the past and all that Smith had put them through. Marty tried to carefully weigh the details in her mind before she spoke. There was no sense in telling him everything.

"So we went to the house where Alice grew up and found a very kind woman living there. She shared with us that she had found a box of personal items in the attic and had mailed them to a woman in Chicago. The woman in Chicago had responded with a letter of thanks, which she gave to Alice yesterday. She was shocked to learn that that woman is her mother—who is alive, or at least was alive a year ago."

"How shocking it must have been for her," Mr. Brentwood replied. "I thought she looked unwell when you returned."

"She's struggling to know what she should do. I suppose we both are, actually."

He shook his head. "What do you mean?"

"My husband has written to me. He wants me to join him in Texas. My sister and her husband want that, as well."

"Alice mentioned as much, but you're needed here. I couldn't run the orphanage without your help." He got up and came around the desk, leaning against it, directly in front of Marty.

She thought for a moment he might take hold of her hands and pressed back further in the chair.

"The children adore you and I know you love them, too."

"I do," Marty replied. "Especially little Wyatt and of course the brothers, Sam and Benjamin. They are so needy and in want of love." Marty stopped short of adding that she knew what that felt like.

As if reading her mind, however, Brentwood confessed his own thoughts. "I think we all are. Orphans suffer such great sorrow in their abandoned lives. When they lose someone precious to them, the loss is overwhelming, and they seek to fill that hole with something or someone who can make it better."

Marty knew he was speaking of himself. She hadn't wanted to believe Alice's comments on Mr. Brentwood's feelings for her, but it was clear the younger woman had been right. Marty knew she had to be forthright with Brentwood. She had to make certain he knew there were boundaries that had to be observed.

However, before she could speak, he did the unthinkable and knelt beside her chair. "I know this isn't at all what you expected, but Mrs. Wythe—Martha—I need you. Since losing my wife, this orphanage has been a daunting task. With you and Miss Chesterfield here, it has taken on new meaning."

Marty shook her head. "I'm a married woman."

He nodded. "I know that. I honor that. I'd never try to compromise your union. It's just that your husband . . . well, he's deserted you. He chose to leave for Texas."

"Because he knew he could find work there," Marty defended. "Mr. Brentwood—"

"Please call me Kenneth." His tone was pleading as his eyes sought hers. "I promise you that I am not suggesting anything untoward. I would never want to hurt you like that. I care about you and your reputation. I can offer you a good home here and only ask in return that you would remain and help me with the orphans. And be my friend."

Marty shook her head. "I will always be your friend, Mr. Brentwood, but I'm Jake Wythe's wife, and we both know that will always come first. Especially given my condition."

He startled and jumped to his feet. "You're with child?"

"Yes." She nodded to emphasize her words.

"He left you here to bear his baby alone?"

"He doesn't know. I didn't know for sure until he was already gone. That's why I can't stay."

It was as if in that moment her decision had been made for her. Marty knew the truth of her own words. She couldn't stay. She needed to be with Jake. Their baby needed its father. Whether Texas claimed another child from her or not, she had no choice.

"I just wanted to let you know what had happened yesterday, and what is going to happen in the near future. Alice and I are going to Texas as soon as my husband sends us the money. I think we both know that it's for the best." She got to her feet. "Now that we've spoken here . . . well . . . everything has changed."

"No, not at all," Brentwood declared, taking hold of her arm. "I'm sorry for my forward suggestions. I truly know the limits of our relationship. It's just that you've come to mean so much to me. You've helped me in so many ways. I swear to you, you're safe here. You don't have to flee me. I won't put myself upon you in a compromising manner."

Marty patted his hand and pulled away. "I know you won't. You're a good and godly man. I don't say these things because I feel threatened by you. I say them because I love my husband. I want to be with him—even if that means going back to Texas. Now if you'll excuse me, I need to get back to the children. It's almost time for their lunch, and then you'll need to take over the classroom."

She walked to the door and paused. Turning there, Marty saw the look of anguish in his expression. "God will make provision for you and the orphanage. He has always done so in the past and will continue to. You just need to trust Him for the answers."

Alice found Marty rocking Benjamin in the front room when she returned from her shift at the diner. The little boy slept while Marty hummed quietly. She was the picture of radiant motherhood, and Alice couldn't help but remember her own mother rocking Simon. How she wished she could remember being rocked in her mother's arms.

"He seems quite at home with you," Alice whispered.

"Yes," Marty replied. "I'm going to miss him."

Alice narrowed her gaze in a look of curiosity. "What do you mean?"

"I mean when we go, when we leave here."

"And are you planning to do so?" Alice came further into the room and took a seat in one of the other rockers. "Have you decided to join Jake in Texas?"

"Yes. I told Mr. Brentwood today."

Alice hadn't expected this news. "And what did he say?"

Marty pushed back a curl on the boy's forehead. "You were right. He has feelings for me. Feelings much deeper than he should. He wanted—begged me to stay. Promised he would never compromise my reputation. I told him about the baby, and even that didn't seem a deterrent."

"I'm sorry, Marty. Sorry that it happened and sorry to have been right. I had hoped that perhaps my thoughts were skewed by my own romantic notions." Alice smiled. "I can be quite the dreamer."

"No, you saw quite clearly and now I must go, even if I hadn't already decided it was the thing to do."

"And when did you decide that?"

Marty shrugged ever so slightly. "I suppose I've known it all along. I've simply delayed acceptance." She smiled. "I'm terrified, but I'm also deeply in love with my husband. I hate that we are separated. I never thought I could feel that way about any man but Thomas, and now here I am hopelessly devoted to another."

"But that's good," Alice replied. "I know he feels the same way about you."

"I hope he still does."

Alice laughed lightly. "Of course he does, silly. He wouldn't be working to send you money for train tickets if he didn't."

For several minutes nothing more was said. Finally Alice glanced over her shoulder and then back to Marty. "Did you tell Mr. Brentwood about me?"

Marty nodded. "I did. I hope you don't mind. I felt we owed him some sort of explanation about yesterday." She frowned. "Did Mr. Smith come to see you today?"

Alice nodded and smiled. "I told Joe and Mr. Bellows that he was giving me a hard time and I feared him. They both acted as my protectors." She giggled. "When Mr. Smith came in, I told Mr. Bellows who he was, and he immediately intercepted the man. I took to the kitchen and told Joe what was going on. He wasn't about to let Mr. Bellows have all the honor. He quickly joined him and then I followed suit. Because no one else was around, I told Mr. Smith quite plainly that I visited my old home and there was nothing to be found."

"You didn't tell him about the box that had been sent to your mother?"

"No. Nor will I. That would only encourage the man further. I did lie to him and I feel rather guilty for it."

"What did you say?"

Alice gazed toward the ceiling. "I told him that everything had been sold or destroyed—burned. I told him that the woman did remember there being some personal papers, but that they had been gotten rid of, as well."

"And what did he say?"

"It's more what he did," Alice countered, lowering her gaze. "He threw a table across the room. I was glad no one else was in the diner. Joe and Mr. Bellows demanded he leave, and Mr. Bellows drove me home tonight. I thanked him and told him I wouldn't be back."

Marty nodded. "It would seem we are committed to leaving for Texas as soon as possible."

"It would seem that way."

Chapter 10

"I can see why Marty is so fond of you," Hannah told Jake. She served him an extra portion of flapjacks and then took her seat opposite him at the table. "You have certainly brightened our days with your stories."

Jake smiled. "I loved my life on the ranch, and the stories are all that keep me going sometimes. I've always known I would one day return to Texas and to ranching. I want to say how much I appreciate that you folks would take me in and give me work."

"You're definitely earning your keep," Will told him. "I could use a dozen men like you."

"It's true," Robert added. "I know you've lightened my workload considerably. Especially since Pa is insistent on overseein' the building of the new hay barn."

"Not just overseein'," Will corrected. "I'm doin' plenty of the buildin'."

"Well, I'm glad to oblige." Jake looked up at the family—his family. Marty's sister and brother-in-law were easy to talk to and work for. He poured a generous amount of syrup over his flapjacks. "You've got a pretty amazing spread here. I have to say it's exactly as I'd have a place."

"We've definitely put a lot of hard work into it," Will replied. "I know your pa put a lot of work into your family's ranch. From what you told me about the location, I figure it to be the ranch owned by the Andersons."

Jake nodded. "Yes, that was their names. I couldn't remember it until you mentioned them. Anderson was a fairly young man. Made a lot of money after the war. Seemed he was from down Houston way."

"Well, I'm sure you could make your way over and meet them if you were of a mind to do so."

He considered it for a moment. "I suppose in time I will. I'd like to know if there's a chance of buying the place back. Not that I'm in any position to do that right now. But maybe one day."

"I know that would mean a lot to you," Hannah said, smiling. "I'll commit it to prayer."

"As will I," Will said before taking a long swallow of coffee.

"You never know how God might provide," Robert added with a grin. "I've seen some miracles around here that had to be His hand."

"Robert's right," Will agreed. "There have been some stretches when we wondered if we'd get through the hard times, but God has always provided a way."

"And He always will," Hannah said.

Jake liked the positive spirit of Marty's older sister. They looked a great deal alike with their blond hair and blue eyes, although Hannah's hair showed definite signs of gray. Being with Hannah made Jake miss Marty all the more. He feared at times he might never see his wife again, but Hannah assured him that Marty would never make light of her marriage vows. Jake said very little in response. He wasn't sure exactly what Marty had told her sister about their marriage. Did Hannah and Will realize Marty had answered his ad in the paper? Did they know she had thrown caution to the wind to marry a stranger—a stranger she didn't love?

"Well, as soon as I can, I plan to send Marty and Alice train tickets to join us here," Jake said between bites. "I appreciate that you would open your home to us . . . and to Alice, too. She's young but very capable. Life's not been any too kind to her."

"You said she was alone in the world," Hannah said, passing Jake a platter of crisp bacon. He took the plate as she continued. "We would never allow for her to be left to the whims of that madman you said was tormenting her."

"I know Marty wouldn't leave her behind, either," Will said. "Between her and Robert, we were always takin' in strays and wounded animals. They both have a heart for helping mend the broken." Will took a sip of coffee. "Besides, my little sister-in-law is even more stubborn than my wife." He motioned toward Hannah, adding, "And I didn't think that was possible."

"Oh, it's true enough," Jake said, laughing. "Marty is more stubborn than a longhorn momma tryin' to get to her calf. I can't say that I've ever met anyone quite as headstrong."

Robert chuckled. "Aunt Marty says it's just a matter of her stickin' to her guns. She thinks if more people would stick to what they say, the world would be a better place."

"I can just hear her sayin' that," Jake agreed.

"I wish she would have come with you to Texas. I hate that she's unprotected in a city like Denver," Hannah interjected.

Jake remembered Marty standing with her shotgun in

hand. Then a flash of memory came back regarding her entry into Denver. "Did Marty ever tell you about holding off bandits on her stage trip into Denver? In fact, she had to drive the stage partway to the next stop because the driver and shotgun had been wounded."

Hannah's eyes widened. "She what?"

Jake laughed. "Well, I could have guessed she didn't share all the details."

"I remember her saying there had been some problems that delayed her trip into Denver," Hannah said, looking to her husband.

Will and Robert both looked more than a little interested and encouraged Jake to continue with his story.

"As I recall, Marty was on a special stagecoach for women only, so the only men around were the driver and his shotgun rider. When they were still a ways out of Denver, some bandits attacked and started firing at them. Well, Marty pulled a revolver from her handbag and started firing back. The shotgun said they probably wouldn't have made it if not for her good shootin'."

Robert laughed. "She can put a hole through a silver dollar at a distance farther than any man I know."

"Well, when the bandits fled and the shotgun got the stage stopped, Marty got out to check on everyone. That's when she found out the driver was unconscious and the shotgun was pert near the same. She hoisted herself up into the driver's seat and drove the team of six on into the next stage stop. She was a heroine, and the papers wrote it all up for everyone to read."

"Sounds like our Marty." Will grinned. Hannah looked less than happy about the news, but said nothing.

Jake shrugged. "I knew then and there I'd found me a proper Lone Star bride."

"But I thought you two had never met before Marty got to Denver," Hannah said, looking at him oddly.

Will laughed. "Sometimes a fellow can take one look at a gal and know he's gonna marry her. I felt that way about you."

Hannah eyed him with a look that suggested he was crazy. "You hated me when we first met."

"Nope, you hated me," Will declared. "You thought I was gonna kick you and your family off the ranch."

Jake was glad for the turn the conversation had taken. He hadn't meant to give away any of Marty's secrets. He'd have to be careful what he said in the future. As talk turned back to Marty and her abilities, Jake decided to refocus the conversation.

"That woman can do just about anything, so I wasn't afraid to leave her behind while I figured things out down here. Besides, she wasn't exactly eager to return. She has a bad taste in her mouth when it comes to Texas."

"She made that clear enough in her letters," Hannah said. "I don't know why she holds such contempt for Texas. The state has been good to all of us."

Shaking his head, Jake considered the matter for a moment. "I know she figures ranchin' to be too dangerous. She doesn't want to lose another husband—she told me that much."

"But fighting off stage robbers isn't exactly safe," Robert said. "Marty doesn't always think about things like that. Life's full of trials and hardships, and they aren't limited to Texas."

"That's for sure. I saw just as many threats in California. Denver wasn't exactly minus hard times, either. Alice's situation was proof of that. I reminded Marty that Alice's father had been killed just carrying papers for the bank, so injury and death wasn't limited to ranch work."

"Oh, and she knows that full well," Hannah said. "My

little sister has always been given to exaggerating. She'll endure something and build it up to be ten times bigger than it actually is. As a child she often told lies—sometimes just for the fun of it. I liked to never broke her of it."

"She did confess that much," Jake admitted. "We had a few go-rounds because of it, but I know she's a good woman and she's trying to start fresh. I won't hold the past against her."

"Nor will I," Hannah agreed. "I just hope she won't hold it against Texas."

"I guess we'll know soon enough," Will said, putting a stack of bills on the table. "I want you to take this money, Jake. You and Robert ride into town and purchase train tickets and get them mailed off to Marty."

Jake looked at the money. "I . . . won't . . . won't take charity. I mean to pay this back in work."

"Nonsense," Hannah declared. "She's my little sister, and I want her here as much as you do. Let this be our gift—to Alice, too. Now finish up your breakfast. Robert, I want you to pick up some things for me while you're in town, so you might as well take the wagon."

The matter was settled and Jake knew there'd be no chance of changing Hannah's mind. He hid his smile and finished off his flapjacks. She was just as stubborn as Marty.

★

"And Ruth told her mother-in-law that she would follow her wherever she went—that her people would be Ruth's people and her God would be Ruth's God," the minister declared from the pulpit.

For Marty, the words seemed to hit particularly close to her heart. Jake wanted her to share in his love of Texas, to follow him wherever he went. He was now with her people, and it was all the more important that she join him. They needed to be a family.

She thought of her expanding abdomen. Few knew of her condition, and she intended to keep it that way. Sam snuggled close to her on one side, and Wyatt edged closer on the other, while four-year-old Benjamin had claimed her lap. Marty couldn't help but wish she could take them with her. When the time came for her to leave, it would be especially hard to leave her three little shadows. The boys were bonded to her, and she to them. She couldn't help but wonder what Jake would do if she showed up in Texas with three additional family members.

A week later, the pastor spoke from the book of Genesis and told of Jacob's leaving his uncle's land to head back to his home. He was afraid of what he would face. He had duped Esau, his brother, out of his birthright and blessing. Now he wanted to return home to be with his family—God wanted him to return home.

Just as you apparently want me to return home.

Marty thought of the train tickets they had received only two days earlier. She and Alice were set to leave for Texas on the morrow, yet Marty still felt apprehensive.

Jacob, in Genesis, wanted to return home and feared the consequences. Marty wanted to be returned to Jake—her Jacob.

Why does this have to be so hard?

Images of Thomas's lifeless body came to mind. He had died with Marty at his side, clinging to his hand, begging him to stay. Marty closed her eyes and other tragedies clouded her thoughts. There had been times when Andy had gotten hurt, when Will had nearly died from pneumonia after riding for days on end in an icy rain. Hannah had known her share of problems, too. She'd nearly died when her youngest daughter had been born breach. There was always a chance of death and dying in life, and Marty knew there was no avoiding it. Not by staying in Colorado. Not by avoiding the ranch.

I'm so afraid, Lord. So afraid. I know trials and problems are everywhere. I look at Alice and I know it could just as easily have been Jake and me getting held up. I don't want to let fear steal my joy, Lord, but . . . well . . . it is, and I don't know how to change it.

"Sometimes God's directions to us seem impossible. Think of Abraham being told to leave his country and his people for an unknown land. Think of Noah being given the order to build an ark—a protection against something no one had ever seen or experienced. Throughout the Bible there are examples of God calling His children to difficult and arduous tasks with seemingly impossible odds. But with God . . . all things are possible."

It seemed with every word the minister spoke, confirmation was at hand that Marty and Alice were doing the right thing.

"Let me say that again," the minister asserted, emphasizing his words. Marty opened her eyes to find him looking directly at her. "With God . . . all things are possible."

She smiled. *Even Texas?*

After the service she and Alice gathered the children around the dinner table, and Mr. Brentwood offered a blessing on the meal. Once everyone was seated, Marty took that moment to make her announcement.

"You heard the story this morning about Jacob returning to his homeland," she began. The children nodded and she smiled. "My husband's name is Jacob and he, too, returned to his homeland—my homeland in Texas."

"Texas is far away," Wyatt declared.

Marty nodded. "It's quite a ways." She paused and looked at Mr. Brentwood. She could see the sorrow in his eyes. Soon she would have to endure the sadness of the children, as well. She steadied herself. "Well, just like Jacob, I need to return to my homeland. My husband has sent train tickets for me and for Miss Alice. We will leave tomorrow."

"You can't go," Wyatt said, reaching out to take hold of her hand. "We need you to cook for us."

The other children nodded and Benjamin looked at Marty with tear-filled eyes. "I wanna go with you. Can I come, too?"

Sam nodded. "Me too. Please let us go with you."

"Me too," Wyatt pleaded. Some of the other children joined in.

Marty felt her heart nearly break at their sweet voices. She held up her hands to still them. "I'm afraid I can't take anyone with me. I haven't the money. I wouldn't be able to go myself if not for others sending the tickets. Alice and I will write to you, however. We won't go away without sending back word. We want to know how you're doing in school and what you're learning. We want to know who Mr. Brentwood gets to cook for you." She smiled, hoping to dispel their fears. "I told him he needed to get someone who makes really good cookies."

Some of the children clapped their hands at this idea, but Wyatt buried his face against Marty's skirt and began to cry in earnest. This caused Sam and Benjamin to do likewise. How could she leave them? Yet there was no choice.

Marty hated the pain she was causing. A part of her wished she'd never agreed to stay on at the orphanage. She had known the day would come when she'd have to go. She had only pretended to believe Jake would give up Texas and return to Denver. Now she had to deal with the devastation their choices had caused to these little ones. Taking her seat in utter defeat, Marty prayed God might ease the children's misery.

"Let us pray and ask a blessing on our meal," Mr. Brentwood said. He began to pray, but Marty didn't hear his words. She had her own prayer to offer.

It's not their fault, Lord. The children have done nothing wrong. They've needed love, and I've given what I had to share. Now I'm taking it away, and they will bear the pain. Oh, Father, it seems so unfair, so wrong. Please help us.

The meal passed in questions about Texas from some of the children who seemed more intrigued by the place than troubled by Marty and Alice's departure. Marty answered the questions and explained to the children about life on a ranch. The girls all envied her ability to have a horse of her own and go riding.

"I'd never want to stop riding," Willeen declared. "I love horses."

"I love them, too," ten-year-old Edith joined in. "When I was little, I used to ride my brother's pony."

There was a great deal of discussion about horses and ponies, riding and being a real cowboy, before the meal ended. The children all helped to clear the table. They each took their own dishes to the kitchen and deposited them in a tub of soapy water before heading off to wash up before their nap.

Wyatt, Sam, and Benjamin lingered in the kitchen for as long as Mr. Brentwood would allow and then tearfully let the man lead them out.

"You'll still be here when we wake up, won't you?" Wyatt asked, pausing at the door. Tears streamed down his face.

Marty nodded. "I'll be here, Wyatt. In fact, I'm gonna spend the day making ya'll a whole bunch of cookies." Her Texas drawl thickened with her emotions. "That way you can eat them and think of Alice and me." Usually the mention of cookies would instantly bring a smile to the boy's face, but not this time.

"I want you to be my mama," he said sadly.

Marty crossed the room and knelt beside him. "I would have loved to be your mama." Wyatt wrapped his arms around her neck and hugged her tight.

"Come on, Wyatt," Mr. Brentwood ordered, pulling the boy away. His expression looked nearly as sad as the boy's.

Marty felt as if a part of her heart went with Wyatt. She got to her feet and wiped her eyes. Just then, Alice put her arm around Marty's shoulders. "I didn't think this would be so hard," she said at Alice's gentle touch. "I love them so much."

"You could adopt them," Alice told her. "You've always talked about doing such a thing."

"I know, but there's no money for it. We wouldn't even be heading to Texas yet except that Will and Hannah insisted on paying for the tickets. And then there's the matter of the baby. I don't know if Jake would consider adopting others now that we're expecting our own. I mean, he was always very positive about adoption before, but he might feel different now."

"You have no way of knowing unless you ask him. Maybe Mr. Brentwood could take Wyatt, Sam, and Benjamin off the list of those children available to adopt. You know, just in case someone comes and wants to take them on."

"I suppose I could speak to him about it. I can't promise anything, but maybe since I'm giving in to what Jake wants, he'll give me what I want in return." But even as she said it, Marty knew that was no way to handle the matter. Marriage was, of course, full of give and take, but it wasn't right to put expectations—demands really—on each other for something that involved the life and happiness of so many.

Turning, Marty broke into sobs and cried against Alice's shoulder. There was no possible way to make this parting easy. Her heart was being torn in two. Without a doubt she would leave a part of herself behind at this orphanage.

Chapter 11

FEBRUARY 1894

Alice dozed to the rhythmic sway of the train car. She couldn't help but feel a sense of relief as the train put first one mile and then several hundred between her and Mr. Smith in Denver. She looked at this as her own independence day. Despite it being a cold February morning and the poor heating in the train, Alice was happier than she'd been in years.

Of course, with one issue behind her, there were others Alice knew she'd have to face. Her mother was alive. That alone caused disturbance to her peace of mind. Not that a part of her wasn't excited to find out if her mother still lived in Chicago and if her brother Simon was alive. Ever since learning about the letter her mother had sent, Alice had looked at the orphanage children with new eyes. Her own brother would be the same age as several of the children.

Does he resemble me? Is he blond and blue eyed? Does he remember me?

She opened her eyes and stared out the sooty window. The

vast open lands stretched for as far as the eye could see. Gone were the snow-covered Rockies. Now scrub and twisted mesquite dotted the sandy landscape. Western Texas looked much as Marty had said it would. Desolate. Dry. Deserted. Marty had also told her that the scenery would change drastically. Texas, Alice had been informed, was such a huge state that it was very much like several smaller states rolled into one. In the east there was an abundance of forest and water. To the south the Mexican and seaside influences were evident. Central Texas held vast farmlands and cattle ranches, as did the north. Western Texas had its share of ranches, as well, with a bit of desert flare in some areas. Alice found it all truly amazing. Marty had been all over the state, traveling with her sister and brother-in-law to purchase cattle or other supplies, while Alice had never been anywhere outside of Colorado.

Glancing at the woman across from her, Alice wondered if Marty had finally found relief in sleep. Marty was so afraid of what Texas would bring.

Please give her peace, Lord. Help her to carry this baby in health and to deliver it in the same. Oh, Father, she needs your comfort. Alice bit her lip and looked back out the window. *And so do I.*

Alice watched the miles race by and thought again of her mother and brother. Marty had wanted her to write immediately to her mother, but Alice hadn't been able to bring herself to the task. Whenever she gave it serious consideration, doubts crept in. Her mother had deserted her. Her mother had taken Simon and left Alice behind. How much could her mother possibly care about her? And if she didn't care, why had she asked after her in the letter to Mrs. Ingram? Why had she written those haunting words?

She is very dear to me, and I hope to be reunited with her.

Could Alice trust that her mother was being honest? Had she only written that in order to sound the part of the caring mother? But what purpose would that serve? These questions and a hundred just like them raced through Alice's mind.

Marty thought she was being immature in her delay to write. She had chided Alice and even threatened to write to Mrs. Chesterfield herself, but Alice had made her promise she'd not interfere.

"This has to be my decision," she had told Marty. "She's my mother—not yours."

Alice looked again at Marty. She felt a sense of security with the older woman. She was like the big sister Alice had never had. Marty had cared for her from the time of their first meeting. She hadn't been concerned with the scar on Alice's face or her lack of references when she'd showed up begging for the job of personal maid to Marty. Instead, Martha Wythe had offered Alice a home and employment.

More than that. She gave me an advocate—a protector—a friend.

Alice knew that no matter what, she would always have the deepest love and respect for Marty because of her willingness to extend grace and kindness to a scarred young woman with no other future.

And now here she was—in Texas. Alice couldn't help but wonder what would happen once they reached Marty's family. She didn't know if she'd return to being Marty's personal maid or if she'd be needed to work elsewhere, but either was acceptable. She felt blessed that the Wythes hadn't just abandoned her in Denver.

"Did you get any sleep?" Marty asked.

Alice was surprised to find Marty watching her. "I slept

off and on throughout the night. I can't say that I'm truly rested, but I know it's been much worse for you."

Marty sighed and straightened in the hard leather-wrapped seat. "I'll be glad to put this trip behind us and sleep in a real bed again."

"Happy, too, to see your family and Jake?" Alice asked with a smile.

Marty nodded. "It's been over a year since I saw my sister. Feels just as long since I saw Jake. I suppose because we parted on such poor terms, the time seems longer than it has been."

"I know he'll be happy to see you again. I've always envied the love he holds for you."

Marty raised a brow. "We fight like cats and dogs despite that love. I wouldn't be envying it if I were you."

Alice glanced around the train car. There weren't too many people sharing the space, but she lowered her voice just the same. "If I could know a love like yours, I would be the happiest woman in the world."

Marty sighed. "I hope I still have Jake's love."

"You know you do. He wouldn't have sent for you otherwise."

"He sent for me because my sister probably made him do so." Marty didn't try to hide her smile. "My sister Hannah is . . . well . . . quite determined when it comes to having things her way."

Alice giggled. "And you aren't?"

A slight chuckle escaped Marty. "I suppose I might as well tell you—she and I, well we don't always see eye to eye. In fact, most of the time we tend to be at odds. It's all in good sport, though. We love each other dearly. Hannah has always been one of the most important people in my life. I suppose I've always wanted her approval, and so I challenge her."

"How is challenging her going to get you her approval?" Alice asked, rather confused by this comment.

Marty shrugged and reached up to straighten her hat. "I suppose it's a sort of game we play. I want Hannah to realize that I'm smart and self-sufficient. Hannah has always held the highest regard for strength and capability. She has no use for women who consider themselves to be too good to work—too refined to lend a hand. She calls them 'fancy window dressings.' Pretty enough to look at but without any other purpose.

"Maybe it's because Hannah had to grow up so quickly. She was supposed to marry when I was born. But her fiancé died in the war, and our father demanded she care for me after our mother died giving birth to me. Our brother, Andy, was just a few years older, so Hannah became mother to us both. She needed strength for that, and she needed us to be strong, as well."

"And was your father also demanding of you?" Alice asked, thinking back on her own father. George Chesterfield had always been a man of purpose, driven to accomplish, less than forgiving of error. She hadn't really thought about the latter until now, but there were many examples that came to mind to prove such ideals.

"My father lost his will to live after losing Mama. Hannah said it started even before that. He was devastated when Hannah's mama died. I think of Hannah as my sister, but she's really my stepsister." Marty paused and watched the dry landscape. "Papa also lost my older brother to the war. Hannah said the war took what little life was left in Papa, and after that he was more reserved. I remember only little bits of him," Marty recalled. "I was sad when I learned he was dead, but I knew it would have been far worse if it had been Hannah who had died."

Alice nodded. "Sometimes I wonder about my father. I know he was deeply injured when my mother left. I remember times when they would argue and he would call her names and make her cry. Usually I went to my room or outdoors and avoided the conflict. I knew no other way, of course. We didn't have relatives or close friends to give me other examples of married life."

She looked out the window. The sun was now bearing down in a crispness that only came with winter days. "Living with my friends after the attack showed me how different life could be. I never heard a mean-spirited word given or names called. Even so, I found it in my heart to make my father's behavior acceptable. I suppose no one ever wants to think badly of their parent—especially when that parent was the only one remaining in their life. Now, knowing that my mother is alive, I have to confess I would like to hear her side of the story."

"I think it would do you good to hear it," Marty said. "At least then you can judge the matter for yourself."

"I think it's possible I've been a fool, Marty." She frowned and twisted her gloved hands. "My father lied to me. He knew my mother was alive. He had her letters. Mrs. Ingram told me there had been a dozen or more that had been kept in his things. How could he lie to me like that?"

"Men do what they think they have to in order to get by. Your father obviously felt it was best to keep your mother from you. Whether that decision was made because he was selfish or trying to punish her, or even if it was because he knew your mother could cause you real harm, I'm sure he acted on the belief that he was doing good for you."

"Good? How could he think it was good to lie?"

Marty shrugged. "Folks lie for a lot of reasons—I ought to

know. But even when I've lied in the past, even when I knew what I was doing would end up causing me trouble in the long run, I always had the best of intentions." She shook her head. "I could always rationalize my decisions."

"I'm so afraid." She sighed and met Marty's gaze. "I'm afraid of what the truth will reveal."

Marty gave her a knowing nod. The expression on her face was almost pained. "I know just how you feel."

★

"So this was Marty's place," Jake stated more than questioned. He and Will had ridden over to the ranch after breakfast, and Jake couldn't help but feel a sense of unease.

"As far as I'm concerned," Will said, "it still is Marty's place. Oh, I told her I'd buy it back, but I didn't actually do the paper work on it. I sent her some money to help out with her needs, but I figured she'd come back one day." He eased back in the saddle a bit and rested his hands on the horn. "Texas is in Marty's blood. She might as well have been born here. I can't imagine she'll truly be happy anyplace else."

"She holds Texas a grudge. And it runs pretty deep." Jake looked at the small ranch house. "She and her man build this?"

Will nodded. "We all did. It was a community effort—a wedding gift. Thomas added to the place a few years after they wed. He built the barn and pens, the outbuildings and such. He was a hardworkin' man—like yourself."

Jake could see the place was sadly neglected. The house needed a coat of paint, as did the barn. Some of the fencing sections had been allowed to give way, and weeds rose up in place of well-groomed flower beds and vegetable gardens.

"I figure you'll want to take it back over. Marty may hold

Texas a grudge, but she's never been one to stay mad for long." He grinned. "As I'm sure you know."

"She endured a powerful hurt here," Jake said, shaking his head. "I wouldn't want her to think she had to live here. Not if it makes her uncomfortable."

"Why don't you just plan to stay on with us for a time," Will suggested. "At least until we're able to mother-up the calves and get 'em branded. Once we have the cows paired with their babies, we can see exactly which belong where. Marty's herd did well last year, and I expect this year will be the same. Last time I checked, most of the cows had delivered and the calves all seemed healthy.

"Anyway, you and Marty can live at our place for the time bein'. Miss Chesterfield, too. The house is more than big enough for all of us. That'll give Marty a chance to ease back in, and I'll have you to help me with roundup."

Jake met the older man's intense gaze. "Thank you, Will. I appreciate what you're doing for me, for us. I don't take any of this lightly. I want to do a good job—to be a good husband to Marty. I know she's worried I'll get myself killed like her other husband, but I don't intend that to happen."

Will chuckled. "Can't say anyone ever intends it to happen, son. However, troubles will come. We've seen it over the years, as I'm sure your family did. Death is a part of life that we have to accept. No sense in frettin' and fearin' it if a fellow knows what lies beyond this world."

"I agree," Jake replied. "I have to say I haven't always lived a life that I'm proud of, but God did get a hold of me and put me back in line."

"You wear His brand," Will said, nodding in approval. "That's clear enough to see. I watched you studying the Bible the other morning, and I've seen you at prayer. We all made mistakes in the past—me included. Or maybe I should say, me especially. God had His hands full with my sorry spirit. But thankfully, He didn't let me go."

"Yeah, I feel the same way. Don't know where I'd be if He had." Jake looked back at the ranch one more time and then turned his horse toward the road they'd come up earlier. "But I know I wouldn't have Marty, and if that were the case, my life wouldn't be worth livin' anyway."

Chapter 12

Robert waited by the buggy while his mother finished saying her good-byes to Carissa Atherton and Jessica. He had agreed to drive Mother over that Sunday afternoon because she'd been worried when the family hadn't shown up for church that morning.

"I hope that you'll let us know if you need anything," Robert's mother told Mrs. Atherton.

"Oh, we're just fine. Tyler's been sicker than this before. I think it's a bad chest cold, but I told him if it worsens he's going to the doctor."

Mother nodded. "This is a bad time of year for it. Just make sure you don't let old Doc Sutton give him calomel. I know the old man is fond of it as a cure-all, but I've read some disheartening things that suggest it's not as good a cure as was once thought."

Mrs. Atherton smiled. " 'The doctor comes with free goodwill, but ne'er forgets his calomel.' " She chuckled. "I remember hearing that when I was growing up. Never liked the stuff."

"Dr. Sutton is nearly eighty, and his notions are so outdated. I heard it said that he still bleeds people on occasion."

"I remember him telling me that I'd miscarried a baby because of the gravitational pull of the earth or the moon or some such nonsense."

Mother nodded. "Yes, I've heard others say the same. Frankly, we need to encourage him to retire and get a younger doctor to take over his practice. I know there are plenty of good doctors closer to Dallas, but we need someone who would be willing to come farther out."

"Well, Tyler won't be getting calomel from me. I can promise you that," Mrs. Atherton said.

"I think it does little good and a lot of harm."

Robert knew his mother had been something of a local healer for years, and people often sought her advice before going elsewhere. He wasn't at all surprised when she told Jessica's mother that she would be happy to help in the matter.

"I have remedies that I know will suit better than that," Mother told the ladies. "Just let me know if you need something."

"I will." Mrs. Atherton's expression suddenly changed. "Oh, I almost forgot. I have that lard I promised you." She turned to Jessica. "Take Robert to the springhouse and show him where that lard is. It's near to fifty pounds," she said rather apologetically. "I hope you don't mind. I put it in one tub."

Robert pushed off the side of the carriage. "It's not a problem."

Jessica turned up her nose. "I find it appalling. Smelly stuff." She led the way to the springhouse but turned and stopped when they were out of sight. "Still, it gives us a few minutes to be alone." She smiled and let her shawl fall away. "Do you like my new gown? I had it made in Dallas. Isn't it just about the most beautiful color you've ever seen? They called it *Samson* and it came all the way from London."

"Looks like green to me," Robert replied with a shrug. "Nice enough. You always fill out a dress real well."

She looked at him and frowned. "You are such a . . . a . . . cowboy."

He laughed. "Well, I reckon I should be insulted, but I'm not. Years of ranching have made that the case. But I still know that green is green, and Samson's a fellow in the Bible."

Jessica stamped her foot. "You can be such a bubbleheaded philistine."

Robert shrugged thoughtfully. "Samson had a bad time of it with the Philistines. Guess it fits that you are, too."

She shook her finger at him. "You know very well that I am only trying to bring a little beauty and culture into your life and into the world around me. Goodness, but you'd think we were at the beginning of the 1800s instead of approaching the end. The 1900s are soon to be here and with it a new modern world."

Sobering, Robert looked at the young woman. So many people expected the couple to marry, yet Robert knew they had little in common.

"Jess, you can have your new modern world. Just leave me Texas."

"But once we're married," she said, giving him a knowing nod, "you'll change your tune. I intend for us to live abroad for a least part of our lives."

"Abroad? And what would I do abroad? I'm a Texas cattle-man." Robert shook his head. "Sometimes I don't think you know anything about me at all."

She came and took hold of his arm and tucked it close to her side. "Now, Robert, don't be such a bore. Of course I know you. I know all about you, and that's why I want to show you what you're missing."

"But that's just it, Jess. I don't feel like I'm missin' a thing."

She pulled back just a bit. "But you've never been out of Texas. I have. I've traveled with my grandparents, and there's so much more to the world than just Texas."

Robert liked the way the sun glinted on her honey-brown hair. She was a striking woman, to be sure, but he wasn't in love with her.

They resumed their walk toward the springhouse. Robert ignored the annoyance in Jessica's tone as she continued to belabor her point. She told him about the glorious big cities she'd visited and all the wonders she had yet to see.

"I know you'll love seeing the world once you're actually doing it," she said, stopping at the door to the springhouse. "You just need to trust me on this."

"Maybe you just need to hear what I'm sayin'." Robert pulled his arm away. "I don't intend to travel abroad or any-where else, for that matter. I'm happy here, Jess. I love the land and the animals. I love what I do. This is my life."

"But it's not what I want," Jessica said.

"Which is why we aren't married," Robert countered.

She frowned at this and began to pout as she pushed back the door. "You're such a mean person sometimes."

"It's not meanness, Jess. It's the truth. I think we've been going two different directions for a long time. I know folks figure we ought to marry each other, but honestly, we don't see eye to eye on much at all."

"You're just scared."

"I'm not scared. I'm tryin' to be honest with you. I don't

want anyone sayin' I duped you. I don't plan to live in a grand house and wear fancy duds. I don't plan to travel or buy priceless bits of junk to put in my house. I just wanna run my ranch and raise a family."

"Well, you'll need a wife to raise a family, and in order to get one, you're going to have to learn to compromise. My mother says that marriage is one big compromise."

"So where does that figure in for you compromising on all these big schemes?" Robert asked.

She looked as if his question confused her. "I'll have children."

"And that's a compromise?" Her comment left him feeling even sadder than when they'd started this conversation.

"Well, children require a great deal of care and attention. It's difficult to travel with them and harder still to have nice things. The compromise will be that I will bear children and endure the consequences."

"Maybe we could just have a houseful of servants to watch over them while we make our way around the world," he replied in a sarcastic tone.

She didn't hear it that way. Instead, she smiled and nodded. "Exactly. That's what I think. A good governess or two and a nurse can take care of the children. Of course, I'll still have to compromise in bearing them."

"You can have that compromise without me. I want to be a father, and when I have children, I want them to be with me."

"You are so difficult." Jessica's words echoed a bit from the interior of the springhouse. She pointed to the large tub of lard. "Take it and go. I hardly think we need to belabor this subject further. You'll understand my point of view in time."

"I don't think time will help me one bit." He hoisted up the lard. "I think you should probably just look to workin' over some other fella. There's bound to be one out there who wants to wear a fancy top hat and cavort with you all over the world—without children. But it ain't me."

She turned and beamed him a smile that he completely did not expect. "Oh, Robert. You do say the funniest things. You know I couldn't be untrue to you."

Robert stopped and put the tub down momentarily. "Jessica, I'm serious. I don't want to lead you on. I'm not the man you want me to be."

She put her hand on his arm once again and leaned close. "But you could be . . . if you wanted to be."

He shook his head. "But that's just it. I don't want to change. We've been good friends since we were little. You followed me around like some kind of lost puppy. I thought you were a sweet little girl, like my sisters. But I wouldn't marry my sister."

Jessica frowned. "So you don't care for me?"

"You know that's not true. I do care for you. That's why I'm not sure—"

She put her finger to his lips. "I'm sorry, Robert. I was too pushy and too insensitive to your feelings. Forgive me." She stepped back and pulled her shawl close. "Now, we'd better get back before our mothers believe us to be up to no good."

Robert felt the muscles in his face tighten. He wanted to say something more. He wanted to tell Jessica that they needed to just forget about marrying and let everyone know they weren't suited to a life together. So why couldn't he seem to get the words out?

He lifted the tub again and followed after her, trying to figure out how he could make Jessica understand without crushing her spirit and causing problems between the families. He didn't want to hurt or disappoint anyone.

Back at the buggy Robert could see that his mother had already settled in for the ride home. He put the tub at the back and strapped it down.

"You be careful now," Mrs. Atherton said. "Looks like we could get a good rain out of those clouds to the west."

Robert gave the sky a glance. "I'm sure we'll be home before then." He tipped his hat at Mrs. Atherton and Jessica before releasing the brake.

They were well down the road for home before Robert's mother questioned him. "What's wrong? Did you and Jessica have a spat?"

He gave his mother a side glance. "Why did you marry Pa?"

She laughed. "Well, I wasn't expecting that question, but the answer is simple. I was crazy with love for him. I couldn't imagine my life without him in it."

Shaking his head, Robert sighed. "I don't feel that way about Jess, and I don't think I ever will."

"What do you mean? I know you care about her. You've been her hero since she was a little girl."

"Maybe so, but Ma, I don't love her like that. It's really startin' to bother me, too. Everyone figures we'll marry. Everyone calls us engaged, and God knows I've never done anything to change their minds."

"Of course not. Why should you? Goodness, Robert, I think sometimes young folks expect some sort of freight train to run them over when they fall in love. But sometimes love just comes along in a quiet and gentle fashion. Sometimes love is born from a lifetime of knowin' each other, and other times from just a few hours. Pray about it, son. You might just be feelin' the pressures of the season. We've got a lot of work to do, and I know you've had a lot on your mind. Don't make rash decisions."

Robert blew out an exasperated breath. *I doubt any-one's gonna let me make any of my own decisions—rash or otherwise.*

★

Marty checked her reflection in the small mirror one more time before deciding there was no way to improve her tired-looking face. She felt exhausted from the long hours on the train. She frankly didn't care to ever set foot on another—at least not for a very long time.

Her stomach growled in hunger, reminding her that it had been over twelve hours since they'd eaten anything. All the food they'd brought with them was gone, and with no money to spare, buying more was out of the question. Jake and the others would probably be there to greet them. Perhaps they would bring sandwiches. Marty certainly hoped so.

"Are you eager to see everyone again?" Alice asked. "I have to say I'm excited to be a part of this adventure."

Marty smiled. "I have to admit I am looking forward to seeing my husband and my family. I'm nervous, too. I want very much for everything to be good. There's no telling how things have gone for Jake since he wrote. He might not get along with my family. They may have even had a falling-out by now."

"Oh, that's silly." Alice shook her head. "I don't think that would ever happen. Jake is a good-natured man. And from what you've told me about your family, well, I think we will all get along just fine. It was so kind of them to include bringing me here."

"My sister is especially fond of helping those in need. She's a good Christian woman. I sometimes wish I could be more like her. I'm afraid I don't have her sensitivity to the needs of people around me. I figure it's because I'm far too self-centered." Marty sighed. "I've tried to be a good person. I really have."

"You have a good heart," Alice said, taking hold of Marty's gloved hand. "You need to stop fretting. No one is perfect, nor will they ever be. The only good thing about us is Jesus. Don't you think He will forgive you for whatever flaws you have?"

"Of course," Marty agreed. "But I know He also wants us to become more like Him. I want that, too, but sometimes I fail so miserably. I can't help but worry about things that seem important to me and don't know how to stop being like that. You'd think for a woman who just turned thirty-six, I would be making some progress."

Alice chuckled and patted Marty's hand. Just then the conductor swung through the car. "We'll be in the station in less than five minutes. Remember, this is just a brief stop, so be ready to disembark. We have a schedule to keep."

The women nodded and Marty could feel the train begin to slow. The grinding sound of metal on metal, coupled with the blasts of the train's whistle, permeated her ears. Her heart began to beat faster. Jake would be there waiting for her. If the rest of the world forgot all about her or was otherwise occupied, Marty knew without a doubt that Jake would still be there. The thought made her smile, and she lovingly put her hand to her waist.

I know he'll be happy about you, too. She bit her lower lip. *But we'll wait just a little longer before we tell him the news. Just in case . . . just on the chance that . . . that you can't stay.*

The train came to a halt and Marty noticed the depot sign. *Cedar Springs. Back where I started. Back in Texas, where I'd hoped never to return.* She grimaced and got to her feet as Alice moved to collect their smaller bags. Her back ached from the long hours of travel. She prayed that was all it was. She'd had a backache the last time she'd lost a baby. She frowned. What if . . .

Marty knew she had to get her heart and mind under control. They seemed to be warring with each other at the moment, and that would never do. She needed to put aside her fears and be strong.

I'm being fretful and silly. I'm just sore from travel, and I needn't create a problem where there isn't one. I'm going to be happy. I want to see Jake, and that's the most important reason for being here.

Jake would know how hard this was on her. Of that Marty had no doubt. But he wouldn't know the full reason for her fears.

"Careful now, ma'am," the porter said as he helped Marty down the train steps.

She glanced for some sign of her family. No one seemed to be around. The entire platform was nearly deserted.

Alice looked toward the baggage car. "I'll see to our things." She smiled at the baggage man, who stood not far from his cart. "Would you assist me, please?"

"Yes'm," the man said, giving her a brief nod. "Pleasure be mine."

Marty tried not to fret at the absence of her family. She knew that any number of things could have happened to delay their arrival. Her stomach growled again.

"Well, whether they get here or not, I'm going to have something to eat."

"Talking to yourself, Mrs. Wythe?"

She turned to find Jake standing only a few feet behind her. Without giving any thought to the public display, Marty threw herself into his arms. "I'm so sorry," she said, breaking into tears. "I'm so sorry for the way I acted. I've missed you so much."

He wrapped his arms around her and pulled her close. "There now, don't cry, Marty. You're here and that's all that matters." He lifted her chin and kissed her tenderly. "I missed you, too."

"I know I'm making a spectacle of myself," she said, meeting his gaze, "but I don't care. I don't like the idea of living in Texas, but I hate the idea of living without you even more. I don't want to ever be apart again."

He grinned. "Me either." He hugged her close and Marty felt her fears give way. Surely God would keep Jake safe. Surely He wouldn't demand another husband from her—or another child.

★

Robert had heard a great deal about Alice Chesterfield. He knew about the attack that had taken the life of her father and left her scarred. Jake had told them about the situation and of the man who tormented Alice for property she no longer had in her possession. But now sitting across the table from the blond-haired woman, Robert felt completely captivated by her.

Alice smiled and answered all the questions his mother had for her. She seemed as patient and relaxed as if they'd all been old friends reunited after a brief separation.

"And is the room to your liking?" Mother asked.

"Oh, it's beautiful and so big. You really didn't need to give me such a large room," Alice answered.

Robert's mother smiled and passed a plate of corn bread in Alice's direction. "Nonsense. It was one of our daughters' rooms, and it wants for someone to enjoy it. This house seems so empty sometimes. I'd love to fill it with people again."

"Well, we're off to a good start with Jake and Marty and Alice," Robert's father interjected. "Marty, I can't tell you how good it is to see you again. And you look quite fit. Colorado must have agreed with you."

"It did," Marty said. "It's very beautiful there, and the air is dry and fresh."

"And it snows . . . a lot," Jake added.

"That's true," Marty agreed. "I have to admit I'm no lover of the cold."

"I'm so amazed at how things are already greening up down here," Alice commented. "February in Denver is never anything but cold, snow, and ice."

"Well, we've had a mild winter—drier than most, but before you came we had a couple of rains. It did wonders for the land," Pa told her. "But you wait. In another few weeks we'll be full of blossoms and greenery."

"And we'll be very busy planting gardens," Robert's mother announced. "I'm so glad you'll both be here to help."

Alice nodded. "I don't know much about gardening, but I'm happy to learn."

"Then we'll have you ridin' and ropin' before you know it," Pa said with a smile.

"I think I'd like that, too," Alice replied, giggling.

Her amusement only served to make Robert all the more fond of her. She was lighthearted, yet there was something very serious about her spirit.

"Don't do it," Marty whispered in his ear.

Robert startled and looked to his aunt for an explanation. She smiled in her knowing way. At the other end of the table the family was already busy chatting about teaching Alice to brand calves, so Robert leaned close to ask. "Do what?"

"Don't make her your new project. She might bear life's

138

wounds, but she's not one of your injured animals, and I don't want to see her hurt."

"Aunt Marty, I have no idea of hurting anyone," Robert replied quietly and leaned back in his chair with a smile. "You should know me better than that."

"I do know you," Marty whispered. "And I recognize that smile on your face. You think you've got me fooled, but I can see in your eyes that you're already making plans."

Robert said nothing but turned his attention back on the meal. He was making plans, but Aunt Marty didn't need to know anything about them.

Chapter 13

"I usually plant corn over here," Hannah told Alice as she and Marty followed her from one plot of ground to another. "I've had some of the orphan boys you sent us last year work on turning up the dirt for me and getting it ready for planting."

"I can't wait to see them again," Marty said, glancing around. "Where are they?"

"Out on the range. We only have two of them with us now. The rest have found homes elsewhere. Hiram and Nate are working with the cattle. They ride like they were born to it and have taken to their duties with ease. They remind me of Andy when he was first learning to rope and ride."

"I'm so glad," Marty replied. She barely remembered the older boys. Her mind however went to thoughts of Wyatt, Sam, and Benjamin. "Those children are so precious. They deserve much more than what they've been given."

"We very much enjoyed working with the orphans in Denver," Alice added. "And the children were quite fond of Marty."

"They just loved me for my cookies," Marty said and laughed. She pulled at the cuff of her sleeve. "I think they'd be glad for anyone who would give them some attention. After all, they're hardly more than babies. They are frightened and so alone. The folks who should be in their lives are either dead or gone. I just wanted to show love to each of them."

"It must have been hard to leave," Hannah said, looking at her sister with great compassion. "I know how attached a person can get to children. Had anyone tried to take you or Andy from my care, I would have protested loudly."

"As I recall, there was that horrible Mr. Lockhart who wanted to send me and Andy to the far reaches so he could have you to himself."

Hannah shuddered. "I try to forget about that man." She turned to Alice. "You aren't the only one to have tragedy and evil men in your past. Mr. Lockhart was the one responsible for killing our father. He caused this family a great deal of harm."

"That's terrible," Alice said. "I hate to hear that anyone else should have to endure the things I've gone through." The look on her face betrayed her fears.

Hannah reached out and touched the younger woman's shoulder. "You are among friends here, and those people can't hurt you anymore. We'll see to that."

Alice looked into Hannah's eyes, and Marty could see that she very much wanted to believe those words. "I feel as if I'm on the run and always will be."

Hannah hugged her close and then stepped back. "You can let that thought go. You are home now. At least for as long as you want to call it home."

Home. Marty looked around her. There wasn't an inch of this place that she didn't know like the back of her hand.

She'd had a wonderful childhood on this ranch. Oh, it hadn't been without its problems and lean years, but they'd had one another, and that had made it all bearable.

Can I learn to be happy here? Can I call this home and know in my heart the kind of contentment that should come from such a place?

She thought of the ranch she'd shared with Thomas. She'd loved her little house. Maybe it would be wise to talk to Will about taking the ranch back. He'd bought it from her—well, he'd agreed to. The paper work hadn't been finalized, though he had sent her a down payment on the purchase. Perhaps she could work something out with him. She knew that Jake would find the spread she and Thomas had worked ideal— just as Thomas had.

"I don't think you've heard a word we said."

Marty looked up to find Hannah and Alice watching her. "I'm sorry. I was off in my own thoughts."

Hannah smiled. "I'm sure it's a challenge to be back and take it all in at once. Jake seems like a very good man. I've enjoyed getting to know him. I was just telling Alice that although you have your own place, I selfishly would like you to stick around for a while."

Marty was surprised by this turn of events. "Stay here? With you and Will?"

"Yes. What's so strange about that?"

"Nothing, Hannah. I suppose I hadn't really thought about it."

"You should. It's been over a year since anyone lived at your place. It's gonna need some attention before anyone lives there again."

Alice gave her a knowing look. "Maybe it would be a good idea, considering."

Marty realized what Alice was getting at. She supposed she should come clean and admit her condition to Hannah. After all, her sister had borne three children and had also acted as midwife for a great many women.

"Considering what?" Hannah asked. She looked from Alice to Marty. "What should be considered?"

"I'm going to have a baby," Marty replied, watching for her sister's reaction.

Hannah's face lit up and her smile stretched from ear to ear. She rushed to take hold of Marty and all but gave a yell of approval. "That's wonderful news! When?"

"Shh," Marty said with her finger to her lips. "Jake doesn't know yet."

"What? But why not?"

Marty shrugged. "I haven't had a chance to tell him. I was too tired last night. Right after supper I fell asleep. I don't even remember getting into bed. I think I fell asleep in the wing-backed chair by our fireplace. Jake must have carried me to bed. When I finally woke up this morning, he was already gone."

"Well, you need to tell him right away. A fella needs to hear that kind of news."

"But . . . well . . ." Marty heaved a sigh. "I'm afraid to get his hopes up."

"Why?" Hannah looked at her oddly.

Marty bit her lip and turned away. "It's hard to get excited when . . . well . . . I could lose the baby. I did before."

Hannah forced Marty to face her. "You never told me."

"I know." Marty shook her head. "I thought it better if you just figured I couldn't get pregnant. Thomas and I were so saddened by the losses."

"More than one?"

Marty nodded. "I don't want Jake to have to go through that. That's one of the biggest reasons I didn't want to come back to Texas."

"I don't understand," Hannah said. "Why would that be a problem?"

"Dr. Sutton told me that miscarriage is common here because we're closer to the equator."

Hannah rolled her eyes. "That old man needs to retire. I was just talking with Carissa about this. It's nonsense. There's no such thing as a gravity pull that causes miscarriage. That's old superstition and nonsense. Women miscarry in the North as well as the South. Some babies just don't get to be born. It's sad but true. We have no way of knowin' why. But I can tell you this, Marty, it has nothin' to do with Texas."

"How can you be so sure?" Marty wanted to believe her sister. She knew the doctor in Denver had told her much the same thing, but it seemed that men of science often told people whatever was the most popular theory of the day. "How can you know that I won't lose this baby, too?"

"I can't know that, Marty. But I do know that only God can create or take a life and that we have to trust Him. It's hard, to be sure, but you won't benefit yourself or the child by worrying and fretting."

"I want to believe that."

Hannah smiled. "Then do. This is a time of joy. You need to let Jake know as soon as possible. I won't stand for you keeping it from him any longer. By the way, when should we expect this little one?"

Marty put her hand to her stomach. "August. Or maybe July. I'm really not sure."

Hannah nodded. "Good summer months for birthing. And I'll help you through it all. Alice and I will help you make baby clothes, and we'll fix up a nursery, and you can just stay here with us. I don't want you to overdo it."

Hannah directed them to start back toward the house. "Now, I want to know everything about your miscarriages. How far along were you? What were you doing when the pain started?"

Marty couldn't get a word in edgewise as they went back into the kitchen. Alice threw Marty a smile but said nothing. There was simply no chance of it with Hannah's animated chatter.

Later that day, Jake invited Marty to go riding with him. She asked Hannah if she thought it would be all right, given her condition, and her sister assured her that many women rode well into their pregnancy.

Marty changed into a split skirt for the occasion and made her way to where Jake already had the horses saddled and ready. She'd grown up riding astride, as many women in Texas did, and was pleased to see that Jake hadn't prepared the feminine sidesaddle.

He helped her into the stirrup and up atop the gentle brown mare before heading over to his own mount.

"I bought this chestnut gelding in Lufkin after getting my first pay. The Vandermarks had some friends who made me a good deal, otherwise I'd still be afoot." He climbed atop the tall horse and smiled. "His name is Bobbin. Not sure why, but the woman who had him told me he knows his name, and she begged me not to even think of changin' it."

Marty couldn't help but smile. "Bobbin isn't such a bad name."

They moved the horses down the lane and headed out toward Marty's ranch. She had been the one to suggest the destination, and Jake seemed pleased with the idea. She didn't know if anyone had bothered to show him the spread or not, but she wanted to talk to him about the baby and about her fears before any more time could slip away.

The ranch house was nearly five miles away, but the day was beautiful, with blue skies that didn't even hint at rain. They talked about the work Jake had been doing, and Marty could hear in his voice a kind of joy she'd never known him to have when they were in Denver.

"So I suppose you don't want to ever consider banking again?"

"Banking?" he asked, looking over from his mount. "Seriously?"

"Sure. Texas has banks, too." She tucked an errant strand of hair back under her hat. "And things won't be bad forever."

"My heart isn't in banking, Marty. I thought you'd understand that by now."

She did understand it, but that didn't mean she didn't hope to change his mind. "You know, the older you get, the harder ranch work is going to be. I look at Will and he's aged a lot just in the last year." Marty didn't bother to add that her brother-in-law only looked better for it.

"I'm trying to keep my focus on what God wants for me," Jake told her. "I feel His presence in my ranch work. That never happened with banking."

"Well, one can hardly argue with the presence of God," Marty muttered.

"Look, I know you worry about my safety, but I've been careful. I never was one for takin' undue risks, anyway," he said with a grin. "That's for your brother. Given the stories your sister and Will told about him, I'm surprised he lived to be grown."

Marty laughed at this. "Andy was always daring. He said

taking risks made him feel alive. He never wanted to be one to die with his boots off."

"And you can laugh about that in a brother but not in a husband?" he asked good-naturedly. "Honestly, Marty, you gotta let me be a man. One day, who knows, we might have sons, and you'll have to let them be men, too."

Marty swallowed hard. They had just reached the ranch, and he'd given her the perfect opportunity to tell Jake the truth about the baby.

"Hmm, would you mind helping me down?" Marty asked. "I'd like to walk the rest of the way."

Jake quickly complied and all but lifted Marty off the horse. He let her slowly sink to the ground and gave her a quick peck on the nose. "You are a beauty, Mrs. Wythe." He went to tie the horses off in a grassy patch and then returned to Marty and offered her his arm. "I do need to confess, I came out here with your brother-in-law."

"I thought Will might have brought you here." She took hold of his arm and began to walk. "He is usually a very thorough man. However, I'd like to return to something you said earlier."

"What's that?" He looked at her with one brow raised.

"You said that I have to let you be a man, and that I would have to let our sons be men."

"Well, you sure don't wanna turn boys into sissies. I wouldn't stand for that. It seems to me that there are already a lot of sissified men—"

"Jake, I'm gonna have a baby," she interrupted.

He immediately shut up and turned to face her. His expression changed almost immediately from shock to sheer joy. He gave a yell loud enough to be heard in Dallas and lifted Marty in his arms.

"Why didn't you say so sooner! Wahoooo! This is the best news ever!" He whirled around with Marty in his arms then set her back on the ground. "When?"

"August. Or maybe as early as July. I can't be sure."

"But that's only about five or six more months. Why didn't you tell me sooner?"

"I only found out for sure after you'd gone. Then there were other things . . . fears that kept me from saying anything—especially in a letter."

He looked at her oddly. "What kinds of things?"

"I couldn't help remembering the times Thomas and I thought we were going to have a little one. I miscarried and lost those babies. I feared the same might come true this time around. Of course, I also thought a lot of it had to do with living in Texas. The doctor here told me that there were a lot more miscarriages due to the heavier gravity because we're closer to the equator."

"That sounds like hogwash," Jake replied.

"That's what my sister and the doctor in Denver said, too. But I couldn't help worry, because the doctor here said otherwise." She shook her head and raised her hands in surrender. "Call me silly or dim-witted. I'm still not sure what to believe, although this is the longest I've managed to carry a child."

"Oh, darlin', you aren't silly or dim-witted. Stubborn, yes. Given to exaggeration? Hmm, on occasion." He laughed. "You don't need to be afraid that Texas is gonna cause you to lose the baby, Marty. Lots of women have babies in Texas." He grinned and the delight was reflected in his eyes. "I can't believe I'm a papa."

"We still have six months to get through," Marty declared.

Jake shook his head. "Nope, I'm already Papa to this little

one." He put his hand to Marty's waist. "I can hardly wait. Marty, you've made me the happiest man in the world."

"But you'd be even happier if I said yes to moving back here to the ranch, wouldn't you?"

He withdrew his touch. "Marty, I can't lie and say that ranching isn't what I wanna do. But, I will say this. If livin' here where you made a home with your first husband makes you uncomfortable, we'll live elsewhere."

Marty sighed. There was no possibility of changing her destiny. Texas and ranching were always going to be a part of her life. She gave Jake a smile. "This place is nice," she told him. "The trees provide cool shade in the summertime. There's a river that flows across the property, and while it gets low in times of drought, it doesn't usually run dry." She choked a bit on the words. "It's a good house, too. Will and most of the men in the community came and helped Thomas build it. It's sturdy. Oh, and there's a wonderful root cellar that's good for storms as well as food storage."

Jake took her in his arms. "You're a good woman, Marty. I promise to do everything I can to make you happy. I love you."

She fought back tears. "I love you, Jake. I was so unhappy with you gone. I'm sorry that I'm so afraid. I don't mean to be. I wanna trust this to God, but sometimes I just remember seein' Thomas lying there . . . the blood . . . the—"

"Shh, let it go. You don't need to be dwellin' on such things, especially now that you have our little one to think on." He smoothed back a lock of hair. "I want you to be happy, Marty. We don't have to live here."

She nodded and reached up to touch his face. "Hannah would like us to stay on with them a while. I told her about losing the other babies, and she wants to take care of me."

"I'd like that, too. It'll be a sight easier to go off and work away from the ranch if I know you're being looked after. Between her and Alice, you'll be in good hands. I'm happy for us to stay put. I just hope one day you'll be ready for us to run our own ranch."

Marty let out a ragged breath. "One day, I will be. I promise."

Chapter 14

"You seem mighty deep in thought," Robert said, coming to sit at the small table by the fireplace.

Alice had positioned herself there to gain a little warmth from the hearth. The evening had turned cool, and the chill seemed to cut clear to the bone. She tugged at the edges of her shawl, feeling rather nervous in the presence of Robert Barnett. "I suppose I have a great deal on my mind," she answered.

"Would you like to play a game of checkers?" He motioned to the board on the table.

"Why not?" She shrugged. "It won't interfere with anything I have planned."

He laughed. "You know, for someone who's just eighteen, you have an old spirit."

Alice looked at him quizzically for a moment. "What makes you say that?"

Please don't make this about my injury and how brave I am to live my life.

Robert shook his head and arranged the checkers on the board. "I don't know. It's just something about you. You've been through a lot, so I suppose that has something to do with it. It just seems that other ladies your age are flighty and immature. They seem a whole lot more interested in the next party or a new dress." He gave a chuckle and added, "And most are completely obsessed with tryin' to find a husband."

Alice couldn't hide her frown, nor did she try to. "Well, it goes without saying, but I'm certainly not doing that."

He cocked his head to one side. "And why not? You're a lovely woman." He smiled. "And just because you're a deep thinker doesn't mean you can't marry."

Alice didn't want to talk about such things. Still careful to keep her face turned to the right so that her scar was less visible, she asked, "What makes you so sure my thoughts are all that deep?"

He chose a red checker and made his first move. "Well, you sure don't talk much, and for a female I find that interesting in itself. Havin' grown up with sisters and a ma who all speak their mind, finding someone like you is a real treat." He nodded toward the game. "So why don't you take a turn at the board and tell me what deep thoughts you were thinkin'."

Alice felt her face grow warm under his scrutiny. She moved her black checker. "I was thinking about my mother, if you must know."

He moved again. "I heard Aunt Marty say you thought she was dead but recently found out otherwise."

"Yes." Alice selected another checker without thought. "That's it exactly. Marty's been after me to send my mother a letter and let her know where I am."

"But you don't want to?" He continued to stare at the board, seeming to ponder his choices.

"I don't know. It might just tip over a big can of worms if I do."

He looked up and smiled. He had the most beautiful eyes, and his face was like a fine sculpture, chiseled in warm flesh tones instead of cold marble. He was the kind of man she'd always dreamed of—before the accident. Alice felt her heart skip a beat.

I've never felt this way about anyone before. Why am I so consumed by this man all of the sudden? Am I falling in love?

The idea startled her. She would never have admitted her thoughts to anyone, not even Marty.

"Might not," Robert said and slid a checker into place.

"Might not what?" Alice asked, forcing the confusion from her mind.

"Knock over a can of worms. It might be a real good thing."

Alice looked at the board for a moment and then glanced to where Hannah was showing Marty some kind of crocheting stitch at the other end of the room. William Barnett had settled in a large chair near them and was reading a book. Even so, it was as if Alice and Robert were the only people in the room. She felt self-conscious and again tugged at her shawl.

"I suppose it just comes down to me being afraid," she admitted. Alice stopped and shook her head. "I really don't know why I'm telling you all of this. I hardly know you."

"Does that matter?" He looked at her as if her words had somehow hurt him. "I wasn't tryin' to pry."

"I realize that," Alice said, softening her tone. "I hope I didn't offend you."

"Not at all. I guess I just find your story to be . . . well . . . interesting. But more than that. It's like a puzzle to be solved. I guess I like to see things put in order."

"So you think I should write to her?"

"Does it matter what I think?"

Alice stopped trying to figure out her next move and folded her arms. "I wouldn't ask if I didn't want your answer."

He chuckled and leaned back in the chair. "Then yes, I think you should write to her. I think you should ask her all those troubling questions and demand answers."

A smile touched the corners of Alice's lips. "Demand answers? Is that what you would do?"

"I'm a man who likes to get right down to the point."

"I don't know if the address I have for her is any good. And she might very well be dead."

"And you'll never know either way unless you write to her."

Alice nodded, knowing he was right. "I have been thinking that same thing. I asked your mother if I could borrow some writing paper. I just haven't been able to make up my mind."

"I can't tell you why, but I don't think you'll be sorry . . . Alice." He paused. "It is all right if I call you Alice, isn't it? We tend to be pretty informal out here."

"Of course." Losing herself for a moment in his blue eyes, she paused. Here was a man with whom she could talk, share her heart, and not feel uncomfortable. She straightened up, no longer trying to hide her face. He didn't look away. "I'd like for you to call me Alice."

"Good. And you call me Robert. We'll be the best of friends, and tomorrow I will take you out riding after I finish my work. *If* I finish. Pa has a way of finding new tasks for me all the time."

She stiffened. "I don't know how to ride."

He gave a low chuckle. "Good thing I do, then. Your lessons will start tomorrow." He moved his checker over one of hers and grinned. "Better get your mind back on the game. I've just taken one of your pieces."

154

More than that, she thought, *you may well have taken a piece of my heart.*

★

Alice looked over the words she d just written, spending some time on the chilly February morning in her room. She'd thought long about what she would say to her mother, and even then the letter had been hard to write.

What will you think when you get this? How can we possibly put aside all the years lost and all the pain?

She held up the sheet of writing paper and began to read aloud.

"Dear Mama,
"*I can't believe you are still alive. When Mrs. Ingram told me the truth, I didn't know quite what to think. About a year after you'd gone away, Father told me you and Simon had died. It's been over a year since you wrote to Mrs. Ingram, but I decided to try this address and let you know that I am alive and well.*
"*I moved recently to Texas with a dear woman named Martha Wythe—Marty. We are staying with her brother-in-law and sister, Mr. and Mrs. William Barnett. They own a large ranch not far from Dallas, near a town called Cedar Springs. I find it peaceful. Having never been outside of Denver, I also find the warmer climate quite agreeable.*"

Alice paused and drew a deep breath before continuing.

"*I don't know how to say the things that are on my heart. I was so hurt when you left, and I've never known what to do with that pain. How does a mother leave her child without any warning, without any word? How you must have hated me. The very thought of that causes me to want to forget about sending this letter, but Marty tells me I must."*

That sounds so harsh. Perhaps I should rewrite it.

She looked at several wadded-up pieces of paper and knew she shouldn't waste yet another piece of Hannah's good writing paper. Maybe letting her mother see the pain was a good thing.

"I won't lie and pretend the past doesn't matter. I won't try to sugar this up so that it goes down easier. Nobody did that for me."

Alice's anger stirred and she fought to push it back down.

"If you desire to correspond with me, you may feel free to do so at the address you'll find at the bottom of this letter. I would particularly like to know why you left and whether my brother Simon is still alive.

"Yours truly,
"Alice"

Taking up the pen, she wrote the mailing instructions and set the letter aside to let the ink dry. A part of her felt good for what she'd accomplished, while another part felt sick. Marty had been after her to write ever since they'd learned the truth in Denver, and Alice knew she would never stop hounding her about it.

She knew Marty was right. It needed to be done. Whether

her mother had a proper explanation or even cared, Alice knew she had to have at least this small contact. She could only pray that her mother was still alive and residing at the same place.

Her thoughts quickly passed from the letter to Robert's promise of riding lessons that afternoon. He was a most incredible man, nearly ten years her senior, as Alice understood from Marty. He was the only son and heir to the Barnett ranching empire, but even if he'd been poor, Alice would have found herself drawn to him.

There was something about the casual way he interacted with her. He didn't seem to care about her appearance. He had never commented on the scar once. No doubt Marty had filled everyone in on her situation prior to their arrival. And if she hadn't, now that they were in residence the story would surely have been told. Even so, Robert made no mention of it.

Perhaps it truly doesn't bother him. Maybe he doesn't care that I'm less than perfect.

A knock on her door brought Alice to her feet. She crossed and opened to find Marty standing there. "We have guests and I thought you should come meet them."

"Let me get my shawl." She picked up a dark blue shawl and wrapped it around her shoulders before joining Marty in the hall. "Do I look presentable?"

"Very much so. You know, I think that scar is fading even faster now that Hannah has you using that special salve she made."

Alice put her hand to her jaw. "Do you really?"

"I do. My sister is a wonder. She knows about all sorts of things like that. You'll like getting to know her better."

"I'm sure I will," Alice said, letting Marty lead her down the hall.

In the large front room, Alice saw two women sitting and speaking with Hannah. She offered a smile but again kept her face to the right. It was a habit she found hard to break.

"Alice, this is Mrs. Carissa Atherton and her daughter Jessica. You and Jessica are about the same age," Marty declared.

Alice looked first to the older woman. Mrs. Atherton's honey-colored hair was neatly tucked and curled into place beneath a lovely hat of plum velvet and black ribbon. Alice thought her one of the most beautiful women she'd ever met.

"It's a pleasure to meet you, ma'am," Alice said, giving a little nod. She turned next to the younger woman, who seemed rather indifferent to the introduction. "Miss Atherton, I'm pleased to make your acquaintance."

Jessica looked her over for a moment. "Mother tells me you are Marty's maid."

"Not anymore," Marty replied before Alice could say a word. "Alice and I are just dear friends now."

Alice heard Jessica give a little sniff, as if disapproving. She wondered if the young woman had been raised to look down on those of less fortune. Alice waited a moment longer and then felt a sense of relief when Marty motioned her to sit.

"We were just having a nice visit," Hannah said, "and I wanted you to join us. We've been discussing plans for several events that will take place in the next few weeks, and I want you to be a part of it."

Marty seemed quite eager to share the details. "One of those events will be Jake's and Hannah's birthdays. Hannah's is on the fifth of March and Jake's is the seventh. We want to have a big party."

"*They* want to have a big party," Hannah corrected.

"And of course Robert has a birthday on the second of

April," Jessica said, smiling. "I do hope we can have a party for him, as well."

"First things first," Mrs. Atherton interjected. "The men won't have time for much of anything until after roundup. We need to think on how we're going to handle that. I was speaking with my sister, Laura, a couple of days ago, and we thought it might be nice to host the roundup at my place. It's pretty centrally located to all the participants, since we'll have the Harpers and Watsons joining us."

"I think that sounds fine," Hannah replied.

Alice had no idea what they were talking about, but it sounded like quite the occasion. She looked to Marty for clarification, but her friend didn't seem to notice.

"So there will be eight ranches involved all together?" Marty questioned.

Hannah and Carissa Atherton nodded in unison, but it was the latter who spoke. "The Reids will be there, the Harpers, Watsons, Barnetts." She paused a moment to count on her fingers.

Marty used that opportunity to explain to Alice, "The Reids are Carissa's sister and brother-in-law and their sons, of course. They have a horse farm with some of the finest quality animals to be had."

Carissa seemed to regain her thoughts. "Of course our family will be there. Then there's the Palmers, the Kirbys, and the Armstrongs. Yes, eight ranches in total."

"Speaking of the Armstrongs." Marty paused and looked to Alice. "Mrs. Atherton's oldest daughter married the Armstrongs' youngest son, Elliot." She returned her gaze to Carissa. "How is Gloria doing? Are they still in North Dakota?"

"No, they were reassigned last year to Fort Assiniboine," Carissa said. "It's located way to the north in Montana. It just so happens that the black Tenth Cavalry was also moved north from its duties west of here. We just had a letter telling us all about it. Elliot was promoted to captain and has very much enjoyed getting to know some of the buffalo soldiers and hearing their stories. Gloria finds life there to be quite taxing, but she has her friends."

"And what about children?" Marty asked.

Carissa shook her head. "She lost two and I think she'd just as soon not have any more, at least for the time. It's such a hard life there. I honestly don't know how she bears it."

Hannah looked to Marty and smiled. "Are you going to share your news?"

Alice saw Marty blush as she nodded. "I'm going to have a baby. It's due in August or perhaps July."

"Oh, that's wonderful news," Carissa said. "I was just telling Jess that we needed some little ones around here. All the children are grown."

"I know just what you mean," Hannah agreed. "I keep trying to convince my daughter Sarah that she and her family should move here. Goodness, I try to talk my brother, Andy, into it, as well. I suppose we shall just have to wait to spoil Marty's baby."

"What of your younger daughter?" Carissa asked.

Hannah shrugged. "Ellie will probably never marry, or if she does, her husband will have to be a very strong man. Ellie is far too caught up in women's rights. She wants education and the ability to vote for every woman. I admire her passion, but I'd just as soon have a houseful of grandchildren." A soft laugh escaped her lips. "I think babies make a house more cheerful."

The topic of babies quickly overtook the conversation, and Alice sat patiently listening as the women planned and plotted regarding Marty's summer delivery. She lost track of the conversation and reflected once again on her letter. If Simon were alive he'd be ten.

I wonder what kind of boy you are. Are you sweet and scholarly? Are you strong and well-mannered? Visions of her brother at the age of five flickered through her mind for just a moment and then were gone. She could barely remember how he looked.

The memory of Robert's face came to mind. Alice loved his strong jaw and full lips. She wanted very much to reach out and touch his cheek and feel the stubble of his beard, the warmth of his skin. Was it possible to fall in love with a man based purely on his appearance? And if one did, was there any sense in it?

I don't even know him. He could be a lazy good-for-nothing. The thought made her smile. Of course he was neither of those things. His family had raised him to be God-fearing and responsible. He was kind and gentle in his nature and very generous with his time.

Otherwise he would never have offered to take me riding.

The Athertons left before lunch, despite Hannah's encouraging them to stay. It seemed Jessica had a dress fitting or some other appointment in town, and they needed to push on. Alice put aside her reflections on the handsome Robert Barnett. She had just begun to help with the cleanup when Marty posed a question Alice hadn't expected. A question that left her feeling sick.

"So, Hannah, when do Robert and Jessica plan to marry?"

Chapter 15

"Are you comfortable?" Robert asked, looking up into Alice's pale, anxious face.

"It seems awfully high up here," she replied from the horse's back.

He chuckled. "I suppose it would, since you aren't used to ridin'." He handed her the reins. "Now take these and hold them firm in your left hand but not tight. Your hand will cramp up on you if you clench the reins."

She took the straps in her gloved hands, as if she were handling a rattlesnake. Robert knew she was terrified and longed to find a way to reassure her. He knew the only way for her to get comfortable, however, was to actually ride the animal, so he quickly mounted his own horse.

"Betsey, there, is a good old gal. She won't go runnin' off with you, so try to relax." He motioned toward the open range. "Let's go up this way and let you get a feel for the saddle."

Alice said nothing. The set of her jaw and her stiff posture

told Robert she was focusing completely on her position. No
doubt she was terrified of falling off and equally certain that
Betsey could feel her tension. This might require a little more
work than he'd originally thought. Reaching out, he took hold
of the bridle. "Come on, Betsey. Let's show her how it's done."

The horses moved forward and Alice reached for the horn
with her right hand. Robert smiled but said nothing. She
still held on to the reins, so he didn't want to discourage her.

"I know a lot of gals ride sidesaddle, but Ma suggested I
train you on the regular saddle instead. Riding astride isn't
always looked favorably upon for women, but I think it of-
fers you more security, and out here with the snakes and
holes and such, I think you need that extra help. This way
if something spooks your horse and she rears, you have the
added advantage of holding on with your . . . uh . . . legs."

"I'm sure you know better than I would," Alice replied in
a tight, clipped tone.

Robert let go of Betsey's bridle and allowed Rojoe to fall
back even with the mare. "The important thing is to keep
yourself balanced and centered. The horse will do the work
if you just keep a few things like that in mind. A horse needs
to know who's in charge, for one."

"He is," Alice said. "Or, I should say, she is."

Robert chuckled. "No. You are. You need to establish that
with the animal as soon as you make contact. Betsey, here, has
been a good horse to train children on, so I have the utmost
confidence she'll be easy for you."

Alice gave a hint of a smile. "I don't think any part of this
will be easy."

"Remember what I told you about holdin' your legs tight.
If you tighten up too much you're gonna wear both of you
out." He thought Alice relaxed the tiniest bit. "Now I'm

gonna show you how to stop her. I want you to gently pull back on the reins."

Alice did so, but as her right hand was still firmly on the horn, she pulled with her left, and Betsey veered toward the left and headed straight into Rojoe.

Robert corrected his mount. "No, you need to pull them straight back toward your waist. You pulled left, so Betsey thought you wanted to turn. Straighten up and loosen the reins again." He watched and waited. "Now, pull straight back and say, 'Whoa.'"

"Whoa!" Alice called out a little too enthusiastically.

Robert smiled. She was such a petite thing, and her nervousness on the back of the fourteen-hand-high mare made him want to just pull her over onto his lap and comfort her like he might a child. Of course, he wasn't thinking about Alice as a child. She was a beautiful young woman, and he had meant what he'd said about her maturity and old spirit. Compared to Jessica Atherton, Alice was far more astute and sensitive. She showed genuine concern for the people around her, and despite her fears and ordeals in life, she had the gumption to get up and try again.

"There now," Robert said, looking at Alice's tight hold, "ease up on the reins a little but keep control."

He heard Alice let out a heavy breath. She looked at him as if to question what was next. He smiled. "All right, now you get us started again."

"Me? I don't know what to do."

"Remember what I told you. Give her a little nudge with your heels. Keep your feet in the stirrups and mostly squeeze with your legs. I'm sorry if this sounds too forward talkin' about legs and such," he said, realizing he was speaking in a most familiar manner with a woman he hardly knew. "If you're too uncomfortable I could just have Aunt Marty or my mother teach you."

"No, I'm not offended."

"But you are very tense. Relax, and don't forget to draw a good deep breath. Sometimes folks forget to breathe while riding and faint off the back of the horse."

Alice grimaced. "I certainly wouldn't want to fall off Betsey. It's a long ways down."

Robert chuckled. "Now, just squeeze with your legs and give a little click with your tongue. She's leg trained so she'll respond to the pressure, but the clicking just lets her know you mean business."

Alice did as he instructed and the mare began to move. "Oh my," Alice said, again going rigid in the saddle.

"Relax. You're gonna be sore when we get done if you don't learn to ease into it."

He had to give her credit. She was trying hard not to be afraid. Alice obeyed his every order and after half an hour, Robert decided she'd had enough.

"Let's walk 'em back. It's not that far. Stop your horse."

Alice pulled back on the reins. "Whoa!" Betsey halted instantly.

"Good. You learn quick." He jumped off Rojoe's back in an effortless manner. Having been riding since before he could walk, Robert felt as if the horse was a mere extension of his own limbs.

Still holding on to the reins of his horse, he went to Alice. Rojoe seemed more interested in the new spring grass than his master, but he quickly complied and followed.

"Now you are going to dismount," Robert told Alice. "It's not all that difficult. Coming down is always easier than getting up there."

"That's what I'm afraid of," she said, looking down.

"Don't be afraid, Alice. I have you."

She frowned and looked back at the neck of her mount. "What do I need to do?"

"Keep the reins in your left hand and slip your boots out of the stirrups," he instructed. She did as he said, looking only a little bit frightened. "Now lean forward, and with your right hand you can grip the saddle or the horn. While you do this, I want you to swing your right leg back over the horse. You're gonna lean against her and then push off to slide down Betsey's side."

He heard Alice's heavy sigh and stood ready to help in case she lost her balance. To the surprise of both of them, however, she managed a perfect dismount the first time.

Robert grinned and patted her on the back. "See? You're a natural."

She shivered. "I wouldn't go so far as to say that."

"Let's walk. It'll warm you up and get your nerves untangled."

He showed her how to lead Betsey, and the two began to move back down the trail toward home. Robert couldn't help but admire the young woman at his side. He wanted more than anything to know everything about her. He wanted her to talk about her mother and brother, to tell him about the night she was knifed. Instead, he said the first thing that came to mind.

"I hear you're gonna help with the roundup cookin'."

Alice didn't look at him but nodded. "I want to be useful. I don't know anything about roundups, but I'm willing to learn."

"This will probably be our last open-range roundup," Robert said, feeling a certain sorrow. "Everyone is fencing these days. Farmers say the open range causes their crops to be ruined and thieves will drive off portions of the herd if you don't keep them under watch. Times are especially hard for folks, so stealing seems like an acceptable way to feed the family."

"Do you lose a lot of your stock?"

"No. We're in a pretty good position. We have good neighbors and we work together. We've always helped one another at roundup, but I know the time is coming when we'll be handlin' these things separately." He shrugged. "'Course that doesn't mean we won't still help one another. I know Pa will always be willing to lend a hand to anyone who needs it, and so will I."

"So you plan to remain in the area?"

Robert grinned. "I do. I have land Pa deeded me when I turned twenty-one. Five hundred acres. I have my own cattle, too. I guess now all I need is a wife and children to make my life complete."

"I understand you are engaged to Jessica Atherton."

It was Robert's turn to be uncomfortable. He hadn't wanted to talk about Jessica. "Not exactly. Folks around here think we ought to be engaged. They've expected us to marry for the last ten years, but there's never been a formal agreement."

"Ten years? But I thought Miss Atherton was my age."

"She is. She's been followin' me around like a puppy since she was little. I think it had to do with her brothers never havin' time for her. They were only a few years older than Jessica, while I was almost ten years her senior. And . . . well . . . I was nice to her."

"Well, you are fortunate to have someone who cares about you," Alice murmured.

For several minutes she said nothing, and Robert was hard-pressed as to how he should respond. Before he could speak, however, Alice continued. "I wrote to my mother. Marty was going to have the letter posted for me today, along with her letter back to the orphanage in Denver."

"I'm glad you decided to write to her," Robert said, feeling much easier about this subject. "I don't think you'll be sorry."

"I hope not. I find myself completely at odds with the decision. I pray in time God will make all things clear."

"He's good to do that. My ma always told me that when I found things were too hard to figure out, I could probably bet that I hadn't prayed on it first."

Alice nodded but said nothing more. They were nearly back to the pens, so Robert decided not to press her further. He reached out and took Betsey's reins. "I'll put her away for you, but next time you're gonna learn to saddle and unsaddle her yourself." He threw her a wink. "I know you'll be just as good at that as you were riding."

★

The weeks passed, pushing the calendar into the first of March, and with it came roundup. Alice learned there was a great deal that happened at such times. She had figured it would primarily be the job of the men, since they would be the ones roping and riding. It seemed, however, that the ranch wives and daughters had just as much to do in order for the event to be successful. Alice found herself cooking and baking days in advance of the actual roundup. There wouldn't be time for lengthy processes while seeing to the cattle, so some foods were prepared and stored ahead of time to make the workload more manageable. When the time arrived to move everything to the Atherton ranch, Alice found herself busy with toting and fetching alongside the other women. Later, she was assigned to cooking beans and helping with the washing up afterwards.

The work was arduous. The men had rounded up cattle from every point of their open ranges. They had a process for what they called mothering-up the calves. This allowed the men to separate out the pairs from the non-producing cows. The cows that were barren would be sold to the feedlot. After the animals were separated, the cowboys would start the process of dividing them up again—this time by brands.

They'd hired extra men to help with the additional tasks of branding, castrating, and treating injuries and diseases, as well as separating out those animals that would be taken to market. Alice had never seen anything like it in all her days. Having grown up in a city, her knowledge of such affairs was completely void. Meat was something to be purchased at the butcher's, and she'd never given thought to exactly what had happened to get it there.

Cooking and cleaning, however, were things Alice was well acquainted with. She found herself amazed at the fast pace of the day. She rose early in the morning, before it was light, and helped Hannah and some of the other women prepare breakfast for the cattlemen and wranglers. The menu was simple but filling. Biscuits and ham steaks, with gallons and gallons of hot, strong coffee to wash them down. The noon meal was usually ham and beans, corn bread, and some kind of sweet treat—cookies, cake, or cobbler. The evening meal was a little more relaxed and spread out. It was during the evening that the men were able to settle in and discuss the day.

Alice liked the suppertime gatherings. There were usually a few of the men who came together and played music. Some of the fellas sang, and on occasion one or two of the wives would join in, as well. Evening meals were the only time Hannah allowed Marty to join them. One of the older hands who'd been left to oversee the Barnett ranch would drive Marty over in the buggy.

Jake always seemed happy to see her, and the two would usually slip off to a spot where they'd share supper alone. Alice was delighted that they were growing closer together. Their start had been rough—there was no doubt about it. Being a mail-order couple was never an easy situation, but they had made good on their commitment, and Alice could only esteem them for it. The key to it all had been their willingness to look to God for help.

"I almost forgot," Marty said, approaching Alice that evening. "This came for you."

Alice looked at the letter Marty held. There was only one person who would be writing to her here in Texas. With shaking hands, Alice took the envelope. It was from her mother.

"She's alive."

Marty nodded. "Read it and see what she has to say."

"Read it here?" Alice asked.

With a shrug, Marty looked around the camp. "Why wait? Nobody here will mind. There is still a little light, and if it's not enough my sister hung lanterns by the cook wagon."

Alice moved toward the wagon. "What if it's . . . well . . . what if the news is bad?"

Marty was right beside her. "Then you'll have friends to stand beside you. Now open it and read it or I will." Marty's determined look told Alice that she wasn't joking.

Alice opened the letter and silently read the few words penned by her mother.

Dearest Alice,

I cannot tell you how happy I was to hear from you and know that you are alive and well. Simon and I are

170

*packing to come immediately and be with you. We
should arrive no later than the tenth of the month.*

> *With greatest affection,
> Mother*

"She's . . . she's coming here." Alice looked to Marty. "She's coming with my brother."

"That's wonderful news! I know Hannah will be delighted to have them."

Alice shook her head. "I . . . can't . . . I don't know why she's doing this." She dropped the letter and hurried away from Marty and the gathering of ranch workers. She had to be alone.

Moving just far enough away to be out of the main circle of light and noise, Alice dropped to her knees in the twilight shadows. The news had left her all but faint. She found it hard to breathe, and her vision seemed to swim.

"Are you all right?"

She looked up and found that Robert Barnett had followed her. She wanted to tell him to go away, but the words wouldn't form in her mouth. Instead, she shook her head slowly.

He knelt down beside her. "What's wrong, Alice?"

For several very long minutes she tried to think of what to say. She should be happy for the news, but instead she felt a sense of fear that she'd not known since dealing with Mr. Smith in Denver. Why should she be so unnerved?

"Alice, what is it? Talk to me."

"Marty brought me a letter. My mother . . . she's . . . alive."

"Oh, that's wonderful news." He looked at her. "Isn't it?"

The shadows fell across his face, and in the growing darkness, Alice could barely make out his features. She knew instinctively, however, that his expression would be one of great compassion.

"I . . . think so. Yes." She nodded. "But . . . well . . . she's coming here."

"Does that worry you?"

Tears formed in Alice's eyes and blurred her vision even more. "I . . . I . . . don't know." She broke down and sobbed with her face in her hands. It was such a relief to know that her mother was alive—her brother, too.

Why am I acting like this? Why this sudden sense of fear?

She didn't look up when Robert moved closer and drew her into his arms. She continued to cry quietly against his shoulder. She could feel his gentle touch and the way he stroked her head like a parent might do for a small child.

"It's the shock of the thing," he whispered. "Shock and relief."

"Well, what in the world is all this about?" The curt, suspicious words of Jessica Atherton caused Alice to snap to attention and all but jump to her feet. She struggled to put as much distance between her and Robert as she could, wiping furiously at her eyes. Tripping over her gown, she struggled to stand.

Robert seemed unfazed. He got to his feet and threw Alice a sad smile before giving Jessica a reply. "Alice had a letter about her mother and brother. You knew she thought they were dead, didn't you? Well, they're both alive and coming here to be with her."

Jessica folded her arms, not looking at all convinced. "A letter? And just how does a person get a letter in the middle of roundup?"

Alice could hear the suspicion in Jessica's voice. She felt bad that she had somehow caused this turn of events. Robert had assured her the couple's engagement wasn't official, but still she didn't like to come between sweethearts.

"Jess, if you must know, Aunt Marty brought it. If you need further proof, Alice would probably show it to you."

"I'm sorry for breaking down," Alice said before Jessica could reply. "I'm not usually given over to crying and such. If you'll excuse me, I need to get back to work."

She didn't want to hear any further exchange between Robert and Jessica. She felt terrible for what had happened. She hoped Robert would be able to set things right with Jessica and the two could go on being as close as ever.

Drying her eyes again on the hem of her apron, Alice went directly to the tubs of hot water and began washing dishes. Roundup would last only another few days, and then they'd return to the Barnett Ranch, and she'd be able to think more clearly about what was to be done.

Chapter 16

Robert had always liked his father's brand. The Bar NT was one folks in the area recognized. The small line over the letters *NT* had been his grandfather's idea—a casual way of putting the Barnett name on each head. For Robert's cattle they had added a small pigtail onto the *T*. It wasn't much, but it definitely distinguished between his head and those belonging to his father.

"Looks like you've got a good increase, son," his father said as they turned the last of the cattle out to pasture.

"I'm pleased," Robert said. "How about you? You gonna get that Angus bull out there breeding right away?"

"That's the plan. Of course our biggest task is going to be working with the other ranchers to get fencing up."

"If Mr. Terry were still alive, he'd tell you it was all a lot of bother for no good reason," Robert said, remembering their former neighbor. His father had bought the Terry ranch when Ted had passed away. Mrs. Terry had moved east to be with her children, but she had died shortly thereafter. Folks had always said the two couldn't be separated for long.

"He would," Pa said, nodding. "I doubt he'd much like the way things have changed. Fencing, registrations, and restrictions—it'd be enough to make him swear, and I never heard that man ever utter a single bad word."

"So I guess you know about Alice's ma and brother comin'," Robert threw out casually.

"Sure. Your ma told me right after the letter came. I'm glad for the gal. It's only right that she have a chance to be with her family. Hannah told her they could stay in the Montoyas' old house for as long as they needed. The gals are all over there cleanin' today."

The Montoyas had been a part of the ranch since the beginning. As his father's foreman and mother's housekeeper, the Montoyas were considered to be a part of the family. His mother and father had always treated them with respect and kindness and taught Robert to never look down on a workingman—no matter his station. When they made the decision to move back to Mexico to be near family, it had nearly broken Robert's mother's heart.

"That's generous of you. I know Alice appreciates your kindness."

His father eyed him curiously. "You and Alice seem to be gettin' along well."

He wasn't sure if his father approved or disapproved by his tone. "Well, I've been teachin' her to ride and showin' her some of the duties I have here at the ranch. Thought I'd ride her over to my land and show her where I hope to build a house."

"And what does Jessica think about that?"

Robert shrugged. "I don't know that Jess thinks anything about it. Why should she?"

Will Barnett's eyes narrowed. "Robert, you aren't toyin' with those two gals, are you? I raised you better than that."

"I'm not toyin' with anybody. Jess is my friend and so is Alice. I can't help it if everybody has a notion that Jess and I are supposed to marry. I've never proposed."

"Maybe not, but neither have you really denied the possibility. I think you'd better be decidin' what it is you want before someone gets hurt."

Robert knew his father to be a man of wisdom. "Well, I've been prayin' about it, Pa. I just don't know exactly what I'm supposed to do. Like I've said before, I love Jess like a little sister. I know her as well as I know my own sisters. But there's something about Alice that intrigues me. I want to know everything about her. I want to spend all my free time with her."

Pa smiled and looked out across the field where the longhorn were happily grazing. "That's how I feel about your ma."

"So what do I do?"

His father took a long moment before answering. "I think you have to let Jessica know that you aren't going to marry her. Then you'll be free to actually court Alice and see if this is the woman God has for you."

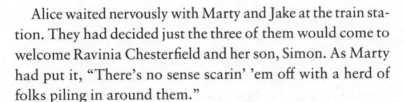

Alice waited nervously with Marty and Jake at the train station. They had decided just the three of them would come to welcome Ravinia Chesterfield and her son, Simon. As Marty had put it, "There's no sense scarin' 'em off with a herd of folks piling in around them."

The comment made Alice smile even now as she watched for her mother and brother to disembark the train. Marty squeezed her arm in support, but Alice found herself feeling strangely displaced. No doubt Marty knew that a part of Alice's thoughts were back in Denver on that horrible morning when she'd learned her mother had taken Simon and gone.

Can I forgive her? Can I put aside my own pain to give true understanding to her reasons for leaving?

"Is that them?" Marty asked. "It must be," she quickly continued. "There aren't any other women and young boys getting off the train."

Alice looked ahead and saw her mother. She recognized her immediately, despite her memories being so foggy over the long years.

Ravinia Chesterfield was a small woman with hair just a little darker than Alice's blond. The boy at her side had thick, fairly long hair the same shade as his sister's, but it was the blue eyes that Alice recognized. It was rather like looking into a mirror.

"Alice!" the boy yelled and disengaged himself from his mother's side. He came running down the wooden platform and threw himself into Alice's arms. "Alice! It's me, Simon. I'm your brother. Do you remember me?" He hugged her close and then pulled back to look her in the eye as if for an answer.

Tears came to Alice's eyes. "I do now."

"Mama told me all about you, and we have your picture. You don't look so different now," he said. "Do I look different?"

Alice nodded. "All grown up." She looked past Simon to her mother.

Ravinia Chesterfield stood in uncertain hesitation. Despite the questions and pain of the past, Alice longed to hold her mother close once again. She moved from Simon and went to her mother's open arms. For several minutes the two women embraced, weeping softly and saying nothing.

Finally Alice's mother stepped back and took a closer look at Alice. She ran her gloved finger along the line of Alice's scarred face.

"Oh, my poor sweet child. What did they do to you?"

Alice hadn't thought of what a shock her face might be. She bit her lip and tucked her right cheek to her shoulder, as she often did. Her mother would have no part of that, however. She lifted Alice's face very gently.

"You have nothing to be ashamed of. Hold your head high."

Alice met her mother's gaze and felt a rush of emotions. Pushing them aside, Alice dried her eyes and motioned to Marty and Jake. "These are the Wythes, the people who took me in and gave me work after I got out of the hospital."

"But now we're all just good friends," Marty said, stepping forward. "I'm Martha Wythe, but folks call me Marty. This is my husband, Jake."

The older woman nodded. "Thank you for being so good to my daughter."

"I'm Simon," the boy announced, positioning himself between Marty and his mother.

Marty smiled. "I suspected as much. You look just like your sister."

The boy's eyes widened. "But she's a girl."

Marty chuckled at this, as did Jake. Alice remained sober, studying her little brother's features. Simon did look just like her. The same cheekbones and nose. Definitely the same eyes. Alice bent down. "They don't mean you look like a girl, Simon. They mean we have similarities in our appearance— our eyes and mouth and so forth."

The boy reached up a hand to feel his face. "But I don't got a scar."

Alice knew he meant no harm by the comment, but it hurt

nevertheless. She reached out to touch his face. "And I pray you never will."

"Does it hurt?" he asked her.

"Not anymore," Alice replied. "It was very painful at first—something I'll never forget."

"Did the police kill the bad guys who did it—the ones who killed our pa?"

Alice shook her head. "No."

"Why not?"

Looking around her at the questioning faces, Alice straightened. "I don't know, Simon. I guess because they never found out exactly who they were."

"That's enough talk about it, Simon," their mother interjected. "I'm sure your sister would rather not speak on something so sad just now. Why don't you go see if you can find our bags?"

"I'll go with you," Jake said, and he and the boy headed off toward the baggage car.

"Are you and Simon hungry?" Marty asked, taking charge.

"No, we ate the food we'd brought along," Mother replied. "Of course Simon thinks he's always hungry."

"I spent time working at an orphanage in Denver, and I know exactly how little boys can think themselves starving to death." The two exchanged a smile at this.

Marty motioned the women toward the depot. "Well then, we have a carriage waiting and a bit of a drive to get to the ranch. At least you picked a pretty day, although my brother-in-law has some concerns about the weather turning bad. Feels it in his bones." She smiled and spoke as if she and Alice's mother were old friends.

Alice felt slightly jealous at their ease. Already she was thinking of the things she would discuss with her mother—

things that had to be said and questions she desperately needed answered.

Marty crossed the depot and led them out the other side to the Barnett carriage. "Why don't we go ahead and settle in while the fellas collect your things."

Alice followed in silence. She wasn't exactly sure what to say or feel. It all seemed very strange. That morning she'd had a million questions to ask, but at the moment not one came to mind. She waited as her mother settled into the backseat while Marty took her place in front. Her mother smiled and scooted to the far side of the carriage.

"There's plenty of room," Mother said, patting the leather upholstered seat. "We'll just squeeze Simon in between us."

Reluctantly, Alice climbed into the back with her mother. She wasn't sure why, but she suddenly felt very awkward and out of place. There was no good reason for it, but the discomfort continued.

"So you live in Chicago?" Marty asked Ravinia.

Alice's mother nodded. "We have two small rooms at a boardinghouse. It's just across the street from where Simon attends school, so I don't have to worry about his having a long walk."

"And how does he like school?" Marty asked. "Is he a good student?"

Alice saw her mother's hesitation. "Well, I can't say that he really enjoys it. He hasn't made good friends in our time there. Most of the neighborhood boys tend to bully him because he's small."

The thought of her little brother being hurt caused Alice anger. Why was it the big and mean folks of the world thought they had a right to cause the smaller, gentler people trouble? Was there no justice in this life at all?

"As for studies, I don't think Simon has a head for it." Mother looked to Alice and smiled. "Don't get me wrong. He's no dummy, that brother of yours. Rather, he's a hard and cautious worker. He'll do whatever I need him to, but book learning hasn't ever appealed."

She turned her attention back to Marty. "Not like it did with Alice."

Marty had turned sidewise in the seat in order to talk to the women behind her. "I found school to be a bore, myself, but my sister insisted it was necessary. I know now that she was right."

Alice's mother gave her a sidelong glance. "I'm sure you continued your studies, didn't you?"

Alice shook her head. "I finished eighth grade and . . . and . . ." She drew a deep breath. "I finished eighth grade. It was enough." There was no sense in telling her mother that in her absence, Alice had felt it necessary to quit school and take care of the house and her father.

Mother seemed to understand her discomfort and changed the subject. "I had always thought Denver a large and dirty town, but Chicago exceeds her greatly. There is so much more activity there, and they are in a constant state of building something new—even with the country in such monetary hardship. The railroads coming through the city and the Great Lakes shipping traffic give Chicago a great many people and problems to handle."

"I've never been to Chicago," Marty said, glancing out the window.

"Then you were only one of a few who didn't make it to the World's Fair last year." Mother clasped her gloved hands together. "It's believed that nearly 27 million people came during the six months the fair was in operation."

"We read all about the fair while in Denver," Alice murmured.

Marty nodded. "Yes, we enjoyed the coverage given it by the newspapers. It sounded quite unusual."

"Oh, it was. They built an entire city—the White City, they called it. A separate area for amusement provided rides and games and sideshows. Goodness, it was quite amazing."

Marty seemed to consider this for a moment. "I take it you and Simon attended the fair?"

"I actually had a job helping to serve food. Simon was allowed to help me with cleanup when he wasn't in school. It earned us a little extra money and allowed me to take Simon on the Ferris wheel. He didn't stop talking about it for months afterward."

Alice smiled at the thought of her little brother's pleasure. She was glad he'd had the opportunity to do something so fun. He would never have known such a thing had he remained in Denver.

Marty motioned back toward the building. "Here they come."

Jake carried a small trunk while Simon managed a large carpetbag. Alice smiled as the boy struggled to hoist the bag up to the carriage. She quickly leaned forward to help.

"That looks heavy," she said, giving him a smile of approval. "Good thing you're so strong."

Simon nodded and climbed up behind the bag as Alice pulled it inside. "I can carry a lot when I'm not wearing this coat." He pulled at the traveling jacket in discomfort. "Mama said I had to wear it on the train, 'cause that's what a gentleman does."

"Well, you'll be happy to know that gentlemen out on the ranch dress a little different," Marty told him. She gave him a wink and Simon smiled.

"Can I ride a horse?"

"Of course you can," Marty declared. "The question is, do you know how?"

Simon frowned and plopped down between his mother and sister. "No. I never got to ride."

Marty reached over the seat and chucked him on the chin. "Don't pout. We have people aplenty to teach you. You'll be a natural in the saddle before you know it. Your sister is even learning to ride."

The boy grinned, and it warmed Alice's heart to see how naturally he related to Marty. She could only hope that somehow, some way, she might find the same openness with him. Of course, he had been the one to initiate their embrace, and he mentioned they had her picture and Mother had told him about her. Had Mama kept Alice a part of their family all these years? It gave Alice a great deal to ponder.

It wasn't long before Jake had the trunk secured and had reclaimed the driver's seat. "Are we set for home?" he asked, calling over his shoulder. Everyone nodded their approval.

"Good. Then we're off," he said and snapped the reins.

Alice sank back into the leather upholstery and said very little. Marty and her mother chatted as if they'd known each other for a long time, while Simon was intent on watching the sights and people around them.

I don't really know either of you. You are flesh of my flesh but complete strangers. How could that have happened in such a short time?

The thought really bothered Alice. Then doubts crept in. She had never really known her mother. At least not in the way she thought she had. The woman Alice knew would never have gone away and left her daughter behind. It was a stone in her shoe to be sure, and like a pilgrim set upon a hundred-mile journey, the rock only served to rub a wound deep and painful.

———————————— ★ ————————————

Robert gave the expectant mare a pat on the rump. "You'll be a mama soon." He left the stall and had just grabbed up some oats when Marty located him. "We've got Alice's family settled in the Montoya house," she declared. "Hannah said to tell you supper will be in an hour."

"Sounds good. I just wanted to check the paint. She's due to foal most anytime." The brown-and-white-blotched horse whinnied softly as if to agree with his comment. He poured the oats into a small feeding trough and then returned the bucket to the wall.

Marty put her hand to her belly. "I wish I were." She laughed. "I know I still have months to go, but I would be a whole lot happier to have my baby here safe and sound."

Robert put his arm around Marty's shoulder. "Ma says the baby will be here before you know it. She's lookin' forward to spoilin' him, too."

"Oh, has she decided it's a boy?"

He chuckled. "I don't think so. I recollect her calling him a her a time or two."

They walked together toward the house, but Marty stopped without warning. "I wanted to talk to you—alone."

"Me? Why?" Robert was surprised by the sudden change in his aunt's tone.

"I guess I'm sticking my nose in where it doesn't belong, but I wanted to ask you about your plans to marry Jessica."

"I don't have plans to marry Jessica."

She looked at him with a stern expression. "That's not what I've been told."

"Me either, but it's the truth," he said, trying to make light of the situation. "Folks have been sayin' that for years, but it don't make it so."

"And does Jessica know this?"

He shrugged and stuffed his hands into his pockets. "I've tried to tell her."

"And what does she say?"

"She changes the subject or makes like it's not a problem. But it is."

Marty's expression softened. Her head cocked to one side. "And why is that?"

"Because I have feelings for someone else."

He wasn't sure it was the right time to share that information, but if anyone would understand it would be Marty. His aunt had always had a way of making him feel at ease, and Robert realized he probably should have talked to her about Alice a while ago.

"Alice?" Marty questioned, as if reading his mind.

Robert nodded and glanced overhead at the thick white clouds. "She's got to me, and I don't know what to do about it."

"You always have been one to take up for the disadvantaged. Are you sure this isn't just another case of your wanting to fix an injured critter?" She smiled and crossed her arms. "'Cause a woman is a whole lot more complex than a cat with a broken foot."

Robert chuckled. "You still remember that?"

"How could I forget? You were only six and so very worried about that animal. I didn't think you'd ever let it walk on its own again. Just kept carryin' it around with you all the time. And, as I recall, the cat wasn't any too pleased about it."

"I suppose it had something to do with being confined in that crate," he replied. "But I know Alice isn't a cat. She's a beautiful woman, and yes, she has been hurt, but I . . . well . . . I love her."

Marty shook her head. "Then heaven help you."

"What would you do if you were me, Aunt Marty? Everyone knows about Jess, and I don't want to hurt her."

"It'll only hurt her more if you don't put an end to it. Being in love with someone else while you're expected to marry another is never a good foot to start out on."

"Sometimes I just want to sweep Alice up and run off with her."

"Then do it. But set things straight with Jessica first, or you'll always regret it."

Chapter 17

With breakfast over and the men off to their chores, the women of the house began their routine. Alice had taken to helping with the ironing and was busy at work in the kitchen when her mother decided to join her.

"You seem happy here," Mother said, taking hold of a nearby chair. She studied the ladder back of the simple piece for a moment. Running her hands along the top rung, she cleared her throat. "I hoped maybe we could talk now."

Alice knew that Hannah and Marty were busy outside and wouldn't be back in for a while. "That would be fine." She put the iron back on the stove. "Would you like to sit?"

"Yes." Mother took a seat without further prompting. "I find that I'm quite exhausted."

Alice noticed that her appearance was that of a woman who'd been days without sleep. Her color was pale and her eyes seemed more sunken today. "Did you not rest well?"

"Well enough." Her mother smiled. "I think the weight of everything is just coming to rest on me."

Alice took a seat across from her mother and folded her arms against her body. Suddenly she felt very vulnerable and wasn't at all certain she could say the things that had been on her mind.

"Alice, I know I hurt you in leaving. But you need to understand why I had to go."

"I'm listening."

Mother looked up and met her gaze. "It wasn't ideally what I wanted. I had hoped that things could be worked out another way." She twisted her hands together. "I don't know where to start, but it's important you understand that I always loved you, and I wanted you with me."

"But not enough to take me with you when you snuck out that night." Alice hadn't meant to reply in such a manner, but now that it was out there she didn't try to take it back.

"You're right to be angry with me. I was angry with myself." She gave a heavy sigh. "I knew you were the light of your father's eye, and he would always treat you well. Unfortunately, that couldn't be said about me or even Simon. You see, your father was a very jealous man. He always seemed to fear someone would come and steal me away from him." She smiled sadly.

"I suppose it was because I was very popular when we courted. I had many suitors, and your father had little patience for his rivals. When you were born nine months after we married, I thought he would finally realize there was nothing to fear, that I was his and we were a family. But, Alice, that wasn't how it was."

Alice frowned. She knew her parents were given to arguments but had never understood why. Now she tried not to form any opinion on the matter before her mother could share her story.

"Your father was involved in some underhanded illegal affairs. I think you know that now, given the things Marty said to me about the envelope you were looking for and the missing gold certificates."

"I know that he was used by someone to deliver forged certificates."

Mother shook her head. "He was the one forging them, Alice. He was in the middle of everything that was going on. He had cohorts, to be sure, but your father was nobody's fool."

"You're saying he willingly did wrong?" Alice leaned forward. "I find that hard to believe."

"I know you do. You always loved him so dearly."

"I loved you, too," Alice threw back. "I thought you loved me."

"I do love you, Alice. I do." Her mother reached out to touch her daughter's hands, but Alice quickly pulled away.

"How can you say that after what you did? You left without warning, and I never heard from you again."

A heavy sadness seemed to wash over the older woman. "I wrote you letters. I wrote a great many. Your father wouldn't let you see them or even acknowledge them, from what I know now. He wrote to me and threatened me—he threatened to see me jailed if I so much as tried to come back and take you away. I felt so bad that I even offered to return to our marriage, knowing that it would be a living hell. But he told me no. He didn't want me back."

"I can't believe that," Alice said, shaking her head. "Papa loved you and Simon. Simon was the son he wanted."

"As I said earlier, your father was a very jealous man."

"What does that have to do with anything?" Alice knew she was letting her temper get control of her. She tried to calm down, but with her mother's next words there was no hope of that.

"Your father didn't believe Simon was his son. He thought I had betrayed him with a business associate."

Alice felt sickened and wasn't sure what to say. Her mother seemed sincere in what she was saying, but this just couldn't be the truth.

"I don't . . . I don't believe you."

Tears formed in her mother's eyes. "That's exactly what your father said to me when I told him that I had never been with anyone but him, that Simon was his son. He knocked me to the ground and walked away, never willing to discuss the matter again."

Alice wanted to scream that it was all lies, but in the recesses of her memories she recalled her father's indifferent treatment of Simon. She had always believed that it was nothing more than favoritism, and since it benefited her, she had given it no other consideration. Especially in light of the way her mother always seemed to compensate and show Simon extra attention.

"Your father wasn't the man you think he was. He was tied up in all sorts of deals and had all manner of evil friends. I feared for our safety, but even more so, I feared your father and what he might do. That's why I had to go. I had to protect Simon from your father's wrath."

"But you didn't see fit to protect me."

"Alice, I knew he would never hurt you. He lived for you. He adored you. There was no question in his mind as to your heritage. But you need to know that I never intended to leave you behind. I had planned to come back for you the next day. I thought I could go to the school and take you from your classroom. I planned for the three of us to board a train for Chicago and stay with a distant cousin there. By putting miles between us and your father, I hoped he would see the error of his ways and make changes. I never intended for it to be the end of our family."

Unable to hear another word against the man she loved, Alice jumped to her feet. The chair spilled over backward and made a loud clatter against the floor.

"I don't believe you. This isn't true. It can't be! You would have me believe my father was some sort of criminal, but he wasn't!"

She left the room without waiting to hear her mother's reply. The things her mother said rang over and over in her ears. And though she longed to refuse them, they burrowed deep into her mind and taunted her.

Mindless of where she walked, Alice crossed the barnyard and made her way down the long drive toward the main road. She fought to control her emotions, but tears began to fall.

I can't believe my father would be so cruel. I can't believe he was so devious and . . . so evil. Surely she's just making this up to make herself look better. After all, Papa can't defend himself.

But even as she considered this, Alice remembered that he had lied to her about her mother and Simon being dead. She glanced heavenward with a single word on her lips.

"Why?"

★

"Looks like it'll be anytime now," Brandon Reid told Robert as they considered the laboring mare. "Legs are out and well positioned. Front legs are white."

"I hope the foal will be a beauty like her mama."

Brandon eyed the horse. "She is a fine animal. One of the best paint quarter horses I've ever bred. She comes from good stock. I'm sure you'll be pleased with her offspring."

Robert gave the mare another look and then smiled. "You know, I'm gonna go get Alice. She's never seen anything like this, and I know she'd enjoy it."

"You know how persnickety horses can be in giving birth. You get an audience in here and she may hold off for hours."

"I know, but . . . well . . . Alice will just sit back quiet. She's not like some women who'd be all fussy and chatty." Robert headed out of the barn toward the house. He knew Alice had planned to iron that morning and would be set up in the kitchen, so he came in through the back entrance.

"Alice?"

"She's . . . not here," Mrs. Chesterfield replied.

Robert found the older woman at the table. She'd been crying. "What's wrong? Is Alice all right?"

She shook her head. "She's upset with me. She stormed out of here about twenty minutes ago."

"Did she say where she was going?"

The woman again shook her head. "I don't imagine she had any particular place in mind so long as it was away from me."

Robert wanted to say something comforting to the woman, but he was more concerned with Alice's welfare. "I'll find her. If she does come back, let her know I'm looking for her. We have a mare about to foal, and I thought she'd like to see it." He didn't know why he felt the need to give her the details of what was happening. Somehow, he hoped it might soften her discomfort to focus on something else.

He left the house and looked around the yard for some sign of Alice. He noted his mother and Marty working in the garden, but Alice wasn't with them. Rounding the barn, he glanced out across the front grasslands and spied Alice walking up the long lane to the house.

Mrs. Chesterfield had said Alice was upset with her. Robert

couldn't help but wonder what had been said in their exchange that would send the normally even-tempered young woman off alone. He decided he'd say nothing about it. In time, maybe she'd tell him.

"Alice!" he called, giving her a wave as he made his way down the drive. "I've been lookin' for you. Belleza is about to foal, and I thought you might like to witness it."

She picked up her pace and made her way toward him. Robert could see that her eyes were red-rimmed, but he said nothing. "It might take a while or it might be quick. With a mare you can never tell." He held out his hand.

Alice looked at him oddly for a moment. "I would like to see the new baby, but I have a lot of work to do."

"Ma and Marty will understand." He didn't wait for her to take his hand, but took hold of her arm. "Come on."

They made their way back to the barn, and Robert tried to figure a way to get Alice to talk to him about what had happened. "That little brother of yours sure has taken to Will. He's followin' him all over the place."

"He seems to enjoy the ranch setting," Alice said after a few seconds.

"And what about your ma?"

She shrugged. "I guess so."

They reached the barn and Robert knew there'd be nothing else said on the matter. "Mr. Reid is here. You met him at the roundup, remember?"

Alice nodded. Brandon approached them. "She's just dropped the foal." He looked worried and Robert couldn't help but tense.

"What's wrong?"

Alice looked at him in confusion, but he didn't take time to explain. Instead, Robert made his way alone to the stall.

There in the hay was a most incredible sight. A pure white foal. Belleza was working to lick the baby's face. Everything seemed perfectly fine.

He turned in confusion. "What's wrong, Mr. Reid? Your voice sounded . . . well . . . you look like there's something to worry about."

Alice and Brandon joined him at the stall. "I don't wanna buy trouble," Reid began, "but I've seen this kind of thing before, so I have my concerns."

"What kind of thing?"

"White foal. You can see the skin is pinkish and the eyes are blue."

"I don't understand." Robert looked again at the foal and shook his head. "Looks like they're gettin' on just fine."

"I've seen this a couple of times before. There's no way of tellin' right away," Reid answered, "but usually this doesn't bode well for the foal. Somethin' happens with the paints deliverin' whites. Not sure why, but we'll know soon enough."

"Know what?" Alice asked before Robert could.

"If we need to put it down."

"Kill it? A newborn?" Robert looked at the man in confusion. He completely respected Brandon Reid's knowledge of horses and knew that he wouldn't say such a thing lightly.

"The next twenty-four hours will tell us what we have to do. Most of the time, though, it seems these paints have problems with white foals not bein' able to digest and pass waste." He watched the baby try to get to its feet. "We'll just have to wait it out."

Alice didn't like Mr. Reid's prognosis of the foal's situation. She knew nothing about horses, but it seemed horrible to imagine that a newborn might be killed. She reached out and touched Robert's sleeve.

"Don't let him harm the foal." Her pleading tone was barely audible.

"I wouldn't do anything to hurt that animal," Mr. Reid replied. "However, if the foal can't process food, it'll be in a lot of pain. The waste will just pack up inside, and then it will die a slow and painful death. I won't have that."

"Neither will I," Robert said, patting Alice's hand. "You wouldn't want that, either."

"Of course not. But . . . I mean . . . isn't there something we can do?"

"Pray," Mr. Reid suggested. "Pray for a miracle."

And that's exactly what they did. First Robert suggested they pray together. Mr. Reid offered up a prayer asking for wisdom and God's will to be done. Robert added that he hoped that will would include the foal being healthy. Alice silently prayed that the baby would live and that God would somehow help her to deal with the information her mother had given her earlier.

She waited in the barn with Robert for the next hour. It was discovered that the baby was a male. A darling little colt that Alice instantly lost her heart to.

Poor baby. I don't even know if you will get to live, and you have no way of knowing, either.

The foal nursed while the couple watched in silence. This was a good sign, Robert had told her, but she knew it wasn't the sign they needed. Robert suggested they go about their business and meet back after lunch. Alice went to her ironing, glad to find her mother had gone to tend to something else. She attacked the baskets of clothes and sheets as if they were enemies to be conquered. By the time Marty and Hannah showed up to start the noon meal, she had things well in hand and was just finishing with a pillowcase.

"Goodness, but I thought that would take you most of the day," Hannah said, noting the freshly ironed pieces.

"I suppose I found it better to focus on this than that poor little colt."

Marty smiled. "Robert told us what Mr. Reid said about it. I hope that he's wrong."

"He could be, couldn't he?" Alice asked hopefully.

Hannah patted her back. "Of course he could. There's always exceptions to every situation. I've seen plenty of pretty white horses in my day."

"Mr. Reid said it was something that happened at times with the paints," Alice relayed.

"He can still be wrong. We have a mighty God who answers prayers, and I'm praying that colt will live."

"Me too," Alice said.

"I think we all are," Marty agreed.

After lunch Alice went to the barn with Robert. The baby seemed to be doing well. He nursed without seeming to notice them, although Belleza was very aware of them. They agreed to come back just before supper and see how things were going.

Alice continued to pray, even as she worked on the evening meal with Hannah. Alice's mother wasn't feeling well and had taken a nap. Marty had gone to rest, as well, and that left the two women alone.

"You seem awfully quiet," Hannah said, interrupting Alice's thoughts. "Is it just the horse or is something else bothering you?"

Alice looked at the older woman and found only compassion in her expression. "I had words with my mother. I'm afraid I wasn't very kind."

"Ah, I see," Hannah replied and picked up a carving knife. "Sometimes that happens. If you care to talk about it, I'm willing to listen."

For some reason, Alice didn't even consider remaining silent. "She told me my father was a bad man. He did bad things—illegal things. That's why she had to leave. I can't believe it. He was always so good to me. Sure, he lost his temper at times, but . . . well . . . she said he was cruel toward her and Simon."

"That had to be hard to hear." Hannah busied herself with slicing up a large roast.

"It was horrible. My father isn't here to defend himself, and I suppose I felt as though *I* should. Now I find myself so confused. I was only thirteen when Mother left. I loved them both so much, but I thought my father was very nearly perfect. I knew I was his favorite, and I thought there was nothing wrong with that because I figured Simon was Mama's favorite."

"Favoritism never leads to anything good. We can see that in our Bible stories about Jacob and Esau, and of course the ordeals of Joseph and his many brothers."

"I know, but when I was younger, it didn't seem to be a bad thing. My mama said it was a big problem because . . . well . . . my father . . ." She fell silent and tried to think how to express the delicate matter. "He thought my mother had been unfaithful."

Hannah looked up. "He didn't believe the boy to be his son?"

Alice nodded. "Mama said he wouldn't believe her. He was jealous of everyone. I don't know what to think. She said he was involved in illegal activities and he had evil people for friends. That doesn't fit my memories of him."

Smiling, Hannah continued to slice the meat. "I think we often create our own image of people, especially after they've passed on. Remember, if your father favored you, then most likely you benefited from his good nature and kindness. If he didn't extend the same to your mother and brother, it wasn't your fault. You mustn't carry any of the blame. Obviously there were circumstances that made the situation unbearable, or your mother would never have made such a daring choice."

Alice considered that for a moment. It was true that it must have been quite perilous to sneak out in the middle of the night—to leave with a small child and no one to help her. She mulled these things over in her mind as everyone was called to supper and Will offered the blessing.

Hannah's words stayed with Alice throughout the meal, even while her brother detailed his day with Will.

"I got to ride on a horse, and it was really big. Mr. Barnett showed me how to put the saddle away and how to brush the horse. It almost stepped on my foot, and Mr. Barnett said if we stayed very long I was going to need a pair of boots." He paused with a big grin. "When Mama's feeling better, I'm going to ask her if we can stay for a long time."

Alice loved the excitement in his voice. She felt a bond with him that she couldn't explain. He was so like her in appearance that she found it hard to believe her father could have ever doubted Simon's paternity. Perhaps jealousy could make a person blind.

After dinner, Marty and Hannah urged Alice to go ahead with Robert to check on the foal. "Don't worry about a thing," Hannah ordered. "I'm going to pop in on your mother and see that she eats something. You go on and see how that baby is doing. Let us know."

Walking alone with Robert, Alice tried not to think about

her mother or father. Instead, she focused on the colt and the man at her side. In the distance she heard a rumble of thunder and noticed dark clouds moving in.

"It's gonna storm," Robert declared. "Hope we get some decent rain with it." He opened the barn door and reached for a lantern that hung on the wall. Nearby a metal box of matches had been nailed to the wall to allow for quick lighting. He struck a match and lit the lantern. Light spilled out across the barn, and Alice made the mistake of looking up to find Robert watching her with a strange look on his face.

"What's wrong?" she asked, putting her hand up to cover her scar.

"Nothing. I was just noticing how beautiful you are."

She shivered and tried to make light of the moment. "Not nearly as pretty as your fiancée."

He shook his head. "She's not my fiancée." The tenderness of his expression hardened, and the magic of the moment passed. "Come on. Let's see how they're doing."

Alice followed Robert to the stall. He hung the lantern on the post and opened the gate. "You stay here."

She nodded and leaned against the stall rail. The little foal seemed quite interested to find Robert in the stall with them. He danced around a bit and backed off behind his mother as Robert approached. Belleza seemed unfazed, however. She knew Robert and it was evident she felt safe with him there. Alice had to admit that she did, too.

"Is he doing all right?" she asked softly.

"I think so. He's frisky and doesn't look to be in any discomfort." Robert worked his way around the mare to better see the colt. The animal did its best to avoid him, and made Robert work to get to him. After maneuvering around the mare, Robert stopped.

Alice couldn't see much of Robert behind the large animal, but just then he started laughing.

"Why are you laughing?" she asked. In such a grave situation, laughter seemed quite foreign.

Robert came around to the front of the mare and gave her face a nuzzle with his own. "It's gonna be all right, Mama," he told the animal. He glanced back over at Alice with a grin. "The little guy is making a mess back there, and I stepped right in it. Best thing I've ever seen."

Alice felt a surge of joy. "You mean he'll be all right? He won't die or need to be killed?"

"No, ma'am," Robert said, coming to where she stood. "We got our miracle."

Relief flooded her and Alice couldn't help but laugh. "That's what you should name him. Miracle." She didn't attempt to turn away when Robert hugged her. The fence between them seemed to make it all very innocent and proper.

"I'll give him the name in Spanish," Robert said. "Milagro."

She fixed her eyes on the white colt. "I think that's beautiful."

Robert smiled and whispered against her ear. "And I think you are."

Chapter 18

Alice sat listening to the preacher share his thoughts on Jesus' teachings on the Beatitudes. She was well familiar with the Scriptures taken from the fifth chapter of Matthew, but her heart wasn't at all on the topic. At least not until the man spoke out on verse nine.

" 'Blessed are the peacemakers: for they shall be called the children of God.' "

She didn't hear much else the man said. She pondered the word *peacemaker* and wondered if that included being the kind of person who put aside old issues and focused on the ones at hand.

Forgiving her mother for leaving her was something that Alice had complete control over. No one could force it from her or keep her from giving it. The past could not be altered, not even in part. If her father was the man her mother declared him to be, Alice could not change that by denying it.

You were good to me, Papa. Why not to them?

Her mother had been sickly that morning, and Hannah insisted she remain behind. No one seemed to question Mrs. Barnett's commands. Even Will just nodded and told everyone he'd have the carriage ready by eight. Hannah remained with Mother, and for this Alice had been grateful. She wasn't yet ready to sit at her mother's side and hear further discussion on her father's failings. Alice had questioned Hannah about her mother's condition—seeking to learn the extent of her ailment. Hannah told her that most likely she was just overly exhausted from the trip to Texas. But Alice thought Hannah had seemed guarded in her response.

Simon fidgeted beside her. It was clear the boy found confinement in his suit coat to be a misery unlike any other. He looked downcast and continued to glance toward the windows. Alice thought to take him out of the service and let him walk a bit, but she didn't want to draw attention to them. She'd never thought to ask if her brother was used to attending church. They weren't an overly religious family when they'd all been together years ago.

After the service concluded, Alice whispered in his ear. "Why don't you go outside with the other children and see if you can make friends."

She didn't have to suggest it twice. Simon darted away like a startled fawn. She smiled and watched him weave his way through the mass of people. Alice stayed by Marty's side, uncertain of what she should do. Her scar made her feel quite self-conscious as she noted several people seeming to study her face.

"When is the birthday party, Mrs. Wythe?" a young woman asked Marty. "I thought it was gonna be right after the roundup."

"We had to postpone it a week, but it'll be next Friday

evening," she assured her. "Have you met Miss Chesterfield, Miriam?"

The young woman shook her head. She was a pretty redhead with a simple taste in her fashion. She looked to be Alice's age.

"Miriam, this is my dear friend Alice Chesterfield. Alice, this is Miriam Palmer. She's the daughter of Mr. Palmer, who participated in the roundup with his sons. Miriam remained at home to help her mother."

"She'd just given birth to my little sister," Miriam announced proudly. "I liked to thought we'd never get us another girl after five boys."

Alice smiled. "I'm pleased to meet you."

"What did your folks name the little one?" Marty asked.

"Edith," Miriam replied. She returned her gaze to Marty. "After my grandmother."

"It's a good name." Marty put her hand to her growing waistline. "We haven't yet thought up names for our baby. Hopefully by the time he or she arrives, we will have sorted it out."

Alice couldn't help but smile. Marty was finally starting to act and think like this pregnancy was something she could carry through to completion. It did Alice's heart good to see her friend brighten at discussions of the baby and plans for the future.

Jake joined them just then. "Will said he needed to help the preacher with something, so we'll be a little delayed in returning home. You feeling all right?"

"I'm fine," Marty said. She smiled at her husband as he put his hand on her arm.

Alice excused herself. "I'm going to go look for Simon."

She exited the church and exchanged greetings with

various people, keeping her head down to avoid their stares. She walked along the front of the church and spied Simon, now jacket free, playing with a couple of the other boys. He seemed content and so she continued her walk toward the cemetery yard.

Reflecting on the pastor's words, Alice strolled among the headstones and thought of her father. How could he have done the things her mother said he'd done? How could he have put Alice in such a precarious position? If what her mother said was true, then he was as much to blame for the attack as the men who carried it out. If the company he kept was corrupt and evil, how could he expect their actions to be otherwise?

She frowned and touched one of the more ornate marble statues. The angel form seemed to glare at her in disapproval. Alice quickly pulled her hand away and looked heavenward.

Why? Why is this happening, Lord? I don't know what to think or to do. I want to be a peacemaker, but I don't understand what that means. Do I just forget that my mother left me? Do I accept that my father was truly evil?

Alice couldn't help but remember the nights she had cried herself to sleep, wishing and praying that her mother and brother would come home. When Papa told her of their deaths a year after their departure, Alice wanted to die, as well. She had been so certain they would return. Father had been very angry about her concerns for them, and at the time Alice thought it was because of her nagging. Now she wondered if it was for the very reasons Mother had stated.

Alice continued to walk amongst the dead and ponder the living. There had to be answers if she was just brave enough to find them.

"You look awfully deep in thought," Robert said, coming upon Alice in the graveyard.

She seemed not to mind his interruption. "I was contemplating."

"Would you care to share what you were thinking about?"

Alice shrugged. "My life. My father's death. My mother and brother being alive. I suppose the quiet of the place led me to such reflections."

He nodded. "I've always liked cemeteries myself. They are, as you say, quiet and good for thinking. I can leave you alone if you'd like."

"That isn't necessary." She gave him a brief smile and glanced all around the yard. "Did you know most of these people?"

"Most," he admitted and came closer to where she stood. "Some not so much as others. Why?"

"I don't know. I suppose because I've always wanted to feel connected, a part of something or someone. My family was torn apart when I was thirteen, and my father kept to himself. He insisted I do the same."

"Didn't you have friends?"

"At school I had a couple of friends, but because of my mother's desertion, I quit school after eighth grade. Most figured that to be an adequate education for a young woman, but I wanted more."

"I think times are changing," Robert said. "Used to be most children ended their education about that time. Boys were needed to help with the work, and girls married or helped their mothers. These days I know there's more of a push to get a full education. I don't mind at all that my folks insisted I stay in school. I went away to college for a year, but found it wasn't for me." He smiled. "My heart is out there on the range, not in a classroom."

"I can understand that. It's beautiful here." She turned to walk away and stumbled.

Robert reached out and caught her before she could fall. To his complete frustration that was the moment Jessica Atherton chose to appear.

"Robert Barnett, I've been looking for you." She eyed him with a raised brow and then turned her attention to Alice. "Miss Chesterfield." Her look was one of contempt.

"I should get back to Simon," Alice said in a most uncomfortable manner. She pulled away from Robert's hold and hurried past Jessica.

Robert waited for whatever assault Jessica might release. She looked madder than a wet cat, and he knew she could be twice as dangerous.

"What are you doing with her? All throughout church I saw you watching her."

"Jess, you need to calm down. Alice and I have become good friends."

"We used to be good friends, but now you avoid me like I should be in quarantine. What is it that's happened between us?" She came to stand directly in front of him, blocking his way to leave.

"Jess, I've told you before, we are friends. You're like a little sister to me. I'd do whatever I could to help you or protect you. You mean the world to me."

Her eyes narrowed. "Then stay away from Miss Chesterfield. I know you feel sorry for her, but you belong to me."

"I don't belong to anyone," Robert countered, "save God. I keep tellin' folks that, but nobody seems to believe me. Furthermore, Alice is staying at our ranch. I can't ignore her or stay away from her any more than I can my folks. Nor do I want to."

"She's an unsightly woman with troubles brewing. I know, because I heard Mama talking to Marty about it just a few minutes ago. Marty said that Alice has had trouble most of her life and now with her mother and brother here, things might even get worse."

"Then I want to be here for her."

"You need to be here for me," Jessica said, sounding child-ish. She stamped her foot. "We were doing just fine until she came here. Now everywhere I go, folks are talking about her. It's Alice this and Miss Chesterfield that. I'm sick of it. You've always cared about broken things, but that dam-aged woman doesn't need to be one of your projects, Robert Barnett!"

"I never knew you to be so heartless and meanspirited." He pushed her aside gently and left her to contemplate her words. It was all he could do to keep from slapping her for what she'd said. He didn't like anyone talking mean about someone he loved—especially not this time.

Back on the ranch, Alice quietly changed from her Sunday clothes and put on a simple cotton blouse and skirt. She and Marty had rid themselves of most of their surplus clothing and now maintained only a few pieces. It sometimes amazed Alice that she had come full circle from a time of well-being with her father to poverty after his death, then to wealth and opulence at the Wythe mansion and finally to this. Life had a way of changing the scenery without a person even realizing what was happening.

A light rap at the door drew her attention. "Come in."

Hannah Barnett opened the door. "I hoped to find you here. May I speak to you for a moment?"

"Of course. What is it?"

"It's about your mother."

"Is she worse? Do we need a doctor?"

"No. I think her condition is mostly one of the heart."

Alice felt herself stiffen. "Why do you say that?"

Hannah sat on the bed and patted the pretty quilt that covered it. "Come sit with me for a minute."

Alice did as instructed but already felt more than a little guarded.

Hannah quickly got to the heart of the matter. "Your mother is discouraged and downtrodden over all that has happened between you two. She wants so much to renew her relationship with you."

"I know, but she said so many things that I just don't understand."

Hannah took Alice's hand in her own. "I know you're hurt and maybe even afraid. Afraid that if you believe your mother, you are somehow betraying your father. Alice, your father is dead. You can't help or hurt him anymore, but you can do both to your mother. She needs you to forgive her. . . . Otherwise . . ."

"Otherwise what?" Alice asked.

"Otherwise, I'm not sure that she'll ever forgive herself."

"So it's my responsibility to make her feel better for her mistakes?" Alice asked in a snide voice. She immediately hated herself for having those feelings. "I'm sorry. That wasn't kind. But sometimes I feel so frustrated by it all. I was a child. I was deserted by the one person I thought would never leave me. I trusted her to always be there." Tears spilled down her cheeks. "I needed her, and she left me to face life all alone."

Hannah pulled Alice into her arms and hugged her close. "She didn't want to. She loved you. She loves you now. Yes, she hurt you and she made a terrible mistake in leaving you. But your father made mistakes, too, and you will, as well. We all make bad choices—decisions that would better be left to rot in the bottom of the barrel. But we can't undo them. We can only move forward."

"I want to," Alice said, trying to regain control. Hannah's warm embrace was like that of a comforting mother, and Alice couldn't help but remember the way she and her mother had held each other at the train station. "I love her so much."

"Then tell her. Tell her that you love her and forgive her. She needs to hear it from you, and Alice, you need to hear it, as well." Hannah let her go and got to her feet. "I'm gonna get the noon meal on the table. Why don't you go spend some time with your mother? I had the men bring her here so I could keep an eye on her. She's in the room at the end of the hall. I'll bring you two a tray to share."

Alice nodded. She wasn't sure how things would go with her mother, but it was worth a try. Escaping the past was one of the reasons she'd come to Texas with Marty. There was no sense in letting part of it go and not all.

She made her way to the bedroom. Mama was resting on the bed, but her eyes were open and she gave the slightest smile as Alice entered the room.

"I was hoping I might see you today."

Alice pulled up a chair close to the small bed. "I'm sorry I didn't come before church."

"That's all right."

Mother looked so small and helpless. Even though the bed was narrow, it seemed to swallow her up. Alice drew a deep breath to steady herself and prayed for strength.

"You look tired," her mother said.

"I was worried about you," Alice admitted.

Her mother seemed surprised by this confession. "You don't need to. I'm just weary."

"I probably added to that weariness." Alice stared at her hands and folded them in her lap. "Mama, I'm sorry that things weren't good between you and Papa. I didn't know. I thought that was just the way husbands and wives treated each other. I had no way of knowing otherwise. We didn't socialize, so I didn't have other families to learn from."

"I know," her mother said in a barely audible voice. "I'm so sorry that you didn't have those people in your life. Given your father's choices, we stayed mostly to ourselves to avoid problems. I always wanted better for you and Simon."

"I think I know that," Alice admitted, "but you have to know how much it hurt when you went away. I thought . . . I thought it was my fault."

"Oh, Alice, no. It was never your fault." Her mother reached out to touch Alice's knee. "Children are never to blame for the mistakes of their parents. I kept hoping that things could be different, hoping that your father would accept Simon and realize I had never betrayed him. I kept hoping . . . until my hope was all used up."

Alice nodded. "I know how that feels. I kept hoping you and Simon would come home, and when Papa told me you were dead, my hope was used up, too."

"I'm so very sorry, Alice. Please know that I always loved you, and I love you still. Please forgive me for not being a better mother."

Something inside Alice yielded to the sincerity in her mother's voice. She reached out and took hold of her mother's hand. "I forgive you. I love you, Mama." Her voice broke and despite her resolve, Alice buried her face in her hands and sobbed.

She felt her mother's engulfing arms. Mama sat up to take hold of her, and Alice had never been happier. She held tightly to her mother's small frame. It was a moment in time that Alice longed to hold on to forever. After a long while, Alice straightened and met her mother's tear-filled eyes.

"I want to know more." She hesitated. "I want to know what was in the box Mrs. Ingram sent you. I want to know more . . . about Papa."

Her mother smiled. "And I want to tell you." She motioned to a bag beside the bed. "I brought most of what she sent. I thought you might want to see it. I also brought your father's letters to me." She licked her lips, and Alice could see that they were dry.

"Would you like a drink?" Alice reached for the glass of water on the nightstand. She wanted more than anything to see the letters and the other things in the bag, but they could wait. Alice handed her mother the glass and waited for her to drink. Once done, Alice returned the water to the table and picked up the bag.

"Is this the bag you were talking about?" Alice asked, knowing it was but suddenly feeling uncomfortable.

"Yes. Everything is in there. I want you to have it."

For a moment Alice only looked at the small cloth bag. She wasn't sure what to say. "I'm sorry for being so upset when you tried to talk to me," Alice began. "It was wrong of me."

"You were hurt—you still are. I can see that in your eyes, and I wish I could take it from you. The scar you bear on your face is only one of many that you have from the past. Deep within you are many reminders."

Alice met her mother's sad eyes and nodded. "It's . . . it's just so hard to think of Papa the way you described. I don't want to think badly of him."

"Then don't. He was a good father in many ways to you. No one can take that from you."

"But he wasn't good to Simon? Or to you?"

Her mother shook her head. "Not at the end. There was a time when I was very happy with him despite his jealous rages. I felt cared for and safe. As the years went by and his suspicions grew, however, it was no longer the same. I felt as if I were in a prison, locked and guarded in my cell. I could have endured that if not for the way he treated Simon."

"Why did you choose to go when you did?"

"Simon had started asking questions, and he didn't understand some of the painful things he heard your father and me say to each other. Remember, you were at school during the day, and Simon was home with me. With your father's growing suspicions that I was being unfaithful, he had taken to coming home without warning. I think he figured to catch me with some lover."

Alice frowned. "I'm sorry."

"Your father was often harsh with Simon. Your brother tried so hard to win his affection, and George would have no part of it. He even started hitting the boy—not for the purpose of correction but out of his hatred."

"That's the part I find so hard to believe."

"You can ask Simon if you'd like. He remembers it well. He still holds his own sorrow for the fact that his father never loved him."

"Just like I bore the sorrow thinking you didn't love me." Alice bit her lip. She hadn't meant to say it aloud.

"But I always loved you, Alice. Always. If you read through

those letters, I think you'll see the truth for yourself. It will be painful, but I want you to know the truth."

Alice looked at the bag and nodded. "I'll read them." And even as she said the words, Alice knew the letters would forever change everything. Without reading a single one, she knew that the things her mother had spoken were no doubt true.

Chapter 19

"Did you speak with the doctor?" Hannah asked Marty. She had just finished washing the breakfast dishes while Marty gathered the ingredients to bake bread.

Marty nodded and placed a canister of flour near a large mixing bowl. "He's the same old doctor he's always been—full of admonitions and cautionary tales."

"He's much too old, and his medicine is outdated," Hannah replied. "You'd do best to rely on me. I don't say that as a matter of pride, but I know how obsolete some of his philosophies can be."

"It would be nice to have a younger doctor come to the community." Marty remembered something her husband had said. "You know, Jake has good friends in the Lufkin area—a married couple and both are doctors."

"A woman doctor—imagine that," Hannah said, drying her hands. "It would be so nice to have a doctor who understands a lady's body. Of course, just having a younger, more up-to-date physician would be wonderful. We had a couple of younger doctors here last year, but they were encouraged to move their practice closer to Dallas.

"Will says with the number of ranches having grown in the area, he hopes to entice the railroad to build a spur out this way. Once in place, he feels certain we can encourage a little community of our own to spring up. It would make it a whole lot easier to get provisions that way."

Marty tried to imagine the expansion of the area and smiled. "We're definitely civilizing Texas."

Laughing, Hannah handed her a dish towel. "I'm glad to have you home, Marty. Not just for the added help." She grew thoughtful for a moment. "It was kind of lonely around here. Once the Montoyas decided to move back to Mexico, well, I didn't have the heart to hire on new staff. I doubt I could find anyone to get along with me as well as they did."

Marty smiled and began drying the dishes. "I remember how she taught me to make tortillas."

"She taught me so much," Hannah admitted. "And I suppose I taught her a thing or two." She gave a chuckle. "We were definitely more like sisters than employer and employee."

"That's how it is for Alice and me. I guess that's why I'm so grateful you allowed her to come with me and to stay here. I appreciate what you've done for her mother and brother, too."

"Family is important. Staying close, whether in distance or just in heart, is something that will see you through the worst of life. It's important to remember that, Marty."

"I will," she promised. Marty hesitated a moment and then decided to move the topic in a different direction. "I wonder if you would give me your opinion on something."

Hannah looked surprised. It wasn't often that Marty asked for anyone's opinion, so her sister was bound to be rather taken aback. She waited a moment for Hannah to regain her composure. "I've been thinking about something for a long time now. I discussed it with Jake back in Denver, but, since I learned about the baby I haven't said anything more to him."

"What are you talking about?"

"You know that I helped out at one of the orphanages in Denver?"

"Yes, I remember."

Marty looked away, bit her lower lip for a moment, and tried to figure out how best to share her thoughts. "Well . . . you see . . . there are these three boys." She turned back to find her sister watching her.

"I want to adopt them." There, it was out. Marty waited for her sister to condemn her desires or at best chide her for her foolish thoughts. When she remained silent, Marty found the courage to continue. "I fell in love with them. Wyatt, Samuel, and Benjamin are their names."

"How old are they?" Hannah began to busy herself with sifting flour.

"Wyatt is going to be eight in July. Sam and Benjamin are natural brothers. Sam is older—he'll be seven in May. Benjamin's just four. His birthday isn't until September."

"Sounds like quite a handful."

Marty smiled at the memory of trying to teach Sam how to tie his shoes. Benjamin had felt the need to learn, too, and Wyatt came along to help instruct. It had turned into a catastrophe. "They can be. But they are precious to me, and I want very much to be their mother."

"How does Jake feel about it?"

"Well, as I said, when I first wrote to you about the older orphans coming here to Texas, I also spoke to Jake about adopting. However, I'm sure he thought I meant to take only one—two at the most. We were financially well-off at that time, and that's not the case anymore. And, of course, I wasn't expecting a child of our own."

"And you're afraid now he won't want to adopt?"

"That and the fact that I had a letter from Mr. Brentwood, the director of the orphanage. Money has been very tight for them. Donations are way down, and all of Colorado is in a horrible state of depression. He's closing the orphanage."

"Where will the children go?" Hannah asked, her look revealing grave concern.

"To other orphanages, I suppose The state runs several, and there are some churches that have their own organizations. But I don't want that to happen to these boys. I want them to be with me—always. Is that wrong?"

Hannah shook her head. "Love is never wrong. It is often misplaced or premature, but I think there is always an element of good and right in it." She smiled. "I think you should talk to your husband about this. Personally, I would love to have children around the ranch. You know that."

Marty had heard her sister express this on more than one occasion. Maybe that was why she had decided to discuss the matter with Hannah first. She needed to see her sister's reaction before speaking to Jake.

"I'll talk to him tonight." Marty felt a sense of relief in making the decision. Hopefully Jake would understand her heart.

A commotion outside drew their attention from the kitchen, and Hannah and Marty went to investigate. Several men were carrying another man, and when Marty saw that it was Jake, her heart all but stopped.

"What happened to him?" Marty heard Hannah ask.

"Horse got spooked and threw him. He would have been all right, but then the horse kicked and caught him square in the head." That accounted for the blood running down his face.

"Bring him in and put him on the dining room table," Hannah instructed. She held the screen door open for the men while Marty tried to regain her breath. It was as if Thomas's accident were happening all over again.

She thought for a moment she might faint. Her vision swam before her and her face felt hot. But even as Marty considered giving in to the sensation, Hannah shook her hard.

"Come on, I said. I need your help."

Marty wasn't sure how, but she managed to follow her sister into the house. The men had positioned the unconscious Jake on the table, and Hannah was already examining him when Marty finally felt her senses return.

"Is he . . . ?" She found it impossible to ask the question on her mind.

Hannah wiped some of the blood from Jake's wound with her apron and surveyed the situation. She opened each of his eyes and then closed them again. Next she listened to his heart, putting her ear against his chest.

Meanwhile, Marty stood helpless. Just as she had all those years ago with Thomas. She could almost see Thomas on the table in Jake's place, only instead of a head wound it was a horrible gash in his abdomen.

"Marty, fetch me some hot water and clean dish towels. Let's get him cleaned up and see if he's gonna need stitching."

For a moment Marty didn't move. She wanted to—meant to—but her feet were fixed in place. She couldn't tear her gaze from Jake's lifeless body.

"Marty! Get me water now!" Hannah demanded.

Hearing her sister's authoritative command shook Marty out of her haze. She hurried to the kitchen and dipped a small pan into the water reservoir. She poured the hot water into a bowl, took up a dozen dish towels, and hurried back to the dining room.

Hannah motioned her to wet some of the towels. "Hand me one after you wring it out."

Marty did as instructed and waited for her sister's next command. When Hannah finally had the wound cleaned, Marty could see that it wasn't all that deep.

"Head wounds always bleed bad, but I don't think he's gonna need stitches," Hannah said. She looked to the men who were standing around waiting. "Looks to me that horse just grazed him. Let me bandage his head, and then you can take him to his room. Marty, go turn down the bed for them. Joe, Bert, remove his boots. Davis, help me get his bloody shirt off after I get the wound covered."

Everyone worked together like a well-oiled machine. Hannah was quite adept at running the household and the men who worked for her. Marty seriously wondered if she could ever be that competent.

Readying the bed, Marty tried not to fear the worst. She prayed, just as she had prayed for Thomas. But this time, she didn't feel quite as afraid. Maybe she was getting numb to all of this. Ranch accidents were everyday events. Maybe in her heart she'd given up hope that the cattle business could ever be safe.

Why would I want to bring children into this?

It was only a matter of a few minutes when the men showed up carrying Jake. Marty got out of the way so they could put him on the bed. Once he was deposited, the boys left to get back to work. It was their way of life, and they seemed to accept it as part of the job.

Marty waited as Hannah checked Jake once again. He moaned softly. "I don't think it's all that bad, Marty. He's already showing signs of coming around. You stay here with him while I mix some salve for his head and get him something for the pain. When he wakes up, he's going to have a doozy of a headache."

Sitting on the bed beside her husband, Marty lifted his hand. She bent her cheek to it and remembered that she'd done the same with Thomas. She shook her head and closed her eyes. "Oh, God, please don't take him from me. I love him so much. I need him so much." She couldn't stop her tears from falling. "Father, I have fought returning to Texas and the ranch for this very reason. I can't bear to lose another husband. I can't lose the father of my baby. Please don't take him away."

"Take who?"

Marty opened her eyes to see Jake looking at her in confusion. "Jake!"

He gave her a lopsided smile. "What's all the fuss about? Who's gettin' taken away?"

Her chest felt tight and Marty gasped for air. "Oh, Jake." She fell against his chest and wept.

Jake put his arm around her. "What's all this? Why are you cryin'?"

"I thought . . . I couldn't bear . . ." She couldn't speak for the catch in her throat. Marty straightened and tried to regain control of her emotions. She replaced worry with anger, something she'd learned long ago helped her to compose herself after a shock. "You scared the life outta me, Jacob Wythe! I thought you were gonna die and leave me here in Texas."

He smiled and shook his head. It was evident that he was in pain as he grimaced, but the smile returned and he put his hand up to her face. "Marty, you worry too much. I'm not going anywhere. At least not until I see if I've got a son or a daughter."

"You better not plan to go anywhere after that, either," Marty scolded. "Here I wanted to talk to you about adopting three little boys, and instead you go get yourself hurt. I don't know what I was thinking, but I think you were mighty inconsiderate, Mr. Wythe. Sometimes I don't think you care for me like you claim."

Jake gave a small chuckle. "Like I said, Mrs. Wythe, you worry too much."

"What's all the shouting about?" Hannah asked as she rushed into the bedroom with a small tray.

"My wife is giving me a mouth-whoopin' for gettin' hurt," Jake replied in a lazy drawl.

Marty got to her feet. "Well, he deserves it. He knows how much something like this scares me. I think it's mighty inconsiderate, given my condition."

Hannah grinned and put the tray on the stand beside the bed. "Sounds like you're being inconsiderate of *his* condition."

"I haven't got a condition," Jake declared. He tried to sit up but fell back. "Well, at least not much of one." He closed his eyes. "Think I'll just rest a bit."

"You've got that right," Hannah said. "I'll tie you to that bed if you don't cooperate."

"You won't have to," Marty said, coming alongside her sister. "If he thinks he's gonna set foot out of that bed, he's got another think coming. I'll sit on him if I have to."

Jake opened his eyes and gave her a half-cocked smile. "I just might test you out, Mrs. Wythe. Sounds like I could be in for a world of fun."

"You'll be in for a world of hurt if you don't do exactly what my sister tells you to do," Marty said.

Hannah shook her head and reached for the salve she'd brought. "I've dealt with children less troublesome than you two. Now, settle down while I redress this wound. I've brought you something to help with the pain, Jake, and don't go tellin' me that you haven't got any. I know that head of yours is hard, but you're gonna hurt for at least the rest of the day. I want you to promise me you'll stay in bed—flat in bed and rest. Hear me?"

"Yes, ma'am," he replied with a wink at Marty. "Can Marty stay with me—maybe read to me?"

"Ha!" Marty declared, hands on hips. "You scare me nearly to death and then you want me to read to you?" All of the sudden she stopped and her hand went to her belly.

"What's wrong?" Jake asked, looking concerned.

Hannah turned to her sister. "What is it, Marty? Are you in pain?"

Marty shook her head. "It's been ongoing. The baby moves all the time."

"That's unusual," Hannah said and looked at her oddly. "You're hardly far enough along to have that kind of movement."

Worry crept up Marty's spine like a tingling snake. "Does this mean something's wrong?"

"Not at all. But my guess is you're further along than you realize. You said you weren't sure if the baby was due in July or August. Maybe it's coming sooner than that. Is it possible?"

Marty considered the matter for a moment. "I suppose so. There was such upheaval what with losing the house and Jake's leaving."

"My guess is this baby may come a month or two sooner than you think."

She glanced over at Jake, who was watching her in wonder. "A month or two sooner?"

"Can I feel it?" he asked.

Marty sat back on the edge of the bed and positioned his hand on her stomach. Just then the baby shifted again, and Jake's eye widened.

"Feisty little fella," he declared.

"Could be a little filly," Hannah said, smiling. "Either way, I think we'd better speed up our work on clothes for the baby."

★

Alice read the last of her mother's letters and sat back in her chair to take it all in. The truth was there on the pages. Her mother had loved her most dearly, had pleaded with Alice's father to be allowed to come back into her daughter's life—only to be rejected.

The letters written by Alice's father had been brief and to the point. They were also ugly and heartless. He had threatened his wife with arrest and ruin if she so much as showed her face in Denver again. He threatened to take Simon from her and have the boy sent far away. He threatened to disappear with Alice so that she might never find either of them again. The words were heartbreaking. He even threatened her mother's life.

Alice could scarcely believe her father's cruel nature. How could he have been so loving toward her and so hateful toward them?

She decided to look through the rest of the papers and items in the bag. There was very little left to her. A small framed picture of Alice, a letter opener, and a pipe were all that remained of her father's personal effects. The other papers proved to be notes he had made for himself and half-

223

written letters that were never finished. Then Alice spied the large envelope at the bottom of the bag. She took it up and wondered if the gold certificates were inside. Opening it, she found a single sheet of paper.

NEVER AGAIN were the only words written.

She had no way of knowing if it was her father's writing or someone else's. The large block letters could have belonged to anyone. It was a mystery that would most likely go unresolved. One thing was quite clear, however. There were no gold certificates, plates, or other counterfeit materials. If there had been, they were long gone. Mr. Smith would never have what he sought, and hopefully that would include Alice's whereabouts.

Chapter 20

The night was perfect for a party. To celebrate Jake's and Hannah's birthdays they had cleared the Barnetts' yard of obstructions, set up a half dozen tables, and made an area for dancing. Hannah and Alice had worked hard to place dozens of lanterns around the area. Some hung from the large cottonwoods, while others were affixed to the fence posts or positioned on creative stands. It definitely lent an air of something special to the party. Parties like this were always a time of great joy. Local ranchers gathered together and discussed the cattle business while their wives swapped recipes and gossip. And, of course, the children entertained one another with games of hide-and-seek and tag.

These are the best folks in the world. Not one of them needs to be cut from the herd. Robert smiled and nodded greetings to the various people who caught his gaze. He loved it here. The heavy humidity of the day had lifted a bit, and now in the cool of the evening, these Texans were ready for a hoedown.

Robert's stomach growled, and he had to admit that most

of his excitement centered around the food. His father and Tyler Atherton had decided to roast a pig, and the aroma of cooking meat had plagued him since yesterday. Not only that, but the tables were all but bowing from a bevy of dishes his mother, Marty, and Alice had worked to prepare. All of his favorites were present: cheesy grits, jalapeño corn bread, corn salad, and molasses baked beans, just to name a few. There were also at least a dozen pies of varying kinds and a chocolate pecan cake. Robert had eaten various renditions of the latter on many occasions and always found he could put away a good portion of the cake by himself.

Then there was the food other folks had brought to share. People had been gathering since early afternoon, and now there were probably eighty or so spread out across the yard, dancing to the tunes the musicians were playing. Inevitably when there was a party, those who were musically inclined knew to bring their instruments without being asked. Tonight they had three guitars and two fiddles. They made for a nice little band and as soon as the skies had grown dark and the lanterns had been lit, they'd begun to play.

Someone took the opportunity to call a square dance, and the crowd split up into paired couples and then squares of eight. Robert decided to take that opportunity to help himself to the food table.

"I don't suppose you've had a chance to speak to Jess yet, have you?" Robert looked up to find Tyler Atherton with plate in hand.

"No, sir. Not yet, but I will." Robert helped himself to a large slice of the roasted pig. "I figure to get her alone tonight and explain it. That way she can have friends around to take her mind off of the matter."

"Could be she'll be all the more embarrassed for it," Mr.

Atherton replied, "but I trust you to be as easy on her as possible."

"Absolutely. I care very much for her." Robert continued heaping food on his plate as Tyler dug into the roasted pig.

Earlier that day he'd managed to speak to Mr. Atherton by himself. Pulling him away from the roasting pig, Robert had spoken his mind. Tyler Atherton had listened without interruption.

"I love Jess," he'd said, "but not in a way that would lead us to marriage. She's like a little sister to me. I would do anything to keep her safe and protected. I would give my life for her, Mr. Atherton, but I cannot marry her."

Mr. Atherton hadn't seemed at all surprised. Robert had always known the man to be rather casual in the way he dealt with life, but he was, in fact, quite astute.

"You're in love with the Chesterfield gal, aren't you?" he'd asked. Robert couldn't deny it and Atherton nodded. "I could see it in your eyes—the way you look at her. Reminded me of how I felt about Carissa. You know, I want exactly that for my Jessica, and if it's not to be with you, then I want her set free to find that person."

Now all Robert had left to do was break the news to Jessica.

The opportunity to do just that came some time later, after Robert's second plate of food. Eating with some of the older ranchers, Robert enjoyed their stories of cattle drives to Kansas and the hardships of days gone by. Reluctantly, he got to his feet and searched the dancers for Jessica. She didn't seem to be among them. He was about to take his search to where the other women had gathered when Jessica approached him to ask for a dance.

"They're playing a waltz," she said with a coy smile. "Wouldn't you like to dance with me?"

All evening Robert had avoided Alice, but now with Jessica standing before him, it was Alice that he longed to dance with. He took hold of Jess and led her toward a quiet spot under a tall sugarberry tree. "We need to talk."

Jessica looked up at him. "Talk?" She gave a tug and broke free of his hold. With great flourish, Jessica whirled in a circle, her skirt splaying out around her. "Isn't this the most beautiful gown? It's perfect for dancing, and I want to dance."

"I know, but this can't wait." Robert knew what needed to be said, but finding a way to do it gently was harder than he'd thought. "Jess, I've been trying to talk to you for a long while now, but you won't hear me out. I talked to your pa this morning—"

Her face lit up. "To ask for my hand? How wonderful!" She looped her arm through his. "And now you've brought me away from the crowd to propose. This is perfect. We can announce it tonight."

He pulled free and took hold of her shoulders. "No! Listen to me, Jessica. I am not going to marry you." He hadn't meant for the words to come out so harsh. He softened his tone. "I will always care about you. Like I told your pa, I would even give my life for you. You're like a member of my family—a little sister who I dearly love. But, Jess, I'm not in love with you."

"But you love me, and out of that a deeper love can grow," she said, smiling.

Robert shook his head. "No, Jess. It's not going to grow deeper."

Jessica lost her smile and fixed him with a stare. "You love her—that scar-faced mousy blonde. You love her, don't you?"

"It's not like you to belittle those less fortunate than you," he reprimanded.

"You love her, don't you?" she pressed.

For a moment Robert didn't say anything. He didn't want to declare his love of Alice to Jessica. What he felt was private and personal. He needed to speak with Alice and share his thoughts with her—not Jess.

"Answer me, Robert. You love Alce Chesterfield."

"I do," he said, blowing out a heavy breath. "I didn't start out to fall in love with her. I wanted to be her friend and help her adjust to life in Texas. I had no notion of anything else. The love just happened."

"But not for me," she said, her voice cracking slightly. "Why can you love her . . . and not me?" A single tear slid from her eye, and Robert reached out to touch it. In the lantern light it glistened for a moment and then faded. She bit her lower lip and said nothing more.

"But I do love you, Jess. Just not that way. Falling in love is a matter of the heart. You can't force it."

"I didn't think you'd have to," Jessica replied. "I thought . . . well . . . I'm pretty."

"Jess, it has nothing to do with looks. You're a beautiful woman. You're smart and talented—everything that a man could want."

"But not for you."

He shook his head. "I'm sorry, Jess."

She lifted her chin, appearing to regain some of her steam. "Not as sorry as you're gonna be." She sniffed. "You'll see. I'll make someone a wonderful wife, and we will travel and be wealthy. I'll be the most beautiful woman in Texas, and he will be the handsomest man."

Instead of making Robert jealous, as he was sure she was trying to do, he smiled and nodded. "I bet you will be. I hope that for you and so much more. I still want us to be friends, Jess. We're practically family."

She started to walk away but then turned back. In her expression Robert saw hurt mingled with anger. "I don't want to be friends with you, Robert Barnett. I'd rather have a rattlesnake for a friend." She stormed off in a huff.

Robert might have chuckled at her reference to the snake if it hadn't been such a serious moment. He watched Jessica approach one of the local rancher's sons. Apparently she asked him to dance, because he willingly followed her to the area where other couples were doing a reel.

"She'll be all right," Tyler Atherton said, coming up behind Robert.

"I hope so. I sure don't like lettin' her down, hurtin' her."

"I heard everything you said, Robert. It takes a big man to be honest in the face of such a thing. I'm proud of you for treatin' her with respect."

Robert looked at the older man. "Thanks. That means a lot comin' from you. My pa says he doesn't respect anybody's opinion more than yours."

Atherton smiled. "We've been friends a long time—gone through a lot together. I feel the same way about your pa." He slapped Robert's back. "And I have a feeling I will always think highly of you, as well. I would have liked havin' you for a son-in-law." The older man squared his shoulders. "Now, come on back to the party. There's still more cake, and I have a mind to get me another piece."

Robert laughed. "I can definitely see the benefit of that."

★

"How are you feelin'?" Jake asked Marty. He knew she'd been worried about him ever since he'd been kicked. He knew that it compounded her worries that he would die like her first husband. "You know I'm concerned that you aren't takin' it easy enough. I know you're thinkin' you gotta get things done because the baby will probably come sooner than August, but you can't do everything."

"I know," Marty replied. "I'm trying to be cautious and take things slow, but there is a great deal to oversee. As for how I feel, I'm a little tired, but otherwise fine. The real question is how do you feel? You know I think it's much too early for you to be out here carrying on with the others."

"Even your sister said I was doin' fine, and it's not like I'm up there square dancin'. Marty, you gotta stop worryin' about everythin'." He put his hand on her stomach. "For the sake of our children, if not for yourself."

"I can't help it. I love you so very much. I don't want to lose you." She stared off at the dancers and musicians. "I know that you're in God's hands, but—"

"But?" Jake interrupted. "But God isn't big enough to handle this? But God won't give you your own way all the time? Grief, Marty, you either trust Him or you don't. I'm not sayin' that we won't have doubts about Him, but I am sayin' that we don't need to. We know He's faithful." He turned her to face him. "Marty, if I drop over dead tomorrow, will you stop lovin' God again?"

She still wouldn't meet his eyes. "I . . . don't know. I don't like to think I would." She shook her head. "I'd like to say my faith is strong enough to get me through anything, but I know better." Finally she raised her gaze to his. "I'm a coward."

Jake chuckled. "Marty, there's no one less cowardly in the world. You are a strong woman, but unfortunately, you think it's your own strength that makes you so. It isn't. We don't do a thang in our own strength, Marty."

"You're sounding more and more like a Texan and less and less like a banker," she told him.

He nodded. "That's who I am, Marty. You gotta let me be who I am. And, you're gonna have to let our boys be who they are."

"Our boys?" She smiled. "So you already plan for a houseful of boys?"

"Didn't you want to adopt three of 'em?"

Recognition dawned on her. "You mean you'd be willing?"

"I love children, Marty. I love the idea of helpin' those needy ones. If you love those children, then I know I'll love 'em, too. I want you to wire Mr. Brentwood and have them sent down on the train."

She threw her arms around Jake's neck. "Oh, thank you. Thank you so much! I've missed those boys more than I can say. I really want them to be a part of our family."

Jake kissed her soundly on the mouth and smiled. "Then that's what I want, too."

Marty reached up and touched the smaller bandage Hannah had put on Jake's wound. "I'll try to be accepting and understanding. I really want to trust God more."

"Then do it, Marty. You've always been a woman who went after what she wanted."

★

Alice found herself watching Robert for most of the evening. She'd been unable to take her gaze from him when he led Jessica Atherton away from the party. However, once she saw him tenderly touch her cheek, Alice knew she had to stop fooling herself. She had fallen in love with another woman's man. The idea sickened her.

"This is such a wonderful place," her mother said, coming

to stand beside her. "I can see why you love it so. I have to say it's nothing like Chicago."

Alice turned toward her mother. "Speaking of Chicago, Mama, I wonder if I might go with you when you return."

Her mother seemed surprised but pleased. "I would love for you to come visit Simon and me in our home."

"No, I meant . . . would you let me come live with you?"

"Well of course," her mother said, taking hold of her arm. "But I thought you preferred it here."

Alice shrugged. "There's nothing to keep me here. I do enjoy it and I love Marty like a sister, but honestly, it would probably be better for all concerned if I were to leave."

Just then Simon barreled into Alice. "This is the best time I've ever had," he said, wrapping his arms around her waist.

Alice smiled down at her brother. "Well, do you suppose you could show me a time like this in Chicago?"

The boy straightened and dropped his hold. "There's nothing like this in Chicago. I want us to move here."

Alice looked to her mother, hoping she would set Simon straight. "Why don't you go on and have some more fun," Mother told him. "We are talking about something serious just now."

"But this is a party," he reminded them. "You don't talk about serious things at a party."

Alice felt bad and nodded. "Perhaps he's right. I probably shouldn't have brought it up just now; you should be out there with the others."

"Go on, Simon. I want you to go play," Mama encouraged. She turned back to Alice and smiled. "It's all right, Alice. We can talk about anything you want—anytime you want. I am so glad to have you back in my life that I could easily spend all of my time with you and Simon and never speak to another soul." Mother seemed to scrutinize Alice for several moments before continuing.

"Alice, you seem troubled about something. What is it?"

"I . . . well. . . ." Alice paused, not wanting to lie to her mother. "Marty and Jake were so kind to take me in when I had nothing—not even references for the job they hired me to do. When the banks fell apart and they lost everything, they still allowed me to stay on with them. I knew it was difficult for them, but they insisted. Now I find myself again having the benefit of someone else's generosity. I guess I just feel that I've overstayed my welcome. I don't want to be a burden to anyone."

"I've seen the way you help out around here. You aren't a burden. I think you more than earn your keep. And they all seem to very much enjoy your company."

"Which is why this is so hard." Alice glanced at the revelers and saw Robert kiss his mother's cheek. How she longed for him to kiss her. "I think we should go before we are no longer enjoyed and useful." She looked at her mother. "But I don't think we should say anything about our plans. At least not until we're ready to leave. Otherwise Mrs. Barnett might feel slighted or believe us to be ungrateful."

"I don't know why she would. She knows I have a home in Chicago."

"I know, but she also said we could use the Montoya house for as long as we liked. Mrs. Barnett is generous to a fault. I don't want to hurt her feelings."

Her mother remained silent for several minutes and then nodded. "If you think that's best, Alice, then I will go along with you. However, have you considered the matter of your train fare? I was under the impression that you had no money."

"I don't," Alice said realizing the problem. "But I'll get it.

234

I'll figure a way." She didn't know how she could possibly make it work, but she was determined to try.

"I wonder if I might have this dance."

Alice turned to find Robert Barnett standing directly behind her. She wanted to refuse him, but instead she found herself nodding in agreement. She let Robert take her to where a dozen or so couples were waltzing.

She looked at him and shook her head. "I don't know how."

He smiled that lazy smile of his and her heart melted. "Then it's time you learned. We enjoy having our get-togethers, and you'll just have to get used to dancin' if you're gonna be around here."

But I'm not going to be around here. I have to leave before you realize that I've lost my heart to you. I have to go before anyone knows how I feel.

"I have to go," she said suddenly and pulled away. She heard Robert call after her, but Alice continued to make her way with great haste to the solitude of the house. It wasn't until she was behind the closed door of her room, however, that she felt she could finally let down her guard. The pain of losing something she didn't really have seemed such a contradiction, but there was no other way to look at it.

I've lost him, but I never had him. So why does it hurt so much?

Chapter 21

For weeks the men planned their trip to Fort Worth and the cattle sale. Knowing they'd be gone for several days, Alice decided it would be the perfect opportunity to leave without any uncomfortable good-byes.

She had been plotting and planning for their escape, but when the time came, she still felt uncertain. She and her mother had spoken several times, but Alice knew her mother wasn't convinced she was doing the right thing. For Alice, however, there was no other choice.

Robert had tried his best to get Alice alone. He continually nagged her to go riding with him or to sit and talk with him in the evening. It was getting harder and harder to avoid him. Alice had even given up going to church, because twice Robert had cornered her after services to speak to her. She felt almost certain that he'd figured out or been told of her feelings for him.

The second night after the men's departure, Alice knew she'd never have a better chance. "We'll leave tomorrow, no matter what," Alice had told her mother. Even now the look of shock on her mother's face was imprinted in Alice's mind.

"Are you sure that's wise? What about money?"

Alice had talked Marty into lending her some money. It wasn't a lot, but it would be enough for train tickets and maybe some food.

The problem, however, was getting away from Marty and Hannah. She knew if either of them caught wind of her plans, they would do their best to put an end to them.

When Marty and Hannah announced they would be heading out just after lunch to work on Marty's place, Alice felt confident God had intervened to help her leave. Watching at the window, Alice jumped into action once the buggy pulled away. That would leave the large carriage, which was exactly what they'd need.

"We must work fast," Alice told her mother. "I don't want any teary good-byes. I've written letters for Hannah and Marty explaining our leaving this way."

"It hardly seems good manners to sneak out," her mother replied.

"We're not sneaking. We're avoiding a scene. I know these people better than you do. They will fuss and fret and nag us to stay."

"Your brother isn't going to like this one bit. He's quite happy here."

Alice looked at her mother in confusion. "Did you come here meaning to make Texas your home?"

"No, I bought round-trip tickets. But seeing how Simon has thrived, I've begun to think about the possibility. Simon has blossomed while here. You have no idea how it was for him in Chicago. He was so unhappy."

"Perhaps with me there, we can find a way to better his life. I'll get a job, and maybe I can earn enough to lavish him with special gifts. Papa used to do that for me."

"And did it make everything seem right?" her mother asked, giving her a look that suggested she already knew the answer.

Alice looked away. "No. I suppose not."

"Alice, why are we really leaving this way? I'm your mother, and I want you to be honest with me."

A lie was on her lips, but one look back at her mother and Alice knew she had to confess her reasons. "I'm in love."

"With?"

"With Robert." She reached up and felt the scar on her face. "He has been so kind to me and never made me feel ugly. When I'm with him, I forget I even have this reminder of the attack." She shook her head, feeling the weight of the world on her shoulders. "I let my heart get carried away."

"And how does he feel about you?" Mother asked.

"I'm sure he feels nothing but friendship." Alice paused, wondering if her mother hadn't yet heard that he was engaged to Jessica Atherton. "He's to be married. Do you remember at the birthday party that one girl about my age, very pretty, and most every man there sought to dance with her?"

"The Atherton girl?" Mother questioned.

"Yes. Jessica Atherton."

"And Robert is supposed to marry her?"

Alice sighed and stopped rubbing her scar. "Yes. They've been promised to each other since they were young. Mama, I don't want to do anything to come between them. I would feel terrible if I caused Robert and Jessica pain. They've been nothing but good to me."

Mother took a seat on the side of the bed. "I see."

"And I couldn't explain that to Hannah and Will. They've

taken me in and treated me like family, just as Marty and Jake have. I couldn't tell any of them the real reason, because I'm ashamed of having let things get out of hand."

Mother nodded. "I suppose you're right."

Alice went to the dresser and pulled out the last of her things. "Hannah and Marty will be busy most of the afternoon. They're going to measure for new curtains and figure out how they want to arrange things when the boys come from Denver. That should give us plenty of time to get to town before the train pulls out of Cedar Springs."

"But how are we to get there?"

"I will ask one of the men to take us. There's always a hand or two around here. I'll tell them that something has happened and you need to return to Chicago immediately. I'm sure it will all work out."

But she wasn't. There were a great many things that could go wrong. The men could change their mind and come home early. Hannah and Marty might have forgotten something and need to return to the house.

I might not even be able to find someone to drive us to the train station. And then what?

The thoughts worried her, but Alice was determined to make things work.

★

"I'm glad we're finished here," Robert told his father. They walked past several Fort Worth storefronts and made their way to the jewelry store at the corner. Robert had already mentioned his plan.

"I'm gonna find the perfect ring for my bride." Robert's grin stretched almost from ear to ear.

"I think I just might pick out a little somethin' for your

mama. I didn't have anything special for her birthday, and this will more than make up for that."

"I'm glad Jake was willing to stay with the others and start the cows for home. I need the time," he said as they approached the brick building, "to have a word or two with you in private."

Robert paused before the jewelry store door. "You and Ma love each other a great deal. I've always admired that. Even when you argue, I can see the respect you hold for each other. It's like you two were always meant to be together."

Father laughed. "You wouldn't have thought so in our early years. Your mama was the most stubborn woman I'd ever met. She would stand her ground over the silliest things."

"Like when she went to help the Comanches?"

The older man nodded. "Took nearly ten years off my life. I thought for sure she'd get us both killed, but your mama has a way with folks—even Comanches. She's stubborn, but she's also the bravest woman I've ever known. Saw her crawl out on a tree limb to rescue a cat for Marty. And it wasn't on some low-hangin' branch, either. I've seen her kill rattlers with a hoe and face down tornadoes and wildfires like she already knew the outcome."

Robert had seen it, too. He saw that same kind of bravery in Alice. Maybe that's why he loved her so much. Despite the attack and all she'd lost, Alice faced life with great determination and strength.

"Alice is like that," Robert said, meeting his father's eyes. "I wanna do right by her, Pa. I wanna give her the things she deserves. I was hopin' you could help me get to work building a house."

"You wanna build right away? You know you two are welcome to live at the house as long as you like. In fact, I had thought about discussin' a change of plans with you."

Robert cocked his head to one side, looking at his father. "Change of plans?"

"Your ma was the one who got me to thinkin'."

Robert almost hated to ask. His mother was well known for coming up with some of the zaniest ideas. "And what did she get you thinkin' about?"

"Well, she reminded me that the ranch will one day be yours. Sooner, rather than later, since we're both gettin' older every day. It seems kind of senseless for you to build a new house elsewhere. She suggested that you two could take the whole east wing for yourselves—that would afford you some privacy. We could tear down a couple of walls in that wing to open things up a bit, remake it with your own sitting room and such."

"But *your* rooms are in the east wing," Robert said, as if his father didn't already know this.

"Yup, but that's where your mama has her plan. Since Marty and Jake will be heading back to Marty's place and Alice's ma will most likely head home before long, the house will be empty again. But you know your ma. She's convinced there will be an abundance of little ones once you and Alice marry. So she thinks it's time to add on again. I thought on it and I like the idea. I can put an addition on the west end of the house for us."

Robert didn't know what to say. He'd never really thought of his parents getting old and settling into an easier life.

"Cat got your tongue?" his father asked.

"I can't imagine you and Ma not livin' in the east wing. I mean, that's all I've ever known. And I sure haven't thought much about the two of you gettin' old."

"Well, it's time you did. I'll be fifty-nine come June. You know as well as I do that I'm slowin' down. I can't ride as long as I used to without causin' my back a world of hurt. The time is comin', maybe earlier than either of us would like to see, when you'll be takin' over."

It took some joy out of the moment to consider his parents unable to do the things they loved. He couldn't imagine his father not sitting on a horse or his mother not gardening.

"Well, we gonna just stand here?" Father asked.

"No, sir." He reached for the door handle, and Father put his hand on Robert's arm.

"Don't go broodin' over this. Your mama and I like to plan ahead. You talk to your little gal about it, and then we can all sit down and have a discussion."

Robert nodded. "I will, Pa. I'll do that first thing."

Just then gunshots rang out. Robert and his father glanced up to see an armed man on horseback holding two other mounts. The man had his neckerchief tied around his face.

The bank's being held up.

Robert looked around to see people scurrying out of the way, taking cover wherever they could.

"Get back," his father said, pushing him around the side of the building. "Stay down. We need to figure out what we can do."

"We don't have any weapons," Robert said. "Our rifles are back with the horses."

"I know." Father looked more than a little irritated at the reminder.

Another gunshot sounded, and shortly after that came the bellowing voice of one of the robbers. "Let's get outta here!"

The man on horseback waited with rifle cocked as his two confederates mounted. Robert could see his father edging closer to the front of the building.

"Pa, we can't do anything." The helplessness of the moment only served to make both men more determined.

But from out of nowhere came rifle fire. Three shots in a row, fast and precise. Each one hit its mark and the men fell from their horses like leaves from a tree. Seeing that, Robert's father bounded out into the street and took hold of one of the thieves' guns before he could shoulder it.

"Thanks for the help," a familiar voice called out.

Austin Todd, the field inspector they'd spent time with earlier in the day, came striding up the street. He wore a determined look and quickly disarmed the other men, who were no match for him. Several armed police officers arrived just then, guns drawn and pointed at Austin.

"Texas Ranger," he told the first officer. The man seemed to relax at this.

"What happened?" the officer asked, looking at the three who were roiling in pain on the street.

"Bank robbery. I think you'll find the money in that bag over there." Austin pointed to the farthest man. Beside him was what looked to be a pillowcase with something in it.

"Anyone else involved?" the man asked.

"I'm guessing the bank personnel. You take over here, and I'll go check out the bank." Austin headed for the building, Robert and his father following after him.

"We saw them but had no weapons. Felt like a fool just crouchin' down there in the alleyway," Robert's father told the ranger.

"It was the right thing to do. If you'd been out there, you could've been shot."

"How did you come to be here?" Robert asked, remembering something Austin had said earlier. "I thought you were headin' to the railroad station, and by the way, when did you become a Texas Ranger?"

"Last year. They incorporated all of us field inspectors into the Rangers. Makes it a whole lot easier." Austin paused at the door.

Robert figured he was making sure there was no one pointing a gun at them.

"Texas Ranger!" he called out. "I'm comin' in, so if you have weapons, put 'em down."

There was no response. The trio made their way into the bank only to find the bodies of the bank manager and his teller on the floor. They were both dead.

"I was headed for my train," Austin said, "then I realized I had forgotten to tend to some other business. Guess God just put me in the right place at the right time." He shook his head at the bloody scene. The look on his face suggested an anger that burned deep and hot. "I should have aimed to kill those murderers."

Two hours later the Barnett men rejoined Jake and the cowhands as they made their way back to the ranch. Jake threw Robert a grin and moved his mount closer.

"Did you get it?"

With the ruckus of the bank robbery, Robert had nearly forgotten what he'd come to town for in the first place. New cows weren't the only thing they had on hand.

"I did," he admitted.

"Then you can 'I do' right away," Jake teased. "I can't tell you how happy I am to see you and Alice gettin' married."

"Well, she has to say yes first."

Robert kept reaching inside his vest pocket to feel for the box. He'd spent a pretty penny on the ring, but he knew Alice would love it, and she was certainly worth it. He smiled to himself and made his plans.

When we get back, I'm gonna find her and tell her that we need to talk. I'll make it sound all serious. Then once we're alone, I'll tell her how much she means to me. I'll get down on one knee and hold up the ring in the box. No, maybe I'll just hold up the ring.

Thankful for the time to figure it all out, Robert said very little as his father related the events at the bank.

Jake seemed more than a little disturbed by the turn of events. "And Marty worries about me ranchin'. I don't suppose she ever thought that bankin' could be just as dangerous. I hope you tell her about the robbery when we get home. Maybe it'll settle her down a bit."

Robert's father shook his head. "There's danger all around us. Marty knows that full well. She always blamed the ranch and Texas for killin' Thomas, but the hard truth of it is that a man could die sittin' at his desk or at the dinner table. Robert and I could have just as easily caught one of those stray bullets. Or the lookout man could have thought us a threat and shot us as a matter of business." He paused.

"Apparently God's not through with us just yet, eh Robert? One thing I know: When I get home I'm gonna kiss my wife for a good long time and then . . . I think I'll clean my guns."

Chapter 22

"What are you saying?" Alice asked the stationmaster at the train depot in Cedar Springs.

"I'm sayin' there's trouble on the line, and there won't be any passenger service out today." He gave her a sympathetic smile. "However, there are other railroads. You could head on to Dallas and catch one of those."

"We've hardly got the money for additional tickets," Alice stated in worry. Biting her lip, she tried to figure out what they should do. By now Marty and Hannah might have returned to the house. She couldn't very well go back to the ranch without creating an uproar.

"Well, I can refund the return passage cost on your mother and brother's tickets. That should allow you to cover costs on another line."

With a sigh, Alice realized this nightmare wasn't going to go away. "All right. But how are we supposed to get to Dallas?"

The man grinned. "That one's easy enough. One of the

Dallas freighters arrived earlier. He won't be takin' anything much back with him. I'm thinkin' you could hitch a ride for free."

She thought about it for a moment. She certainly had no way to get the Barnett carriage to take them. The driver had been hard enough to convince to bring them here in the first place. "Very well. Where can we find the driver?"

After getting instructions on where to locate the man, Alice returned to where her mother and brother waited. Simon was in an ill temper. He was decidedly upset that they were leaving Texas. He had whined and complained all the way to the train station, reminding Alice that she couldn't take her colt with her on the train nor could she take any more riding lessons from Robert. Now played out, Simon sulked beside their mother.

"There's a problem, but I believe we have a solution." Alice told them what had transpired. Her mother turned over the train tickets and received the money due her before they went in search of the freight man.

The trio approached just as the driver was ready to pull out. He was an older gentleman with gray at the temples. Alice summoned up her courage. "Excuse me."

The man looked down from his seat and smiled. "What can I do for you, little gal?"

"Our train has been canceled because of problems on the line. The stationmaster said you might be willing to take us to the Dallas station. However, we don't have any money."

"Oh, that's quite all right." He set the brake and climbed down. "I'll take you just for the company. Been a long time since I talked to a couple of pretty ladies." He gave Alice's mother a nod. "I'm Roy James—no relation to Jesse James." He guffawed as if it were the most priceless of jokes.

"Mr. James, this is my mother, Mrs. Chesterfield, and my brother, Simon."

He again nodded toward Alice's mother and smiled. "You can call me Roy, ma'am. Let me help you up. You can sit with me while you young'uns ride in the back."

Alice's mother looked hesitant, but Alice gave her arm a pat. "That will work just fine for us." Her only concern was managing to get out of Cedar Springs before someone from the Barnett ranch showed up to stop them.

Once they were settled, Mr. James put his team in motion. He smiled over at Alice's mother. "So, headin' home or goin' to visit?"

"Home," Mother replied.

The man looked straight ahead. "Got your man waitin' for you to return, eh?"

"No. I'm widowed."

Roy James beamed her a smile that could have brightened a dark room. "Widowed. That's quite a coincidence. I'm a widower myself."

And with that Mr. James began a nonstop conversation with Mother that made Alice smile, in spite of her worry. It seemed the man had taken an instant liking to her.

★

Robert didn't like the way his mother looked when she greeted him at the door. He knew immediately that something was wrong.

"What's going on?"

She glanced at his father before saying, "The Chesterfields have gone."

"That must have been difficult for Alice. Is she all right? Should I go talk to her?"

"She's gone, Robert. All of the Chesterfields have gone."
He shook his head. "Why? When?"

His mother sighed. "Marty and I went over to her place after lunch to measure for curtains. While we were gone, they left. Joe said Alice came and got him and said it was imperative that they get to Cedar Springs right away."

"But that doesn't make sense. Why would they just leave like that without a word?"

Mother held out a folded piece of paper. "Alice left a letter for me and Marty and one for you."

Robert took the paper with trembling hands. This couldn't be happening. Not now. Not when he'd put everything right and even bought the ring.

He unfolded the note and read the lines to himself.

Robert,

By the time you read this letter I will be on a train to Chicago. I am sorry that I wasn't able to say good-bye in person, but I couldn't bear the thought. You see, I've fallen in love with you. I know that probably comes as a shock, and believe me I didn't set out to do so. I wouldn't come between you and Jessica for all the world, which is why I have to go. I'm so sorry. I feel just horrible about it all.

You are by far and away the best man I've ever known. You made me feel as if I weren't damaged goods, and for that I thank you. I hope you will be happy in your marriage to Jessica. She's a beautiful woman with much to give.

Yours,
Alice

He looked up and fixed his mother with a stern look. "She says she had to go because she loves me. That doesn't make any sense at all. She doesn't want to come between me and Jess, but I've told her more than once that we aren't engaged."

Mother reached out and touched his face, as she often did when she wanted to calm him. "She probably felt guilty. In her letter to me, she mentioned feeling that she had disrupted our family and changed our plans. She felt that she and her family had become a burden."

"But they hadn't!" He crumpled up the letter. "I'm going after her."

"Son, she probably caught the evening train. It's too late for you to stop her now."

Robert hadn't considered that. "Did she ever tell you what her mother's address is in Chicago? I could go there and bring her back."

"I don't have it. Perhaps Marty does," his mother suggested.

He didn't wait to hear more. "Aunt Marty!" he yelled at the top of his lungs.

Stomping through the house, he continued his search. "Aunt Marty!"

Marty poked her head out of her bedroom. "Goodness. What is all the yelling about?"

"Alice is gone."

"I know. She left me a letter and her Bible." Marty shrugged. "I can't tell you how sorry I am."

"Sorry isn't what I came for. I want her mother's address in Chicago."

"I don't have it. I don't recall ever even seeing it. When Alice learned the truth about her mother and sent her a letter . . . well, I never asked." She pushed open the bedroom door. "Jake, did you ever see an address for Mrs. Chesterfield?"

Jake was sitting at the end of the bed and pulling off his boots. "No, can't say that I did."

"That's just great. Now I'm gonna have to go to Chicago and scour a city bigger than Dallas to find her."

Marty took hold of his arm. "Robert, what did Alice say in her letter to you?"

"That she had to go because she loved me and didn't want to come between me and Jess." He gave the door a fisted punch. "But she didn't come between us. There was no 'us.'"

"Alice was always very sensitive about hurting people. She couldn't bear the thought that she might cause someone pain. I'm sure she felt any delay or doubts you might have in marrying Jessica were her fault."

"But they weren't, and she didn't even give me a chance to tell her that. I can't help what folks assumed, including Jessica. I never proposed to that girl, and I told her weeks ago that I couldn't marry her."

Marty looked perplexed. "Why didn't you tell Alice?"

"I tried, but there was never a chance. I'd ask her to go for a walk with me or go ridin', but she always refused and kept her brother or mother with her so we couldn't be alone. I figured when I got back from Fort Worth, I'd show her the ring I got her and propose—even if I had to do so at the dinner table."

"That would have been something," Marty said with a hint of smile. "Well, what are we to do? We don't have any way of finding her mother, short of perhaps hiring someone in Chicago. There's no sense in your going up there blind. We could send a wire and have them intercepted on the way."

"That's a good idea." He turned on his heel and headed back through the house. Despite the late hour, he was determined to go to Cedar Springs and start the process.

251

"But it's so late," his mother said. "Why don't you wait until morning? That train won't get to Chicago for at least a couple of days."

"Your mother's right," Father agreed. "The stationmaster will have closed things down, and you won't be able to find out exactly what connections the Chesterfields will be making."

"I could go to his house." Robert didn't like the idea of delaying. "It's not like hundreds of people catch the train here. He's bound to remember what their plans are."

"Robert, listen to reason. Get cleaned up and have yourself something to eat." His mother motioned to the stove. "We kept food warm for you. Eat and then get a good night's sleep and head out early in the morning."

He knew she was right but hated to admit defeat. To delay his search made him feel that Alice was slipping beyond his reach. He started to refuse her suggestion but finally agreed. "I guess morning will be soon enough."

Mother smiled. "Of course it will be. You'll see."

★

Alice swallowed back an angry retort as the stationmaster in Dallas explained that the train had pulled out only minutes ago.

"When is the next train?"

"Headin' north? Tomorrow," the man informed her. "Best if you take a room for the night."

"I can't afford that," Alice declared. "I have just enough money for our tickets."

"One of the pastors here takes in folks from time to time. He and his wife have spare rooms." The man smiled. "They'd most likely put you up for the night. You could leave most of your things here if you like. I can lock 'em in the office and then you wouldn't have to carry them all over town."

Alice knew there was no other choice. She took the name and address of the parsonage and asked for directions. The stationmaster cheerfully related the information, which further frustrated Alice. How could anyone be so happy in the face of her sorrow? How dare the world go on turning when her heart was clearly breaking?

"We will take only what we need for the night," she told her mother. "Pack it all here in my bag, and I'll carry it. We have a bit of a walk."

"Pity that Roy didn't stick around," Mother replied. "I know he would have driven us. Do you know he asked to call on me?" She gave a laugh. "I would have said yes if I lived here."

"We can move here, Mama," Simon insisted.

"Well, either way," Alice said, taking a few things from her bag to make room for her mother's and brother's articles, "we have to go to Chicago and get your things." She knew full well that once they were in Chicago there wouldn't be money enough to return to Dallas.

The reverend Goodman and his wife, Ophelia, were an older couple who lived not far from the station. They were kind and easygoing and instantly welcomed the sad trio into their house.

"We've got a couple of extra rooms," the pastor told them. "And we believe it a part of our ministry to offer them to folks in need."

"We thank you for that," Alice's mother said. "We were to have taken the train from Cedar Springs to Chicago, but apparently there was some sort of trouble on the line. The stationmaster sent us here to Dallas, but the train we might have taken had already departed. So we find ourselves rather abandoned."

"Well, you are no longer orphaned," the man declared. "Ophelia and I are happy to help. Now, are you hungry?"

"I am," Simon said. His misery had only deepened with each new problem.

"We could all stand a meal, if it's no trouble," Alice replied. "We have no money, however."

"Nor would we take any." Mrs. Goodman *tsk*ed. She moved to take the single bag that Alice had brought. "Let me show you where your rooms are. You can wash up, and by the time you return, I'll have supper for all of you."

With a weariness that seemed to grow by the minute, Alice followed the woman. She longed to be back at the Barnett ranch, enjoying an evening of checkers with Robert and some of Hannah's tasty cinnamon rolls.

I can't let my thoughts take over like that. I have to put Robert from my mind.

Though it seemed an easy enough task, Alice knew it wouldn't be as simple to put him from her heart.

Later, as she shared a bed with her mother, Alice stared in the darkness at the ceiling. She couldn't sleep in spite of being exhausted.

"Why don't you share your heart with me," Mother told her. "It might help."

"I'm sorry," Alice said. "Did I wake you?"

"No. I've been awake and praying for you. I know you're deeply troubled. Are you sure this is the right thing to do? Leaving, I mean."

"I'm only certain of one thing, and that's that I love Robert more than life."

"Then perhaps you should return and give him a chance to speak his mind. Seems to me he cares for you, as well."

"But if he does, it would mean I came between him and his intended." Alice contemplated the matter further before speaking. "It would mean . . . well . . ."

"It would only mean that you fell in love with him without any thought to hurting anyone else. I know you wouldn't have set out to cause harm. You were never that kind of a child, and I can't believe for one minute that you've become that kind of woman."

"I'm not, but I can't help thinking how messed up everything has become. Why would God let me fall in love with someone—someone who doesn't care about how hideous I look—and then take him away?"

"First of all," Mother said, rolling to her side to face Alice. "You aren't hideous looking. You are a beautiful young woman with a scar. But that scar does not define you. Everyone has scars to bear. I have mine. And your father left me with a great many. Although you can't see them.

"And second, I'm not convinced that running away from a problem is the proper way to resolve it. I felt at first, selfishly I must say, that you should return with us to Chicago. But upon reflection, I'm not at all convinced. I can't help but think God has put these delays in our path to give you time to reconsider."

"But I can't stay and watch him marry another," Alice replied.

"Who says you will? What if Robert feels exactly the same way about you that you feel about him? Wouldn't it be better for him to end his engagement to someone he doesn't love and marry the woman he really loves? How fair would it be to Jessica Atherton if he married her only because he could not have you for his wife?"

"I don't know, Mother. I have no answers, only questions. I don't know anything anymore."

Her mother reached out and pulled her close, as she had done when Alice was a child. The warmth of her mother's arms gave Alice a moment of comfort.

"Then pray about it, Alice. Pray and ask God to show you the answer. He has already seen tomorrow, and He knows exactly what you need and to whom you should be wed. Pray on it tonight and see if you have an answer in the morning."

★

Robert tossed and turned in his bed all night long until finally he pushed back the covers and got up. There was no sense in pretending he could sleep. By the time the tiniest hint of light showed on the horizon, he was saddled and ready to ride.

"I'll be back as soon as possible," he told his father and Jake before putting his heels to Rojoe's flank.

All the way to Cedar Springs, Robert kept thinking about the wasted time. *If the bank robbery hadn't taken place, we would have been home much sooner. I might have been here to stop her—to show her the ring and convince her of my love.*

The miles seemed endless, but it gave him more than ample time to pray. He'd tried to pray during the night. Every time he woke up, he issued another plea to God. But he didn't feel as though his prayers went any higher than the ceiling.

"I know you're with me," Robert said aloud, glancing heavenward, "and I know you hear me. So why do I feel alone in this?"

The cloudless sky offered no reply, and even Rojoe seemed to ignore him. Why was it that God let people find each other and fall in love, only to separate them again?

"Why, Lord?"

There was still no answer, no comfort, no understanding. Robert tightened his grip on the reins. He had to find her. She was already such a part of him that Robert felt as if he'd lost a limb.

"I need your help, Lord. I need to find Alice. I need to tell her that I love her."

Chapter 23

"So there we were," Will related at the breakfast table, "about to go into the jewelry store, when shots sounded from the bank across the street. Robert and I ducked into the alley-way to figure out what we might do to help, but we had no weapons."

"And I'm certain that wouldn't have stopped you," Hannah said, shaking her head.

"Well, we were tryin' to figure things out when two of the robbers ran out from the bank to the man holdin' the horses. They mounted and just then three shots rang out, and they dropped like dead weight."

"Were they dead?" Marty asked. The thought of such a thing gave her the shivers.

"No, they'd only been wounded. A Texas Ranger we know got 'em."

"All three of them taken down by one man?" Hannah asked in amazement. "He must have been a very good shot."

"His name is Austin Todd, and he plans to pay us a visit

this fall," Will interjected. "He's interested in buying a small piece of land so he can build a house. He doesn't want to ranch or farm but also doesn't want to live in the confines of a town. Thought I'd take him around to some of the various ranches and see if anyone wanted to sell him some acreage. He's going to look at a parcel we have as well."

Marty tried to ignore the conversation but found herself hopelessly drawn in once again when Will mentioned the bank manager.

"He and the teller had been shot and killed by the two bandits who robbed them. They both had families."

Hannah passed her husband a platter of ham steaks. "That's so sad. Such a violent end to a person's life."

Marty grimaced. The uneasiness she'd felt at the start of the conversation was magnified by the comment regarding the bank employees. She pushed the eggs and grits around her plate but had completely lost her appetite.

"I don't care to ever endure such a thing again," Will admitted.

"I'm with you," Jake agreed. "When you told us the story on the trip home, it made me glad we don't live in a city. I doubt I could ever live there again. Too many people and too much noise. Not to mention all the added dangers."

Hannah raised her coffee cup and took a sip before responding. "I lived in a city once. Nothing good came from it. I prefer the life we have here."

Marty thought about Denver and all that she had known there. If a person had plenty of money to spend, the city could be quite entertaining. On the other hand, the poverty she'd known in the months before leaving convinced her that without adequate funds it was sheer misery.

She hadn't really considered the problems of the city in comparison to her life here in Texas. Marty had to admit there was a peacefulness here that spoke to her spirit. Perhaps Texas wasn't to blame for her sorrows. Just then the baby moved as if in agreement.

"Seems with the economy continuin' to be bad," Will continued, "folks are gettin' more and more desperate. I imagine there will be quite a few more bank robberies before it's all said and done."

"I have to admit," Jake threw in, "there were several times in Denver when I had grave concern about our little bank. Anywhere you have money, you'll also find someone who wants to take it away. When everything started fallin' apart financially, we had so many angry customers that we all feared for our lives."

Marty's head snapped up at this. "You never told me that."

"I didn't want to worry you." Jake gave a shrug. "There wasn't anything you could do to help."

"But I should have known about the danger." She pushed back her plate and got to her feet. "I'm not hungry. Please excuse me."

Marty moved as quickly as her expanding figure would allow. She departed through the kitchen and out the back of the house with no real destination in mind. All she knew was that she had to get away from the conversation and the idea that Jake's life could have been taken at any moment during his bank work.

I was so sure banking was safer than ranching and now this. Why does life have to constantly threaten us with death?

"I'm sorry, Marty."

She turned to find Jake had followed her. Looking at him as if truly understanding him for the first time, Marty drew a heavy breath and let it out. "I never realized. I've been such a fool."

"I didn't want to frighten you. You were already so much against ranchin' because of the dangers. I figured you'd have a real hard time of it if I told you about the bank's situation."

"I should have known. I knew that things were bad, that men were rioting because they couldn't get their money. Grief, I knew people were abandoning their children, so why wouldn't they also kill and rob?"

Jake reached out and touched Marty's cheek. "Danger is everywhere. It's a reality we have to face no matter where we live or work. I don't want you livin' in fear, Marty. The Bible says that perfect love does away with fear. I know my love isn't perfect, but God's love is, and He's the only one who can do away with your fears."

"I know," Marty said, shaking her head. "But it's so hard. I love you and I love our child. I love Wyatt and Samuel and little Benjamin and can't wait until they are with us. I love my family. I can't bear the thought of losing any of them."

"Marty, folks die every day. Family and friends aren't immune to death just because we love them. But we know that death can't hold us. By givin' our hearts to Jesus, we have eternal life with Him. He's the door into heaven. If we don't go through Him, we can't get in. But you and I, we've already been accepted. There's a place for us up there." He glanced at the cloud-strewn skies. "It might take a little while before we can join up with our loved ones, but it won't be forever."

Marty nodded, knowing he was right. "I suppose death has always seemed like . . . well . . . the end. My mother died when I was born, and I never knew her. When I lost my father, I never thought about seeing him again. I just knew he was gone, and that seemed final."

"But you will see them again one day. They loved Jesus

just as you do, just as I do. Death isn't the end of anything. Instead, it's a beginning."

She gave Jake a smile. "You always seem to know just what to say to make me feel better."

He pulled her into his arms. "That's my job." He kissed her lightly and then put his hand on her stomach. "Baby's gettin' mighty big. Sure lookin' forward to this little one."

Marty marveled at the love he clearly held for their unborn child. "Me too."

"Have you been thinkin' on names?"

She nodded. "I have a name in mind for a girl. Johanna— after my father John and sister Hannah. Then maybe Frances for a second name—after your mother."

"I'd like that name very much. You know my middle name is Frances—after her." He smiled and tried the name out. "Johanna Frances. Has a good strong sound to it. But what if this is a son?"

Marty considered the matter for a moment. "I still wouldn't mind using the name John."

"I wouldn't, either," Jake replied. "I was thinkin' maybe we could call him John Jacob."

"That's a perfect name. John Jacob Wythe." Marty leaned forward and kissed Jake. "That way he would be named after you, as well."

"I was thinkin' more of him bein' named for my grandfather and father, but you're right."

"I usually am," Marty countered.

He chuckled and finally released his hold on her. "I don't know about that, Mrs. Wythe. I seem to recall several occasions when you were dead wrong."

Marty's gaze traveled across the distant pasture land. "I can't imagine what you're talking about, Mr. Wythe."

———————— ★ ————————

"Are you sure they haven't been here?" Robert asked the young man at the ticket counter.

"I haven't seen anyone like that around here. Stationmaster might have seen them earlier, but he had to leave. Word came that there was a death in the family. Closed the window down until I could take over. Had a bunch of angry folks, even though it wasn't much more than ten minutes."

"I am sorry about that, but I'm desperate to find my friends." Robert looked around the Cedar Springs depot. The place bustled with activity, but there was no sign of Alice or her mother and brother.

He turned back to the ticket window. "They were headin' to Chicago."

The man nodded. "Well, they could get there any number of ways. There's still one train due out late this afternoon that's headed north. They might be taking that one."

"What time does it depart?"

"At 5:45. Heads north to Kansas City. They might take it and change trains there. Why don't you come back then. Maybe they'll be here, waiting to board."

There was really nothing else he could do. If he left to go in search of them, Robert had no idea where he would start. There were numerous hotels and restaurants. He didn't have time to visit them all.

"I think I'll just stick around here until then," he said. "Thank you for your time."

Robert crossed to the waiting area and took a seat. The gentleman across from him offered a newspaper.

"I've already read this, if you'd like to take a look," the older man declared.

Robert took the paper. "Thank you. I'm much obliged."

He looked through the pages, trying to focus on anything but the worry in his mind. What if they'd arrived in time to take the train out the night before? The stationmaster didn't think that possible, but what if they had?

The minutes ticked by as slowly as any he'd ever known. People came and went, seemingly with no cares at all. A group of gentlemen stood at one end of the room smoking cigars and discussing something that seemed of great importance. A woman with a brood of children took a seat not far from the ticket window and immediately began to share food from a basket. It reminded Robert that he'd not eaten since the night before.

He checked the clock. Still another hour to go. He tried to relax and refocus on the newspaper, but it was no use. He didn't care about the local happenings or comments on the ongoing financial troubles. He had no interest in various sales offered by Dallas merchants, and he certainly didn't care about the opinion of the editor. Folding the paper, he handed it back to its owner.

"Thank you."

The man nodded and smiled. "Where are you headed?"

"I'm not," Robert replied. "I'm waiting for someone."

"Ah, I'm Kansas City bound myself."

Robert nodded, but had no desire to keep up with the small talk. "If you'll excuse me." He got to his feet and headed outside for a breath of fresh air.

Clouds had begun to build. It looked like they might be in for a storm before nightfall. Robert didn't like the idea of having to return to the ranch in the rain. If he managed to find Alice and her family, he'd suggest they wait it out until morning. It was getting much too late to travel all the way home.

Pacing the depot platform, Robert tried to think of what he'd say to Alice. It was important that she understand his heart. He didn't want her thinking she'd done anything to come between him and Jess.

As if anyone could come between two people who truly loved each other.

A whistle sounded from one of the locomotives several tracks away. A freight train moved forward ever so slowly. The rail yards seemed just as busy as the depot. Robert looked at his pocket watch. Half an hour. In half an hour he would be with Alice again. In thirty minutes he would propose to the woman he loved. At least he hoped as much.

But what if she isn't taking this train? What will I do then? No one has the address for her mother's place in Chicago. I don't even know what train she might be on so I could wire ahead and have her return to Texas.

There was no sense borrowing trouble. If they didn't show up, Robert knew he would figure something out. He wasn't going to lose Alice—not if he had anything to say about it.

I'm just gonna keep a positive attitude. I'm gonna expect the best.

But in thirty minutes nothing had changed. Robert returned to the waiting area to search for Alice, but she wasn't there. More passengers arrived by the minute to board the train, but none of them were Alice. By the time the 5:45 pulled out, Robert felt his hopes drain away.

There was nothing left to do but head back home. Dejected, Robert exited the depot to find it had begun to sprinkle. His stomach growled. The hollow feeling seemed appropriate.

Chapter 24

"I wrote my friends in Diboll," Jake announced. "The two docs I was tellin' you about. One's a lady doctor."

Hannah smiled. "Good. It's about time we had a few of those."

"Well, since you talked about the old doc in Cedar Springs, I thought I'd put out the word that we could use a couple of younger doctors. I don't know if they'd ever consider leavin' Diboll, but I figured it was worth a try. I don't want Marty to be without a good doctor."

"Oh, you shouldn't fret, Jake. Women have been having babies without doctors for centuries. I've even known doctors to refuse deliveries because that's something a midwife could handle. If I were you, I'd just relax. I've delivered babies before, and I'm sure I can deliver this one just as well."

Jake hated that he sounded ungrateful for the care Hannah had given her sister. "Oh, I know you're well trained. I've been real impressed with the way you take care of everybody around here. I hope you'll forgive me for implying otherwise."

Hannah handed him one of the freshly baked cookies she'd just taken from the pan. "Jake, there's nothing to forgive. You're just being mindful of your wife's needs. I admire that. And frankly, I would like to have a lady doctor around."

Marty entered the room with her nose up in the air. "Do I smell your cinnamon sugar cookies?" She spied the pan and gave a squeal of delight. "Oh, I did. You have no idea how much I've craved those."

"You should have said something," Hannah chided. "I would have made you a batch every day."

"And I'd be four times this size," Marty replied, patting her abdomen.

"You're a perfect size, and cravings are natural for expectant mothers. Here, have a cookie. They still need to cool, but I'll put a stack of them on a plate for you, and you can eat to your heart's delight."

Marty took the cookie and bit into it. A look of satisfaction and pleasure filled her face. "Mmm, just as I remembered."

Jake had already devoured his cookie and was hopeful that Hannah would hand out more right away. She seemed to read his mind and did just that. Jake offered no resistance.

"So when should we expect the boys?" Hannah asked Marty.

"Almost anytime. We sent the money. In fact, we sent extra to make sure the boys had what they needed. Mr. Brentwood is making arrangements for them. He doesn't want them to travel by themselves, so he's trying to find someone to accompany them. He said he might be able to secure a chaperone within the week."

"That's wonderful. We should have your place completely ready for their arrival. Although I do wish you'd stay here until the baby is born."

"It's not like you're that far away," Marty replied. "You told me first babies are usually long in coming, so I should have plenty of time to send Jake or someone else to fetch you."

Jake knew that Marty had her heart set on moving the boys right into their new home. "I think I'd best get back to work. I promised Will that I'd have that new pen built by the time they came back from the Reids' with those new geldings."

He cast a glance at Marty. "You doin' all right?"

She smiled. "I'm doing just fine. Stop worrying."

He nodded and made his exit without another word. Approaching the new pen, he could see that the other men had been hard at work. It was nearly complete. The worst job had been digging postholes. After that, the rest almost seemed easy.

"You fellas made good progress," he said.

"Had to, since you ran off," an older man named Bert declared. He threw Jake a grin. "But I guess if I had a pretty wife about to have a baby, I'd wanna check up on her, too."

Jake knew that Bert had once worked for Marty and went to work for William when she moved to Colorado. He rather hoped the man might want to return with them to Marty's ranch. He was going to need all the help he could get, and Bert knew the ranch better than anyone else.

"Say, Bert, you ever think about leavin' this place?"

Bert straightened from his work. "Leave the Barnetts'? What'd you have in mind?"

"I know you worked the Olson ranch after Marty was widowed. I wondered if you'd like to come back and work for me. I don't have much money just yet, but your room and board would definitely be covered. Marty and I plan to sell off a few head this fall, so I could give you part of that in wages owed."

Bert took off his hat and wiped his brow. "I reckon I'd be

right honored to come back. Always enjoyed the work there. How quick were you two plannin' to return?"

"Soon. We want to get settled in before the orphans we're adopting arrive."

Nate, one of the boys who'd come to live with the Barnetts the year before perked up at this. "Who's coming—if you don't mind my asking?"

"Not at all," Jake replied. "There are three of 'em. Wyatt is the oldest. Then there's Samuel and Benjamin."

"I remember Wyatt but not the other two. I know they're going to love it here. I never had a real home until the Barnetts took me in."

Jake couldn't imagine not having a close family connection. "What happened to your folks?"

The sixteen-year-old shrugged. "My mom died when I was young, and my pa just sort of drifted. I was passed around from one family to another. We didn't have no other folks. Finally one of the families learned that my pa had died of typhoid fever. They decided enough was enough and turned me over to the orphanage."

Jake thought it sad to have been so unwanted. "How old were you?"

"Eleven."

"Most folks would have found a boy like you to be an asset. You could have easily helped out with the workload, if nothing else." Jake realized that sounded as though the boy were only good for labor.

Nate didn't seem to notice. "There wasn't much for me to do in the city. I was in school during the day, and when I came home there were chores to do, but not like here. Most of the folks who took me in were poor as church mice, and I was just another mouth to feed."

"Well, I'm sure glad you came to Texas. Down here folks know the value of a young man like you. I'm sure you've more than earned your keep. I heard Hannah say that you two were a real pleasure to have around."

Bert joined in at this. "Him and Hiram are two of the best greenhorns I ever had to train. He learned quick and that's always good."

"I'm glad you and the missus are adopting those boys. It'll be good for them to have a real home and somebody who cares about them." Nate picked up a long rail. "I'm gonna need help attaching this to the corner post."

Jake pulled on his gloves and followed the boy to where the rail would be secured. Listening to Nate's story had touched him in an unexpected way. Marty had told him stories about the children, but they remained just that . . . stories. Now it all became much more.

Jake hadn't really considered how adoption might affect the lives of those children. He'd only considered how it might affect his life and Marty's. It shamed him to think that he'd not even thought to find out the story of each of the boys. Where had they come from? Who were their people, and how could they just abandon their children?

★

The sound of a wagon drew Marty's attention to the front window. The large freight wagon pulled to a stop out in the drive, and Marty could see that Mrs. Chesterfield was sitting atop with the driver.

"Goodness, Mrs. Chesterfield is back," she announced when Hannah came to investigate.

"Are Alice and Simon with her?" Her voice betrayed hopefulness.

Marty could see the two climbing down from the wagon. "Yes! I'm so glad. This will mean the world to Robert." She flung open the door and made her way outside.

"Alice!" Marty went to the younger woman and embraced her. "I thought I might never see you again."

The driver helped Mrs. Chesterfield from the wagon. She seemed quite pleased with herself, and Marty wasn't sure if it was the fact that they'd returned to the ranch or the company of the driver.

"Roy James, ma'am," the man announced, tipping his hat as Hannah came alongside. "No relation to Jesse." He chuckled heartily, and Marty found that she instantly liked the man. "I drive freight outta Dallas to Cedar Springs and beyond. Headin' up Denton way today."

Hannah extended her hand. "I'm pleased to meet you. I'm Hannah Barnett. Why don't we go inside and I'll prepare some refreshments."

"I'd be pleased to do so," he declared.

Marty remained with Alice as the others made their way into the house. "What in the world were you thinking?"

"You got my letter, didn't you?"

"Yes, and your Bible. Grief, Alice, you nearly sent me into labor," Marty said in a stern reprimand. "Don't ever do that again."

"I don't know that I can remain here," Alice answered, "but I knew I had to come back and try to explain my heart to Robert."

"You won't have to explain much. The poor man went half mad when he learned you were gone. He took one look at your letter to him and was ready to charge off in search. We finally convinced him to wait until morning. He hasn't returned yet."

"He came looking for me?" Alice asked in disbelief.

"Yes, silly. He's half over the moon in love with you."

Alice's mouth dropped open and her eyes widened. "He is?"

Marty laughed. "I guess love truly is blind, but the answer is yes. He had fully planned for the two of you to talk things out when he returned from Fort Worth with . . ." Marty decided against mentioning the ring Robert had purchased. "With the others," she finally added.

"That means I destroyed his chance for a life with Miss Atherton." She shook her head. "I never meant for that to happen. I didn't set out to fall in love. It just happened."

"There was never going to be happiness for Robert if he married Jess. He knew that, and so did she. They ended any possibility of that weeks ago."

"But he said nothing."

"You weren't listening," Marty insisted. "He tried on more than one occasion to get you alone. He said you went out of your way to avoid him."

Alice nodded and dropped her gaze to the ground. "I did. I thought if I stayed out of his way, kept myself from any hint of intimacy, that we'd both be better off for it."

"And were you?"

Alice let out a heavy breath and raised her head. "No."

"Well, you're back now and that's all that matters. I don't know when Robert will return, but when he does, I hope I'm around to see the reunion. It's gonna be a doozy."

With Alice at her side, Marty made her way into the house. Hannah had already seen to it that a plate of her cookies was positioned on a side table and was just returning with a tray holding tall glasses of sweet tea.

"Mr. James, will you drive all the way back to Dallas tonight?" Hannah asked. "You don't have to, you know. We can put you up." She offered him tea and he took a glass.

272

"No, ma'am, that won't be necessary. Like I said earlier, I've gotta make my way up to Denton. I've got friends up that way, and I'll spend the night with them."

Hannah nodded and served the others. When everyone was settled with a glass and cookies, she finally took a seat. "Well, I'm glad you were available to bring our friends home."

"I had the pleasure of their company on the way to Dallas, and when they looked me up this morning, I couldn't help but assist them in returning. The company is the best I've had in years." He turned to Mrs. Chesterfield and winked. The woman blushed and looked at her hands as the man added, "I hope to share it again."

Hannah looked at Marty and smiled. It was easy enough to see that the older couple was already sweet on each other.

"I'm gonna go out and see your horse, Alice," Simon announced. He held a cookie in each hand. "I'll bet he's gotten bigger."

"Simon, we've only been gone a day." Alice sat down beside Marty on the couch and sighed. "You'd think we'd been away for weeks."

The boy shrugged. "Well, I hope we aren't gonna leave again. I want to stay here forever."

Mrs. Chesterfield shook her head as Simon barreled out of the room. "I swear that boy has the energy of a wildcat. He wears me out, but it does me so much good to see him happy again." She looked to Hannah. "I was wondering if maybe you could use a housekeeper."

Hannah nodded. "I'm sure I could use the help. If Robert has his way, he'll marry Alice and start having a family before we know it, and I'll want all the free time I can get to spoil my grandchildren."

Marty looked at Alice. She was clearly embarrassed by the declaration but said nothing.

From her position by the window Marty could hear a rider approaching. She leaned forward to glance out and saw it was Robert. She couldn't help but grin. "Oh, this ought to be really good."

The others looked at her in confusion, but it was Hannah who posed the question. "What are you talking about?"

"Robert just rode in."

The room went silent. All gazes shifted to Alice. The younger woman was biting her lip and twisting her hands together. Marty reached over and stilled her hands.

"Remember, he's just as much in love with you as you are with him."

Alice said nothing and even the boisterous Mr. James remained quiet. It was as if the entire house held its breath in anticipation of Robert's arrival. They didn't have long to wait.

"Ma!" he called at the top of his lungs. He was coming in from the back of the house from the sound of it.

Marty squeezed Alice's hands and dropped her hold.

"Ma, are you sure you don't have Mrs. Chesterfield's address in Chicago? I couldn't find—" He fell silent the moment he stepped into the room.

Marty watched his face as he caught sight of the party gathered there. She might have laughed at her nephew's stunned expression, but without warning he crossed the room and pulled Alice up from the couch. Then without so much as an explanation, Robert hoisted her over his shoulder like a sack of beans and headed for the door.

"We need to talk," he declared.

Once the couple was gone from sight, the entire room

erupted in laughter. "She's in for it now," Mrs. Chesterfield said. "Did you see the look on her face?"

Hannah shook her head. "If I'm any judge of people, I'd say Robert is in for it, as well." She shrugged and held up her glass of tea in a toast. "I guess we're to be in-laws. Here's to us."

Ravinia Chesterfield raised her glass. "To Robert and Alice."

Chapter 25

Alice had the wind knocked from her when her body hit Robert's rock-hard shoulder. His strides only made matters worse as he stormed out of the house and across the yard. He headed in the direction of the river and ranted all the way.

"I can't believe you would go runnin' off like that. Scared a dozen years off my life. I never in my life seen a woman more stubborn and irritatin'. Here I was half sick with worry and wonderin' how in the world I was ever gonna find you in Chicago, and you just turn up here pretty as you please."

Alice tried to comment, but it was hard enough just to get her breath. "You . . . don't . . . have . . . to—"

"And how many times do I have to tell you that there's nothin' between Jessica and me. Just because folks expected us to marry didn't mean we were gonna marry. I tried to tell you that I felt nothin' for her except brotherly love. But you wouldn't listen."

Again Alice tried to speak. "Robert . . . you need . . . to . . . put me . . . down."

"You know, it just never fails to amaze me how folks can get their minds made up about a thing and not let it go. I put an end to any weddin' plans weeks ago. I wanted to tell you, but you kept avoiding me. I swear you were harder to corner than a badger."

He finally stopped, and Alice could see they were at the ravine above the river. Several cottonwoods shaded the sun and made a rather pleasant setting. Alice struggled against Robert's hold, and he finally put her down.

Fixing him with a stare, Alice gulped in air. However, he didn't give her time to comment. "I don't love Jessica Atherton. For your information, I've loved you since we first met. You did something to me deep in my heart." He thumped his hand against his chest. "I know Marty was worried that I only cared about you because you'd been hurt—" he paused, shaking his head—"but that wasn't the reason."

Alice decided it was better to remain silent and let him speak his mind. His face seemed to contort between expressions of love and anger. Alice thought him the handsomest man she'd ever known, even with the two-day growth of stubble on his face. Truth be told, she'd loved him from first sight.

"I love you because of who you are inside. You're thoughtful and kind, gentle and lovin'. I've watched you with your brother and seen how you came around to forgivin' your ma. You brood over Marty like a mother hen to her chicks. I've seen you work, too. You've helped my ma in more ways than one."

He began to pace before her. "When I found out you were gone, I thought I was gonna be sick. I read your letter, and when I saw that you loved me, too, it only made me all the more determined to find you and set things right. Instead, I chased all over the countryside only to lose any sign of you. Do you know how I felt when I realized you were probably already on your way to Chicago?"

Alice started to answer, but Robert continued his tirade. Turning, he pointed a finger at her. "Well, it wasn't good. I can tell you that. Fact is, it liked to have killed me. I hate big cities, but I hated more thinkin' that I'd never see you again."

With her hands on her hips and her brow raised in question, Alice finally had a chance to speak. "Are you done?"

Robert seemed surprised by this. He started to comment but then closed his mouth and knelt on one knee. "Not quite." He fumbled in his pocket, and when he extended his hand toward her, Alice could see he was holding a ring.

"Will you marry me?"

A smile formed on her lips. He really was the man of her prayers. "I thought you'd never ask." She reached out to take the ring.

But instead of giving it to her, Robert rose and slipped it on her finger. He started to embrace her for a kiss, but Alice held him back. "I've never been kissed by a man, and I'd like to wait until we're married."

Robert studied her face for a moment, and Alice wasn't at all sure what was going through his mind. He reached up and tenderly ran his hand down her scarred face.

"I've held back from that kind of intimacy, as well. Never thought I'd meet up with someone who felt the same way. I'd be honored to wait." He took hold of her hand and kissed the back of it in genteel fashion. Lifting his head, he gave her a lopsided grin. "So long as you don't keep me waiting too long."

"How about a few weeks?" she asked. "We could marry in June."

"Why June?"

"That will give my mother time to collect her things in Chicago and get moved down here. She's going to work for your mother."

"Truly?" He chuckled. "Well, looks like we'll have all our family around us." He stopped and frowned. "You know I don't intend to live anywhere else, don't you? This is my home, and Pa told me that he wants to rearrange things right away so that we have the east wing of the main house to ourselves."

She smiled. "I wouldn't want to live anywhere else. Texas and this ranch suit me just fine." Now it was her turn to frown. "But what if Mr. Smith tracks me down here? There's still that complication to contend with I don't trust him to give up just because we left Denver."

"If he shows his sorry face around here, I'll deal with him," Robert said in a most protective way.

His declaration warmed Alice's heart. She would finally truly be safe and happy. She gazed back across the field toward the house. "I suppose we should go tell them we plan to marry."

He took hold of her arm. "I think they probably already know, but it can't hurt to make it official."

Alice paused and looked at the man who would be her husband. "I love you, Robert."

He grinned. "And I love you, but if you keep lookin' at me that way I'm gonna haul you off to the justice of the peace right now."

★

That evening at the supper table the conversation was all about the changes that would be made to the main house.

"I think maybe we should keep Ravinia and Simon in the

Montoya house," Robert's mother said. "Alice can live there, too, of course, until she and Robert marry." She glanced at her husband. "Couldn't we just build ourselves a little place—maybe over by the river?"

"I suppose we could."

Robert looked at his bride-to-be and then to his parents. "I don't want you to go to all that trouble and expense. Alice and I talked about it, and there's no reason we can't all live under one roof."

Marty put her fork down. "You know, he's right."

"Well, we wanted to afford them some privacy," Mother replied. "After all, they need time to get to know each other without a lot of folks hanging over them."

"Might I offer a solution?" Mrs. Chesterfield asked.

"Of course," Father said.

Robert winked at Simon, who was fidgeting in his seat, anxious for dessert. A tremendous feeling of relief washed over him as he realized everything would be exactly as he'd hoped. He offered a silent prayer of thanks.

"What do you think about that, Robert?"

He looked to his mother in confusion. "I'm sorry. I didn't hear what was said."

Father laughed. "Better get your head outta the clouds, son. There's a lot of work to be done before that weddin'."

"I was just prayin'. Thankin' God for His mercy . . . and for Alice."

She blushed at this and put her attention on the food. Mother quickly picked up the discussion. "Ravinia has suggested that she and Simon live here in the house for at least the first year, while you and Alice take the Montoya place."

Robert grinned. "I think that would work out well for all of us. Thank you, Mrs. Chesterfield."

"You can start calling me Mother Chesterfield, if you'd like."

"I'd like that very much." He glanced at Simon and smiled. "And you're gonna be my little brother. I always wanted a brother." Robert then took pity on the poor boy. "But, Ma, I think if you don't serve up that custard pie, Simon is gonna waste away." Everyone laughed except Simon, who was nodding most enthusiastically.

After dinner, while the women cleared the table, Robert and his father had a chance to talk. Robert relished these times. They'd always been close, and he couldn't imagine doing anything without his father's support.

"So, do you approve of my marryin' Alice?"

Father seemed surprised by this question and narrowed his eyes. "Haven't I made that clear? I think Alice is a fine woman. She's gonna fit into our family just right. Fact is, she's everything I ever prayed your wife would be."

"You prayed about my wife?"

"Don't sound so shocked," Father replied, easing down into his favorite leather chair.

Robert took a seat, as well. "I guess I never thought about it."

"Well, since you'll no doubt be a father one day, you ought to give it some thought. Prayin' for your children is something you do on a daily basis. You pray for their safety and health. You pray for their happiness. You pray they'll make good decisions. And you pray for the people who will touch their lives, especially when it comes to a spouse."

"And you've been prayin' about mine."

"Since the first day you were born."

Robert shook his head. "I never knew."

Father chuckled. "Son, you don't know the half of it, but one day you will."

"I know that I want to be as happy as you and Ma have been. I've never seen two people more suited to each other. Folks are always sayin' it's like you were meant to be together from the beginnin' of time."

"I like to think so, too. Your mother completes me. I didn't even know that something was missin' until I met her. She's caused me no end of grief at times, but also no end of love." He paused and rubbed his chin. "You know, there will be times of grief and anger. You can't avoid those things in life."

"I do know. But I also remember your tellin' me that when we belong to God, we don't have to bear those things alone. I want to be a good husband to Alice."

"Then stay close to God, son. If you're right with the Lord, everything else will fall into place. It doesn't mean there won't be ups and downs, but He will be a strong support in times of need."

Robert knew that support already. His faith was a stronghold in which he found security and love.

Alice appeared at the opening to the dining room. "They've kicked me out of the kitchen and said I should spend some time with you, Robert."

He got to his feet and crossed the room to take hold of her arm. "Why, I'd be plumb pleased to spend the evenin' with you. Why don't we go on out to the barn and take a look at your colt?"

"I would enjoy that very much."

"Now, don't you two go gettin' carried away," Father warned. "I know a thing or two about rolls in the hay."

Robert looked at him in mock horror. "You and Ma—rollin' in the hay? And I thought my folks were respectable."

Father laughed. "Respectable, yes. But with a flood of

282

feelin's for each other. Now, you two go on before I change my mind. I could always find a chore for you to do, Robert."

"Yes, sir!" He pushed Alice toward the door. "We're movin'."

The night skies held an abundance of stars. The earlier clouds had moved out, and now there was nothing to keep them from seeing the vast expanse of the heavens.

"It's so beautiful," Alice said, gazing upward. "I've never known anything like this."

"I never want to know anything else," Robert said softly. "Except for you."

She trembled slightly, and Robert worried that she would catch a chill. "Are you cold?"

"No," Alice whispered. "Just overcome by my heart and the way I feel about you. I never thought true love would come along for me after the attack. Oh, I hoped it would. Your aunt and I used to talk about there being a good man somewhere who wouldn't mind my scarred face."

Robert stopped and turned Alice to face him. "When I look into your eyes and see the love you have for me shinin' back, I don't see the scar. You are an incredible woman, Alice. I wanna have children with you and grow old with you. And when I die, I wanna be buried next to you."

"I feel the same way," she said in a barely audible voice. "I'll never want for anything more than that."

★

Jake and Marty retired to their bedroom. The day had been quite productive, and Marty was more than a little tired. She yawned and rolled her head to ease the tension in her neck. Jake led her to a chair and had her take a seat. He began kneading her sore muscles.

"The house is nearly ready," he told her. "Once I hang

those curtains for you, we'll be ready for the boys. I hope goin' back there won't be too hard on you."

Marty shook her head. "I thought a great deal about that. When I went there with Hannah, I took some time to just walk around the place. I have to admit I was worried that I'd only be able to think of Thomas, but it wasn't that way.

"We had a good life there and I know you and I can have a good one there, too." She closed her eyes and enjoyed the feel of Jake's skillful hands. The tension drained away and made her all the more sleepy, but she wanted to assure Jake that all was well.

"I realized something as I walked around the yard."

"What was that?"

"I missed the place. I missed my flower beds and garden. I missed the trees we'd planted. I felt a sense of coming home. It took me completely by surprise, but it comforted me in a way I hadn't expected."

"That's how I felt in comin' back to Texas. At least in the beginning." He stopped and came around to the front to kneel down beside her chair. "Texas was my home, and I spent the last few years longing to return. When I got down here, I thought that I could finally be happy. But I wasn't."

Marty hadn't expected this declaration. "Why not?"

He gave her a hint of a smile. "Because you weren't here. That's when I realized that my home wasn't really Texas anymore—it is with you. I've given it a lot of thought, Marty, and if you don't want to stay here, we won't. After the boys and the baby come, if you're of a mind for us to move elsewhere, we will. But I wanna be ranchin' no matter where we go."

Marty touched his cheek, and love for her husband swelled within her heart. "You would do that for me?"

"Yes. That and so much more. I want you to be happy, Marty."

She pulled him close and hugged him as best she could. "I am happy, Jacob Wythe. I'm happy with you, and I'm happy to remain in Texas."

Chapter 26

"The train is late," Marty declared. She had argued with her sister and husband, insisting that she accompany them to Cedar Springs. Neither thought her in any condition to take the long ride, but Marty wouldn't hear of not going.

"Those are my boys, and I will be there to welcome them! If you won't take me with you, I'll saddle a horse and ride there." She had stood her ground, and finally everyone gave in and let her accompany them to town. Marty knew they understood she would do exactly as she had threatened.

Now, as she paced the depot waiting area, Marty could only focus on the clock. "Why are they late? You don't suppose there was trouble on the line, do you?" She looked to Jake for an answer. "Should we inquire?"

"Marty, you've got to settle down. You promised you'd take it easy," Jake reminded her.

"I'm just walking back and forth," she said. "It's warm in here. I think I'd be more comfortable out on the platform."

"So long as you stay out of the sun," Hannah commanded. "I won't have you overheating and getting sunstroke just as you're about to gain three sons."

Marty nodded and started toward the door. Jake was instantly at her side, helping her. "You really should have stayed home. I don't know what got into me lettin' you come along."

"Well, it's not like you could've stopped me," Marty said, giving him a stern look. "I still know how to hitch a buggy or ride a horse, and I truly would have done it."

Jake laughed. "I can just see you and your expanding middle up atop a horse. But I know how stubborn you can be, and I doubt it would surprise me if you tried it. But if you try it before you safely deliver my son or daughter, I'll put you over my knee."

It was Marty's turn to laugh. "With all this extra weight I'm carrying, you'd be sorry for it."

"You're still no bigger than a mite," he replied, shaking his head. "And I don't think I've ever seen you quite so beautiful."

Just then the train whistle could be heard off in the distance. Marty ran to the edge of the platform to look down the track. She might have fallen over if it hadn't been for Jake's quick thinking.

"Marty, you seem bound and determined to get yourself hurt. Now, step back here. The train will be here soon enough."

The air was heavy and damp with humidity, and the sun made everything seem unbearable. Marty wasn't about to say as much, however. The last thing she wanted was Jake ordering her back into the depot. She allowed her husband to lead her away from the edge of the platform.

"I hope they're all right. I hope the trip hasn't been too hard on them."

"I'm sure they're fine, Marty. Mr. Brentwood found that woman who was willing to travel with them, and I'm sure she managed quite well."

The locomotive engine came into view, chugging and puffing thick black smoke. The whistle sounded again, and Marty could barely keep herself standing still. She had thought about the boys since Jake had agreed to adopt the constantly m. She knew the boys would be half out of their minds with excitement to take the trip and to gain a mother and a father.

The train approached the station. The engine and coal car passed by, as well as the mail car and several baggage cars. It seemed to take forever to stop the behemoth, but finally it came to a rest with the passenger cars neatly positioned beside the platform.

The conductor descended from the steps of the car and placed a little step stool on the ground. "All off for Cedar Springs. Next stop Dallas."

Marty pressed forward despite Jake's hold. "Do you see them?"

"Not yet," he replied.

She craned her neck to see around several people who had come to board the train. "I can't see anything. Maybe we should get closer." She knew that there would most likely be more passengers getting on the train than debarking, but even so, she wasn't about to be pushed aside.

"Excuse me," she told one stocky older man. "My children are coming off that train."

And then she finally saw them. Wyatt stepped down first, aided by a porter. Next came Samuel and finally Benjamin, who was being carried by a middle-aged woman.

Wyatt saw her first and came running. "Mama!"

That single word hit Marty like a ton of bricks. She was his mother now. Wrapping her arms around the little boy, Marty began to cry. "I'm so happy to see you."

Samuel and Benjamin followed suit until Marty was being hugged from every side. "I can't believe you're finally here. Oh, how I've missed you. And look, you've all grown so much since I left."

Wyatt patted her stomach. "You growed, too, Mama."

She laughed but tears welled in her eyes. "I'm going to have a baby."

"Do we really get to ride a horse?" Samuel asked, pulling away. He frowned. "Why are you crying?" Wyatt and Benjamin stepped back, as well, and awaited an answer.

Marty smiled. "These are tears of happiness."

"Are you really going to have a baby?" Wyatt asked.

She nodded. "I am, and it will be your little brother or sister. I'm going to depend on each of you to be good big brothers."

Benjamin hugged her again. "I'll be good," he promised.

"Ahem." Jake cleared his throat. "I'd kind of like to meet my sons."

Marty regained control and wiped her eyes. "Boys, this is your new papa. He's a good and fair man, and he already loves each of you dearly."

The boys were shy in meeting Jake. Wyatt was the first to step closer. "I'm Wyatt," he told Jake. "I used to have another papa but not anymore."

Jake squatted down and offered Wyatt a smile. "I'm mighty glad to meet you, Wyatt. I've always wanted a son."

"I'm Sam, and this is my brother Benjamin," Samuel introduced.

Jake nodded to each of them. "I hope you all know how

much we want you to be part of our family. You boys are mighty special, and I'm gonna do my best to be a good pa to all of you."

"I'm Sarah Mitchell," a woman declared from behind the boys. "Mr. Brentwood paid my way to Dallas if I would accompany the boys here." She smiled, and Marty went immediately to the woman.

"Thank you so much for bringing them. I've missed them more than I can even tell. Would you like to join us for lunch?"

"All aboard for Dallas," the conductor called.

The woman glanced over her shoulder. "I've got to return to the train. My mother lives in Dallas, and she's not been well. Mr. Brentwood's advertisement for a companion to these children was an answer to our prayers." She handed Marty a small traveling case. "This is all they have, but I'm sure you knew they'd arrive with very little."

Nodding, Marty took the case, only to have Jake quickly retrieve it from her. "Thank you, Miss Mitchell," he said.

"It was my pleasure. They were quite excited about the trip, but they are good children." She smiled at the trio. "Boys, I hope you enjoy your new home."

With a little wave she turned toward the train. Marty watched the woman climb the steps and disappear into the train car. How strange to be so grateful to a complete stranger who shared only a few moments in her life.

"Well, I'm bettin' you boys are hungry," Jake said. "We've got plans to have a meal at a little place around the corner. I'll put your case in the wagon, and then if you like, we can walk there while Marty and her sister, Hannah, bring the wagon."

This met with everyone's approval, and Jake led the way back through the depot and out a door on the opposite side. Marty followed close behind and saw her sister waiting near the exit. Jake paused and introduced the boys to their new aunt. Hannah embraced each of them. She didn't seem in the least concerned that her action would put anyone off.

"I'm very happy to meet all of you. I'm your aunt Hannah."

"Do you have horses?" Samuel asked.

Hannah laughed. "I do, and I'll be happy to show them to you when we get back to the ranch."

The warmth of the day started to overwhelm Marty. She felt flushed and then dizzy. "Jake, I think I need to sit down."

He handed the case over to Hannah and quickly took hold of Marty. "I told you comin' here was too much for you, but you wouldn't listen." He helped her to a chair. "Next time I'm not takin' no for an answer."

"Mama, are you sick?" Wyatt asked. The boys crowded around her in worry.

"Your mama is gonna be fine," Jake assured them. "She's too stubborn to be sick."

"Come on, boys, let's bring the wagon up close so your mama doesn't have far to walk." Marty was grateful that Hannah took charge. She hated that Jake was right and the trip had proved more than she should have undertaken. She knew it would only worry him if she mentioned the pains she had started to have.

Alice busied herself with laundry while awaiting the return of the others. Her mother was otherwise occupied with entertaining Mr. James, who had just stopped by on his way back to Dallas. He laughingly had told them it wasn't out of his way and seemed only right, but Alice knew better. She couldn't help but smile to herself. Her mother and Mr. James had become quite close, and even Simon seemed to like the man.

She may very well get hitched before I do. And wouldn't that be something?

Alice and Robert had set the date of their wedding for the twenty-third of June, and that day was fast approaching. Of course there had been so much work to do in preparation that Alice didn't have time to be bored and worry over such matters.

With Hannah and Marty's help, she and her mother had designed and sewn Alice's wedding dress. Being a practical woman, Alice hadn't wanted to worry about an elaborate white gown and instead settled on a sensible gown that could be used again and again.

After all, the country was still suffering, and even here at the ranch they needed to tighten the belt. Hannah and Marty had insisted there be a big wedding celebration at the ranch, but Alice would have been just as happy to marry Robert in a small family ceremony.

"Alice, come see what Robert's doing," Simon called from a pen near the barn.

"I'm busy hanging the laundry. Can't it wait?"

"Nope. He's riding one of those new horses, and it's throwing him all around."

Alice felt her heart jump to her throat. Leaving the basket of clothes, she hurried to where her brother waited. "Where?"

"Over behind the barn," he said, pointing. "In that big pen they use for working with the horses." He looked at her as if she should know this already. "He's just started riding the new bay."

She didn't wait to hear any more. Making her way to the pen, Alice whispered a silent prayer for Robert's safety. She didn't want to be a widow before she got the chance to be a bride.

Clasping her hand to her mouth, Alice caught sight of the event. Several of the ranch hands were standing at the sides of the pen. A few were sitting atop the fence, and all were cheering Robert on in his endeavors.

Alice could hardly bear to watch. The gelding was not happy to have a rider and was doing his best to eliminate him.

"Isn't it great!" Simon declared more than asked.

"I thought Robert said they were already saddle broke." Alice didn't see a thing about this horse that spoke of being trained in any way.

"Mr. Reid taught them to wear a saddle, and now Robert's going to teach them to allow a rider." Simon told her. "He said it's always hard to get horses used to having someone on their backs, and they have to do this to get them trained. Sometimes it takes a long time, and sometimes just a short time." Simon grinned up at his sister. "Robert's teaching me all about horses."

The bay bucked a few more times, but Robert held fast. Alice found it hard to breathe as she continued to watch. Was this what it would be like to be a rancher's wife—always worrying about the dangers her husband faced? No wonder Marty had been wary of returning.

Finally the horse seemed to realize who was in charge and settled down. Robert walked it around the pen several times and then encouraged it to speed up to a trot. The bay responded well, and the ranch hands nodded their approval as Robert passed by.

After another fifteen minutes of working with the animal, Robert finally halted the bay and climbed down. "He's a good one," he declared. "I think he's gonna make a fine cow horse. He learns fast." Robert relinquished the reins to Nate, who in turn led the horse off to another pen.

"Where's the roan?" Robert asked.

Alice swallowed the lump in her throat. Was he going to do this again? She shuddered and moved away from where she'd watched the affair. She didn't care to see it again.

She finished hanging the laundry, all the while thinking of the dangers her beloved had to face. Robert loved this life. She knew that full well, and it would not suit either of them if she were to voice a complaint.

"Lord, I don't mean to be afraid," she whispered as she headed into the house. "It's just that I'm not at all familiar with living on a ranch. Help me not to be afraid. Help me to leave Robert in your hands."

She felt tears come to her eyes and chided herself. "You're being silly, Alice. You don't want anyone to see you like this, so you have to get a hold of yourself."

Drawing in a deep breath, Alice paused at the back door and gazed around the yard. Despite the dry conditions, recent rains had caused most everything to green up. There was still a considerable amount of dry, brown vegetation strewn across the landscape, but it was the refreshed grass that caught her eye. She let out her breath in a slow steady manner and felt a sense of peace settle on her.

The thought of Robert getting hurt still troubled her, but Alice knew that as a rancher's wife she would have to be strong. Maybe stronger than she'd ever had to be before.

Inside the house, Mother was finishing up the final sweeping. The vision brought back memories of days long past when the older woman had done things in a similar fashion in their own home. For a moment, Alice could only watch. She thought of how hard it had been to accept her mother's still being alive and the deceit of her father. Now, however, Alice felt only joy at having her family back.

Mother spied her watching and halted her work. "Is something wrong?"

Alice smiled. "No, I was just remembering when I was a little girl and you would sweep our house. It seems like a thousand years ago instead of just a few."

"I remember teaching you to make strawberry jam," her mother said, leaning on the broom. "It is one of my favorite memories. You were only nine. Do you remember?"

She did. It had been such a wonderful experience. It was really the first time Alice had done much of anything in the kitchen. "I loved sampling the jam." She laughed. "I remember you worried that none of it would make it to the jars."

Mother chuckled. "I think you ate as much as you canned."

Alice sobered. "I'm sorry you were so unhappy, Mother. Those days seemed fairly pleasant to me. I knew you and Father argued from time to time, but I figured that was what married folks did. I'm sorry that I couldn't have somehow made it better for you and Simon."

Putting the broom aside, Mother came to take hold of Alice's arms. "That was never your job. Besides, it's in the past. We must let go of the awfulness of those ways in which we were wronged and look to a better future. If not, we are destined to bring even more sorrow upon ourselves."

"I'm glad you came here. I'm glad you're back in my life," Alice said and hugged her mother close.

The sound of an approaching wagon caused both women to end their reminiscing and instead head to the front door. Alice could see that it was Hannah and the others. She smiled at the sight of Wyatt, Samuel, and Benjamin hanging half out of the wagon in order to take in all the sights.

"Whoa." Jake stopped the team and set the brake.

"Is this going to be our new house?" Wyatt asked, standing in the back of the wagon.

"No," Hannah replied from the front seat. "This is my house, and you're going to rest up here a bit before heading to your home."

Alice came to the wagon as Jake helped Marty from the well-cushioned place he'd made for her in the back. Marty looked rather tired, and Alice hoped she would lie down before endeavoring anything else.

"Alice, would you help Jake put Marty to bed?" Hannah asked, as if reading her mind.

"I will. I was just about to suggest the same."

"I'm really all right. I just got a little warm. I'll be fine," Marty protested.

Jake would hear none of it. "You're gonna take a nap, or I'm gonna tie you to the bed until you do."

Alice put her hand over her mouth to suppress a giggle. Marty started to say something, but Jake held up his hand.

"Save it, Marty. You aren't gonna win this fight." Then without warning he lifted her in his arms and headed for the house.

Alice hurried on ahead to pull down the bedcovers. She barely managed the task before Jake placed Marty gently atop the clean sheets.

"Now, stay there while I go fetch you somethin' cold to drink. Your sister said there was sweet tea in the cellar." He looked to Alice. "Make sure she stays put."

Already Alice was removing Marty's shoes. "Don't worry. She's not going anywhere."

Marty gave an exasperated sigh and crossed her arms like a defiant child. "Now you have everyone against me."

Jake rolled his eyes and Alice couldn't help but smile. It

wasn't going to be easy to keep Marty from overdoing it, and both of them knew it full well. Once Jake had gone, however, Marty surprised Alice by asking for help.

"Can you unbutton this blouse? I can't bear the heat of it anymore."

Alice quickly complied and soon had Marty undressed down to her lightweight shift. With Marty resting, Alice took up a cloth and dipped it into the water bowl atop the dresser. She came to the bed and began to wipe Marty's face and arms. The older woman offered no resistance and instead thanked Alice for her care.

"Jake worries too much. Hannah, too," Marty said and then closed her eyes. "But I think I will take just a little nap."

Alice smiled and finished her ministering. "I think that's a good idea."

★

Later that evening Marty climbed back into the wagon with Jake's help. The pains had stopped once she'd rested, and for that Marty was grateful. It worried her to think that her stubbornness might have brought the baby too early.

"When are you going to have the baby, Mama?" Wyatt asked.

"Oh, in another few weeks," Marty replied and reached out to ruffle his hair.

Benjamin curled up next to her as Jake moved the team out and headed for home. "Mama, will we have a big bed?"

"No," Marty told them. "Your papa made you each your very own bed."

"We don't have to share?" Samuel asked in amazement.

"Nope. You'll have a bed all your own. But you three will

share a room. At least until we can afford to add on to the house."

"We can share," Wyatt declared. "We can share real good."

Samuel nodded in agreement. "We have to share. We're brothers now."

Marty chuckled and touched the boy's face. "That's right. You are brothers, and together we are a family."

Chapter 27

"You may now kiss your bride," the preacher announced.

Alice trembled as Robert took hold of her and pulled her close. She closed her eyes in anticipation and then felt his warm lips on hers. A spark of passion grew into a flame. She wanted the kiss to go on forever. She wanted always to remember this moment in time.

But as quickly as it started, it stopped and Robert pulled away. Alice could barely hear the crowd of onlookers cheering them. Her heart beat so loudly in her ears that it drowned out nearly everything else.

People soon began to surround them, offering congratulations and well-wishes. Alice found herself separated from Robert as the ladies moved in around her, commenting on her pale blue gown and her carefully styled hair.

"I think the lace trim on your bodice is perfect," Laura Reid said, reaching out to touch the modest neckline. "So fine and delicate."

"She looks like an angel," Hannah declared. "When she said she didn't need a fancy wedding dress, I wasn't sure I could approve. After all, it is the rage."

The ladies around her laughed. "Since when have we Texans worried about what the rest of the world thinks?" Carissa Atherton questioned.

"I like the pleating in the bodice," Hannah pointed out. "It took hours of tedious work, but it came out beautifully."

The others agreed while Alice craned her neck to find where Robert had gotten off to.

Since the wedding had taken place midmorning, everyone was now prepared to celebrate with a spread of food that Hannah and some of the other women had been busy making all week.

Alice wasn't a bit hungry, however. She wanted only to be left alone with Robert. She wanted to again feel his lips upon hers. She felt her cheeks grow hot and looked around, almost worried she'd spoken her desires aloud.

Little by little the crowd thinned, and Robert came to reclaim her. Alice allowed him to lead her to the head table. He helped her to take a seat before offering to get her food.

"You sit tight. I'll fetch a plate for both of us."

She nodded her approval and couldn't help but watch him as he walked away. He was her husband. They were really and truly married. Alice marveled at the thought and reached up to touch the scar along her jaw. It might have been her imagination, but the scar felt less prominent. Maybe it really was fading, as Marty had suggested.

The thought of Marty caused Alice to search for her dear friend. She finally spotted Marty standing away from the others near one of the cottonwood trees. The grimace on her face suggested she was in pain. For a moment it didn't register, and then all at once Alice feared the reason.

Leaving her place of honor, Alice hurried across the yard to where Marty stood. "Is it the baby?"

Marty looked up, her face pale and her mouth tightly clenched. She nodded, drew a deep breath, and then straightened. "It started just before the wedding. I didn't want to say anything. It's your day, after all." Her features relaxed. The pain had apparently passed.

"Is it too early?"

"I don't know. Hannah has insisted that I was further along than I originally thought." Marty gave her an apologetic smile. "I'm sorry to spoil things."

"You aren't spoiling anything. But you need to get to bed. Come, and I'll help you." Alice looked around for Hannah.

"Oh, don't make a fuss. I don't want everyone knowing. Jake will—" Marty gasped and bent over, clutching her stomach.

Alice couldn't take any more. "Someone, please come help me. Marty is going to have the baby!"

Jake was first to reach them, with Hannah close behind. Several other people followed until nearly everyone had gathered to see what assistance they might offer. Hannah ordered people around like a well-trained general.

"Jake, get her into the house and help her out of her gown. Ravinia, put more water on the stove and then get that stack of towels I set aside."

They quickly obeyed, and Alice could only stand helplessly watching as Jake carried Marty away. Robert seemed to understand and put his arm around her waist.

"Alice, she's in good hands. My ma is the best midwife around these parts."

"I believe you. I just wish there were something I could do to help."

"There is," Carissa Atherton announced. "You can go on

with your wedding celebration. Marty would want you to do so. Now come. The birthing will probably take some time."

Reluctantly Alice allowed Robert to lead her back to the table. Carissa took over as hostess, and soon had everyone's focus back on the festivities. Alice found it almost impossible to eat despite the wonderful array of foods set before her. Robert didn't seem to have any problem at all, and after he'd cleared his plate, he started in on hers. He spoke casually with those who came to speak to them, while Alice's mind was on the delivery of Marty's baby.

"I can't stand not knowing what's happening," she whispered to Robert when they were finally alone.

"I understand, but this is our wedding day, and I'd really like for you to share it with me." He smiled and patted her hand. "You know Aunt Marty wouldn't like it if she knew you were neglecting me."

This made Alice smile. She could imagine Marty chiding her quite severely. Just then Simon came up to the table with Wyatt, Samuel, and Benjamin in tow.

"They're worried about their mama," Simon declared. "I told them she'd be done having the baby pretty soon. That's right, isn't it?"

Alice could see the hopefulness in the boys' eyes. She nodded. "That's right. Sometimes babies seem to take forever, but other times they come real quick. You boys just need to pray and ask God to watch over your mama." She gave them a smile. "Everything will be all right."

Two hours later, Alice's mother appeared at the door. It seemed that everyone noticed her at once, and silence blanketed the yard. She smiled and made her announcement.

"It's a girl."

Cheers erupted from the crowd, and several of the attendees

rushed toward Ravinia Chesterfield to learn more. Robert, however, took the opportunity to slip away with Alice.

"Where are we going?" she asked as he led her away from the party.

"Anyplace where we can be alone," he said.

He pulled her behind the smokehouse and drew her into his arms. Without giving her a chance to protest, Robert pressed his mouth to hers. A charge like lightning shot through her, and Alice wrapped her arms around him as if she might otherwise drown.

The kiss seemed to go on forever, and Alice lost all thought of anyone but her husband. When he finally lifted his head, Alice found herself almost faint.

Robert grinned like a little boy who'd just gotten away with a prank. "And that, Mrs. Barnett, is how to properly kiss your husband."

Her senses returned and Alice smiled. "Behind the smokehouse?"

He laughed. "I hid here for many a questionable deed. I tried my first smoke here. I figured no one would know, 'cause the smokehouse was in use. My pa caught me just the same. I came here once when I stole cookies that my ma had forbidden me to eat. I don't know why I figured she'd not notice them missin' off the plate. She never said a word about it, however, but when I was half sick from havin' eaten too many, she just smiled and gave me castor oil."

"Goodness, I had no idea you were such a hooligan," Alice said, unable to hide her amusement. "I don't know if I would have married you had I known."

Robert nodded most soberly and tightened his hold on her. "That's why I didn't tell you." He kissed her again, but this time it was brief and left Alice longing for more.

"Come along, Mrs. Barnett. I'm sure we'll be missed if we don't return, and I, for one, don't want my pa comin' in search of me."

Alice quickly agreed. "Neither do I, Mr. Barnett. I wouldn't want to scandalize him."

Robert laughed heartily and drew her alongside him. "I don't know how I ever enjoyed life before you came here, but I have a feelin' it's only gonna get better. Ma once told me that Pa was a blessing from heaven, and that's how I feel about you. God knew the kind of wife I needed, and He brought you right to my doorstep."

Alice leaned closer and smiled. God had known her heart and her desires, too, and He had given not only her mother and brother back to her, but brought an entirely new family, as well. Most important, God had given her a man who would love her despite her scars.

"And just where have you two been?" Robert's father asked with a raised brow.

Robert gave him a sheepish grin. "I was just showin' Alice around—behind the smokehouse." His father roared with laughter, and Alice felt her cheeks burn with embarrassment. There would be no keeping secrets in this family, and maybe that was for the best. Secrets had a way of coming between folks, and Alice wanted nothing to ever come between her and her beloved. Smiling, she gave a sigh and prayed that this moment in time would last forever.

Tracie Peterson is the award-winning author of over one hundred novels, both historical and contemporary. Her avid research resonates in her stories, as seen in her bestselling HEIRS OF MONTANA and ALASKAN QUEST series. Tracie and her family make their home in Montana. Visit Tracie's website at www.traciepeterson.com and her blog at www.writes passage.blogspot.com.

Books by Tracie Peterson

www.traciepeterson.com

LONE STAR BRIDES

A Sensible Arrangement • A Moment in Time

LAND OF SHINING WATER

The Icecutter's Daughter • The Quarryman's Bride
The Miner's Lady

LAND OF THE LONE STAR

Chasing the Sun • Touching the Sky • Taming the Wind

BRIDAL VEIL ISLAND*

To Have and To Hold • To Love and Cherish
To Honor and Trust

SONG OF ALASKA

Dawn's Prelude • Morning's Refrain • Twilight's Serenade

STRIKING A MATCH

Embers of Love • Hearts Aglow • Hope Rekindled

ALASKAN QUEST

Summer of the Midnight Sun
Under the Northern Lights • Whispers of Winter
Alaskan Quest (3 in 1)

BRIDES OF GALLATIN COUNTY

A Promise to Believe In • A Love to Last Forever
A Dream to Call My Own

THE BROADMOOR LEGACY*

A Daughter's Inheritance • *An Unexpected Love*
A Surrendered Heart

BELLS OF LOWELL*

Daughter of the Loom • *A Fragile Design*
These Tangled Threads

LIGHTS OF LOWELL*

A Tapestry of Hope • *A Love Woven True*
The Pattern of Her Heart

DESERT ROSES

Shadows of the Canyon • *Across the Years*
Beneath a Harvest Sky

HEIRS OF MONTANA

Land of My Heart • *The Coming Storm*
To Dream Anew • *The Hope Within*

LADIES OF LIBERTY

A Lady of High Regard • *A Lady of Hidden Intent*
A Lady of Secret Devotion

RIBBONS OF STEEL**

Distant Dreams • *A Hope Beyond* • *A Promise for Tomorrow*

RIBBONS WEST**

Westward the Dream • *Separate Roads* • *Ties That Bind*

WESTWARD CHRONICLES

A Shelter of Hope • *Hidden in a Whisper* • *A Veiled Reflection*

More From Bestselling Author Tracie Peterson

To learn more about Tracie and her books, visit traciepeterson.com.

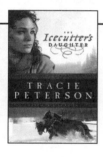
◊ BETHANYHOUSE

More Romance You May Enjoy